M000315088

In Accord

No Frills
<<<>>>
Buffalo
Buffalo, NY

Copyright © 2013, 2014 by Kristin Chambers

ISBN: 978-0-9910455-0-1

Printed in the United States of America.

This novel is a work of fiction. Names, characters, places and incidents are either the product of the author's imagination or are used fictitiously. Any resemblance to actual events, locales or persons is entirely coincidental.

All rights reserved. No part of this publication may be reproduced, stored in a retrieval system, or transmitted, in any form or by any means, electronic, mechanical, photocopying, recording, or otherwise, without the written prior permission of the author.

Cover design by Greg Kellog
Photograph by Mark Chambers

No Frills Buffalo
119 Dorchester Road
Buffalo, NY 14213

For more information visit
Nofrillsbuffalo.com

Readers praise for IN ACCORD

Upon reading the synopsis of this book I was immediately captivated and intrigued by what the pages of this novel would hold. The separate endings that each of the characters writes are all interesting and different enough from each other to keep each new take fresh. All the characters are very believable and bring a different flavor to the table of the story that keeps you interested and wanting to know the rest of the story. I really liked the idea that someone is writing about a book club and it doesn't come off as the stereotypical older American's getting together over tea. While that does hold its place and is a comfort for many, this book goes far beyond the Sunday afternoon discussion of the typical classics. I loved how the personal lives played into the renditions that each of the characters made to the end of the story. Overall this is worth reading and caters to all types of readers.
Reviewed by Chris @ LIVE TO READ

http://livetoread-krystal.blogspot.com/2014/04/in-accord-by-kristin-chambers.html

New novelist Kristin Chambers' IN ACCORD is a skillfully braided story of friendships and questions that change lives. Four women, bonded since their children's births and through life's turns, comprise a book club aptly named In Accord. The women challenge themselves to re-write an ending to a recent book they'd read that had troubled each. The main characters of the story-within-a-story are a couple each concealing an infidelity. Their story deflates rather than concludes and leaves the In Accord women disappointed. As each sketch out an ending more reflective of their personal sensibilities, lives explode. The symmetries of reaction, the echoes and reflections, make reading this story feel kind of like looking down a hall of mirrors. A very satisfying read!
–*Amazon reader Nancy C. (Napoli, NY)*

5.0 out of 5 stars **Definitely worth it!**
I enjoyed this very much. The characters and references I was familiar with made for an interesting story line. I found myself

wanting to know more about the characters. I liked the way the story and Mariners Cove intertwined. Amazon reader T. A. "Tyzee" (Buffalo, NY)

In Accord... we learn about the intricacies of marriage and raising children, how cancer can be a devastating illness, and how each woman realizes that friendship can be a wonderful thing and that they need to make some changes in their lives to be happy. Told with humor, compassion and love, this is a great story. I love how the author intermingled each of the women's stories into a novel that is definitely un-put-down-able. If you love a great women's fiction novel than you cannot go wrong with this one. *Kathleen K. "Celticlady" (Rhinelander, WI USA)*

5.0 out of 5 stars **Excellent read! I couldn't put it down!** The author is perceptive regarding the lives of the characters and the book is very well written. I couldn't put it down. I loved all the Western New York references. *Reader Judy G. (Buffalo, NY)*

5.0 out of 5 stars   **Worth being tired for.......**

My four year old refuses to sleep through the night. When I made a conscious decision to be tired for several days until I finished this book, that says that the book was wonderful. It was easy to find bits of yourself in each of the women, and see their stories as your own. Kristin captured the essence of the relationships between the women and their families. Loved it! *Amazon reader Alisha G. (Avon, NY)*

5.0 out of 5 stars **Clearly drawn, interesting characters...**

I love the premise. As a member of a book club that has been meeting for 17 years, I know that it is often the case that a novel's ending can leave a reader feeling unsatisfied, sometimes even downright angry. In this book, the women who make up the In Accord book club decide to do something about it...Kristin Chambers' novel is engaging and relevant. She has a gift for writing lively and realistic dialogue. Set in Buffalo, New York, it pays homage to the City of Good Neighbors, as well as to beautiful Chautauqua County. In Accord is a good read; I'm going to recommend it to my book club. *Amazon reader Deb M. (Bemus Point, NY)*

5.0 out of 5 stars **Warm, funny and all too true!**

I so identified with this group of women-all drive the same car, live in the same city, are in the same book club, have families. Yet each has her unique voice, and finds her voice throughout the course of the story. The premise...allows each woman to pilot her course through a month of trials, routine, relationships and self-discoveries while considering what a satisfying ending is. Bravo to Kristin Chambers for understanding real women of today! *Amazon reader "clancy6"*

5.0 out of 5 stars **Great book!**

The writing in this book was free and easy, quickly drawing me into the story. Not only were the scenes vivid and the story interesting, but the characters were realistic. I highly recommend this book. Amazon reader **Emily** (IN, United States)

5.0 out of 5 stars **Great read**

The narratives of the four friends were so authentic to some of the experiences in my own life that it felt almost too close to home. Kristin Chambers meticulously examines the ebbs and flows of female friendship, marriage, and the experience of middle adulthood. Powerful, heart-centered storytelling. Being from Buffalo, it was also great to see our city showcased in such a way. Would love to see a sequel of what comes next for Maggie, Hannah, Ellen and Julie. *Amazon reader Phoenix (Buffalo, NY)*

Dedicated to my brother, Mark Chambers, who was the first to believe in my story and was unflagging in his loving confidence that I could, and should, write it.

In Accord

Kristin Chambers

1: Reasons to Celebrate

Four Hondas, grimy with road salt, snugged up against the dark brick wall of the tiny Thai restaurant. Inside the restaurant's midnight blue main dining room, the four women who owned those cars celebrated Julie's thirty-ninth birthday and rejoiced over the news that Maggie's bone scans were clean. Talking quietly but laughing freely, the four occasionally touched one another on a hand or a shoulder, and gestured with the animated familiarity of old friends. If one of the men at the bar had been studying them, he would be struck by the rich gold and emerald colors of Maggie Brinkman's turban, and that Julie Johnson, in spikey blond hair offset by a conservative sweater, seemed to lean in to the words of her companions, not saying much herself. Then he would appreciate Hannah Feldman's wide, generous smile, which often seemed particularly directed toward Ellen Palmer, the one with the lustrous brunette hair and muscular shoulders.

Having quickly enjoyed a second glass of white wine, Ellen headed toward the powder room tucked into the back of the cozy diner. She eyed the beautiful red orchids displayed on low room dividers, giving the dining areas the illusion of privacy. Then her eyes fixed on a man seated at the furthest table, facing away from the bar. Something about his military posture held her attention, even as she silently scolded herself for staring. He sat opposite a plumpish, carefully coifed woman who frowned at her half-eaten salad. Dim restaurant lighting gave the man's bald head a slightly greyish sheen and washed out the colors in his plaid button-down shirt. Without seeing his face, she was struck by the sheer ordinariness of the two: a middle-aged couple having a modest meal in a suburban eatery. They weren't talking or even looking at each other. They were both just parked there. *Every bored, middle-aged couple*, she thought, mentally fast-forwarding her life ten years.

By the time she rejoined her friends, the ordinary couple had left, and the room was crackling, electrified. Unnoticed by the other diners, three men at the bar had been watching every move of the balding man. When he finally paid his check and drove away, the three descended upon his table, their latex-gloved hands silently depositing every object that might have touched his fingers or lips into antiseptic evidence sleeves. They vanished quickly without a word to the other patrons or the perplexed wait staff.

"What the hell was that? Weird!" cried Maggie, vigorously stirring cream into her coffee. Her gold loop earrings jangled as the turban encircling her head shifted to reveal her peach-fuzzed head. "Dammit!" She struggled to reposition the wrap.

Ellen grinned, trying to telepath *it's fine* by gesturing at her own head and adding a thumbs up in one smooth motion.

Hannah ran her fingers though her own thick, curly black locks. "Your hair is growing in great."

"Ick, I look like a damn cancer billboard."

"You *don't*. And so what? The important thing is that you're *here*." Ellen answered.

"Don't you know you look fabulous?" Julie asked, surveying Maggie. "When are you going to ditch those head wraps, anyway?"

Maggie loosened the turban and dropped it to the dark tile floor. "Now?"

Clinking goblets, they cheered. It had been a grueling, long road.

"So," Julie tilted her head toward the back of the restaurant where the three men had been so interested in the bald man's dinnerware, "That felt weird. What do you think it was all about?"

"Some kind of crime investigation," opined Hannah, who could always furnish an answer.

"Looks like our tax dollars at work," Maggie complained. "Does it really take *three* guys to clear one table?"

"That couple was so *blah*," Ellen added. "What on earth could either of them have possibly done to justify grabbing all their shit like that?"

Julie laughed. "From where I sat, it looked like they mostly wanted *his* stuff. I'm thinking maybe he's a pedophile? Or a sex trafficker?"

"Un-fucking-likely," Maggie touched her head self-consciously. "He was so old and washed-out, he looked like he'd died already and his wife hadn't bothered to tell him!"

"Didn't they just arrest an *81*-year-old perp out in Blasdell?" Julie reminded them of a recent news report of a very elderly child molester in a nearby suburb, leading everyone to wrinkle their noses.

Dessert arrived – mango sticky rice, coconut cake, and crunchy fried bananas – with extra plates for sharing, and the friends returned to celebrating Julie's birthday and Maggie's new lease on life.

"To you." Ellen tipped her glass to each of her friends. "To friends, to health, to happiness, to coconut cake!" She briefly held Maggie's glance, strong but scared, and caught her breath. Maggie desperately needed health on her side.

"I'll drink to that," added Hannah. "The holidays are over, the kids are finally back in school, Maggie and Julie are getting on their feet, everything's going to be okay, I just *know* it."

"I'll toast to all of it." Julie raised her glass again and took a minuscule nibble of fried banana.

Fourteen years of celebrations, tears, and unflagging support in the trenches of motherhood cement these women. Their firstborns had all arrived within the same year, bonding their group with a powerful elixir of sleep deprivation, colic, cradle cap, and nursing, fussing, and teething woes, as well as bursts of joy and pride at the first smiles, first words, and first steps of each adored baby. Over the years, they coached each other through delicate negotiations with in-laws, celebrated new births and birthdays, struggled with new jobs, and tried to figure out the changing terrains of their marriages. They kept one another from going mad; struggled with wanting or needing to be career women while caring for and obsessing about their own children; faced down Maggie's devastating bouts of cancer and a horrible accident that nearly killed Julie's son; and watched in furious frustration as Julie's marriage dissolved in the stink of her husband's affairs.

These days, Ellen, Maggie, and Hannah talk or text most every day. Ellen and Julie jog together four days a week in Delaware Park. All four of them meet for brunch every Sunday. And several years ago they formed their own little book club which meets monthly. They called it the *In Accord Book Club* because each, over the course of a single month, had purchased Honda's eminently sensible family car, the Accord. Now they spend huge chunks of their lives in those cars driving their children to soccer or dance or karate, or whatever, so the kids won't roam free on urban or suburban streets.

They were nervous about the streets for a reason. There were thirty years when women in Buffalo sensed with sickening certainty that they didn't actually know who was on the street, stalking, hunting. Even in this "city of good neighbors," where extraordinarily generous strangers push each other out of snowdrifts and open their thin wallets for kids who have cancer and adopt flea-infested Chihuahuas from neurotic hoarders, even given all of that, a cloud of anxiety hung over the city. Since the early '80s, when news of a serial rapist first made the local papers, parents were hyper vigilant about their daughters' whereabouts. *Don't jog on deserted bike paths. Don't walk alone anywhere, ever. Don't take shortcuts over the tracks in Riverside.* And any woman, out by herself, even walking to her car in her own neighborhood in the middle of the day, felt a stab of fear if a man came alongside her, just innocently walking faster than she.

The fear faded after the attacks stopped for over a decade. People assumed that the monster had moved, or (better) been imprisoned for some other crime or (best) had died, hopefully of some painfully debilitating and disfiguring disease. But then, on the anniversary of the killing of a university student, a middle-aged mother running alone in the middle of the day on a suburban bike path was strangled. Everyone was on edge again after her body was discovered. She had fought hard for her life. There was precious little comfort in learning that she had been strangled but not raped.

The book club friends finished celebrating the birthday and the fantastic cancer-remission news, paid their tab, and made their way through a gathering storm back to their families and obligations.

A few days later, Ellen was up at five for her morning jog when she caught the news on early television: the alleged bike path rapist/murderer, now identified as Artemio Sanchez, had been arrested and linked to his crimes by DNA evidence gathered after he dined at a local restaurant. With some urgency, she texted her friends: TURN ON TV

Julie, preparing to join Ellen for a run in the park, texted back: Whoa

Within seconds, Hannah's text arrived: OMG. OMG. Bastard. Was he the creep at the restaurant?

Ellen: Yup

Julie: 4 real?

Hannah: OMG

Their texting was suspended as each stood transfixed in front of her flat screen watching the excited anchor repeat the bones of the story again and again, as very little else was known. The bike path rapist had left DNA evidence at a restaurant, enough to confirm that he was the serial killer who had terrorized Buffalo for so many decades. The district attorney had already lodged two murder counts against him with more pending. Footage of a stunned and haunted-looking, fattish, balding man in orange prison garb and shackles replayed in an endless loop in the background.

Mesmerized, Ellen texted: Sorry, Jules, can't run, can't take eyes off TV.

Julie replied: I know. See you tonight!

Hannah followed: Yes. See you!

Several hours later, Maggie awoke from a stoned and groggy sleep and read the text chain. Index finger tapping furiously, she *replied all*: HOLY SHIT! WOW! S O F'g B! See you all later, can't wait.

That evening, the book club women planned to discuss a recently published novel that revealed, in delicate and nuanced layers, the pathology of a high school shooter, his many victims, his devastated family, and his clueless friends. Reading it had made them all nervous. But when they finally gathered, they could talk of little else than how close they had been to a similar monster and how un-monster-like, how ordinary, how bland, he appeared. It was a huge relief to have his vicious siege truly be over, but it was equally surreal to know that he had lived among them, dined among them, even brazenly jogged in a run commemorating one of his victims. *How could no one have suspected?* It seemed inexplicable.

Time, however, moves only forward. Eventually, Artemio Sanchez became a footnote in Buffalo's history, just one of yesterday's horrid news stories, as the tight-knit group tended to their daily lives and their mutual friendships. The shadow of the fear he inflicted lurked in their collective memory. It made itself known in odd little self-protective tics, like always double-checking the back seat of their cars before getting in, never parking in closed underground garages, and never getting on an elevator alone with a strange man. Tics became habits, passed on to daughters like old family recipes.

2: Three Years Later

Although a Buffalo October is typically perfect, this day's forecast was mixed and unsettled, calling for early sun followed by gale force winds, periods of calm, and a precipitous drop in temperature. It was as if Lake Erie was having a fulsome temper tantrum. The four friends, gathering at Hannah's for their monthly book discussion and food fest, were too busy to keep tabs on the forecast.

Turning her metallic beige car onto Crescent Avenue, Ellen sang along to *You're So Vain,* a happy smile softening her face. Remnants of early evening sunlight glinted off the reds and golds of the maple-tree-lined street, lending it an arched majesty admired in the neighborhood. The wind barely rustled in the leaves. Book club gatherings were a social high point for her. Despite calling their group the *In Accord Club,* the women were seldom of one mind about anything. That was what made it so attractive to her. She hustled to reach Hannah's at the appointed hour and then, as always, faced the challenge of finding parking. Finally a bulky Ford van pulled out halfway up the street. "Mine!" she whispered as she eased into the spot, noting with satisfaction that she was early. Gathering her purse, phone, and book, she confirmed that there were no strange men loitering on the street and hopped out. The faint aroma of chocolate snaked through the evening air, drawing her up the wooden steps and onto Hannah's wide Victorian porch. Ellen filled her lungs with a deep, slow, yogic breath. Book club nights seriously challenged her willpower. She breathed a quiet mantra: "No carbs for you, no carbs for you, no carbs, no carbs, no carbs," as she crossed the porch and rang the bell.

Jerking the door open, Hannah's fourteen-year-old daughter, Zoe, scowled through puffy eyes and mascara-streaked cheeks. She tossed her pretty head to motion Ellen into the foyer, turned without a word, and stomped up the stairs. Ellen held her breath, knowing it was a faux pas to acknowledge this child's chronic unhappiness. Zoe had turned into an emotional minefield, always upset about something, from understandably noxious events such as betrayed confidences to not finding the perfect white gym socks washed and paired in her bureau drawer. Softly, Ellen lobbed a neutral "Hi, Zoe" to the teen's departing back and entered the well-lit foyer.

As always, Ellen was struck by the rightness of it: the polished antique tiger-eye maple secretary topped by photographs of a young Hannah and her husband Simon, hopeful, fit, and sexy. A single dried silver hydrangea blossom in a slender silver vase. The Japanese print on the wall by the curved mahogany staircase leading to the bedrooms. There was none of the clutter and disarray of her own home: the piles of mail and stacks of magazines; shoes orphaned near doorways by her husband, William; her two sons' sports gear and school papers strewn about; her own blouses needing a quick ironing, draped over the backs of dining room chairs.

Ellen noted that she was the first one there.

"Hi, Hullo! I guess you didn't check your phone this afternoon," Hannah called cheerily from the kitchen. "I texted everyone to come a half hour late because I had an emergency after school." Ellen arched her eyebrows. Things were *always* coming up in Hannah's world.

Hanging up her jacket, Ellen checked herself quickly in the hall mirror and adjusted her face to show more smile. Her hair, with new "sun-kissed" highlights obscuring a few strands of grey, swished on her shoulders in a simple, flattering cut. Fading freckles, the price of so many adolescent hours spent in the summer sun, splashed across her high cheekbones. After refreshing her lip gloss, she wandered into the kitchen. "Saturday, I'm getting a new phone. My old one doesn't hold its charge anymore so I missed your message. Let me help. Can I cut some vegies or something?" she eyed the red peppers piled by the sink.

"Thanks," Hannah smiled. "Next time, I'll text *and* email you. You look great, by the way. Sticking to that no carbs thing, huh?"

"Yes!" Ellen relaxed her shoulders, turned on the water, and began to scrub her hands. "So, dare I ask what's up with Zoe? She looked upset."

"Something!" Hannah pushed curly dark tendrils off her forehead. "Lately, she's just impossible. She absolutely refuses to talk about it, whatever *it* is. My first guess is she's having shit with a girlfriend, but could be a boyfriend. Or maybe it's hormones, or something to do with the moons and the tides." Hannah coughed. "The environment, needy children somewhere in the world. *What-effing-ever.* She's taking us all on her crazy ride. Simon's ready to pull his hair out."

"*Really*, Hannah?" Ellen grinned. "If I recall correctly, Zoe's always been a bit of a handful. Remember when she refused to wear a bib and tugged on that cute one with Pooh and the honeypot on it until she rubbed the back of her neck raw?"

"I'll never forget that. No bibs ever, after that. But the worst was how she wouldn't nap except in my lap. God!"

"How about whole bit with everything having to be pink? And zeroing in on you whenever you talked on the phone, she had special radar for that."

"NO crayons, only markers. She had to be like Beth and the big kids."

Ellen raised her hand. "On her behalf, I remember how she laughed more than most kids, that really wonderful *hahaha* that you could hear from all over the house, do you remember?"

"I do, I do! And, she got such a kick out of dressing up."

"Oh, yeah! Bride's veils, and tutus and capes, all mixed together!"

They were both chuckling now. "So did you finish *Mariner's Cove?*" Hannah wiped a tear from her eye.

Delicately removing the seeds from the peppers, Ellen nodded. "Yes! And let me say, I object to that ending. *Very* unsatisfying. You?"

"I was up 'til three in the morning, finally finished it."

"Oh, wow, you must be exhausted."

"Nothing new there. But that conclusion sure let me down, another book that crashes and burns in its last chapters. Maggie's going to be really pissed that we've spent time on a book like that. She gets particularly offended over novels with dumb endings."

"Since the cancer, she gets really upset about time being wasted on anything," Ellen agreed.

"Good point," Hannah stopped to cut brownies and arrange them on a platter. "Actually, everybody was disappointed in that last one. And here we go again."

After the two friends finished prepping the refreshments, Hannah went upstairs to say goodnight to her little boy, Matthew. Ellen wandered into the ultra-modern family room, which she found incongruous in this wonderful, rambling Victorian house.

When Hannah and Simon purchased the house, ten years ago, they had been charmed by its gorgeous stained glass windows, stunning oak woodwork, and cozy rooms. Its disjunctive layout seemed perfect for children's games of hide-and-seek or adult candlelight dinners. And it was perfect for those things. But time inexorably wore away their enthusiasm as the flaws of the old house became apparent, like fault lines in an earthquake zone. The handsome alcove off the living room with the built-in oak desk couldn't accommodate a computer *and* a printer and had only one functional outlet. The bathrooms and closets were comically small by today's standards. Windows and wiring had to be replaced. The family room was added after Matthew's birth four years ago. This room was built for functionality, appointed with sturdy modern leather furniture, and heated by a gas burning fireplace that copied the look of an old wood stove ("But none of the mess," Hannah was pleased to note). Ellen settled into the nearest comfortable chair, propped her feet out on the ottoman and began to idly leaf through her copy of the book.

3: Mariner's Cove

Mariner's Cove was a novel chosen on the strength of its author's stellar reputation and the pleasure the club had found in her earlier works, discovering characters who swung at the curve balls life threw at them with sly humor and feminist irony. However, no one had previewed this particular selection, a slim volume with a lovely, artful dust jacket promising "the refreshingly frank voice of Alysen Tomas in a new novel about the complicated, joyous and agonizing re-emergence of a long-lost love." The fact that the story takes place in western New York provided further inducement for choosing it.

The story launches in a wannabe upscale restaurant, Mariner's Cove, which boasts a wide wooden dock jutting into Chautauqua Lake, a 17-mile-long lake that was once a water route for Jesuit explorers and French fur trappers. It is rimmed by old vacation cottages and new million dollar estates. Only a two-hour drive south from Buffalo, the lake long served as a vacation destination for families on a budget. Maggie and Ellen each visited there as children and have fond memories of rides on the Chautauqua Belle, fishing for walleye, roller skating at Midway

Park, and eating at an iconic restaurant with a wooden dock jutting into the lake. It's almost home turf.

The story opens with a man and a woman seated together at Mariner's Cove celebrating their twenty-fifth high school reunion. During the hot, hazy summer before these two left for college, they had been each other's first lovers. The woman, Claire, had fallen in love. But during his first semester, Charles had given himself over to a heady mix of drugs and politics, quit school, hitchhiked west, and dropped everything related to his "bourgeois" life, including Claire. Nothing in her life, not marriage, not a child, not even a career, enabled Claire to successfully bury the deep ache of losing him. She nursed it constantly, like a jagged tooth.

Their reunion led inexorably to a yearlong affair that ended abruptly when his wife confronted him with suspicious credit charges. Claire was devastated again, just as she had been at eighteen. "I felt like shit on his shoe," she complained to her sister.

When she was just thirty, Claire's sister Paula received a devastating diagnosis of Parkinson's disease. Paula was not married, and her disease quickly slammed the door on independent relationships; she moved into a group home. Reluctantly, but increasingly, she became dependent upon Claire and Claire's husband, Philip, for loving company. And so she was devastated when, on a group-home outing, she spied Philip stroking and holding the hand of an adoring young woman who was not her sister.

"Claire would die if you told her," Philip had pleaded when Paula confronted him. "I will break if off immediately, I promise, please don't tell!" Philip had seemed so sincere, so contrite, that Paula agreed to hold his secret.

When Claire admitted her affair with Charles, Paula already knew that Claire's husband was an adulterer, too. But as a woman of her word, she honored her vow. Thus, Claire's and Philip's infidelities remained a secret that silently fouled the marriage. Over time, each built mental break walls against their memories of passion, of hope, of escape. *Mariner's Cove* didn't quite conclude on that note, however. It offered an epilogue in which Claire again chose stability and the quiet death of stasis over truth or freedom.

Ellen reread the epilogue and shook her head, feeling profoundly irritated:

> *As Claire pulled into her driveway, she could see the flickering TV screen through the front window, familiar and faintly comforting. Her husband, Philip, was home. She hoped he had turned up the heat so the house didn't feel like a crypt. Once inside, she saw the usual pile of mail on the counter: bills and circulars, an invitation to a fundraiser, plaintive pleas for funds from too many worthy non-profits. At the top of the pile was a faux hand-addressed envelope with the return address of her home town. The envelope had been stamped with the words: "Reunion Gala! Register early!" It must be approaching*

time for the thirtieth, she realized. Would Charles show? She banished the thought, feeling as if a live cinder were burning the flesh at the back of her throat.

Philip sidled up behind her and kissed her lightly on the crown of her head. Looking over her shoulder at the envelope in her hand, he said, "Yeah! Looks like time for your high school reunion. You going? Want to see who's still standing?"

"Uh, no, don't think so," Claire said softly. "I'm not really in touch with anyone and I don't have much interest."

"Well, suit yourself but it's perfectly fine with me if you want to go." Philip could be unexpectedly gallant, Claire thought, but knew she would be staying far away from Mariner's Cove this year. Maybe she and Philip could go to the shore instead, take a real vacation like people who had actually figured out how to have fun together. She imagined proposing it later but gradually decided no; *going to the shore would be a lot of bother, plus there's no way they would truly enjoy it.*

And thus, Mariner's Cove ended. Ellen set the book down and closed her eyes.

4: In Accord

"Hell-looo! Hell-looo!" Ellen startled awake to the cheery greeting of Maggie, who ushered herself in while Hannah was still upstairs. Arriving on a fierce gust of wind, Maggie's new suede jacket swished as she unwound her bunchy paisley scarf and changed from boots into thick, colorful hand-knitted socks. When Ellen entered the vestibule to greet her, she immediately noticed that Maggie's beautiful auburn hair was growing out much wavier than it had been before the last round of chemotherapy. Maggie smiled, her wide green eyes sparkling. "I'm a mess," she proclaimed, running her fingers through her unruly mop. "That crazy wind just about blew me over, no small feat," she patted her roundish belly and laughed again. "Look at you, you skinny bitch! How do you do it?"

Reflexively sucking in her abs, Ellen stammered for a reply as Hannah descended the open staircase, loudly chirping back up to her little boy, "Nighty, night. Nighty, night. Don't let the bedbugs bite!"

"Holy shit," Maggie grabbed Hannah in a warm embrace. "So good to see you! But are you kidding me? How is that darling little boy ever going to get to sleep if he's picturing getting *bit* by some kind of nasty little bug hiding out in his bed?"

"It's a *verse*," Hannah protested, grinning. She took Maggie by the shoulders and looked frankly into her face. "You look fabulous, girl. How are you feeling?"

"Other than totally depressed that fucking, fucking winter is about to land on us, I'm great." Maggie's pallor was gone and her full lips sported a fresh coat of deep red lipstick. Her wide silver bracelets jangled as she smoothed her hair.

The doorbell announced Julie's arrival. Flushed from fighting the wind, Julie shivered in the doorway and gratefully stepped inside. Her short spiky blond hair always looked as if she'd just been in a wicked gale, but even so, she looked flustered. "Hey, it's scary out there!" she cried. "What in heaven's name is going on?"

With Julie's black jacket and a hanger in her hand, Hannah called upstairs to her husband. "Simon?"

After a brief pause, a deep masculine voice floated down from the second floor, "Y-eesss?"

"Could you see what's going on with the weather, please? Everybody's getting bashed by the wind. Is something dreadful about to happen?" She smiled broadly at her friends. "It's one of his obsessions. He's got a whole little weather station up there, so we might as well make use of him."

"On it!" he called down cheerily.

Gathering first in the kitchen, the women choose herbal tea or coffee and nibbled on stuffed mushrooms, chocolate brownies, and apple tarts. Conversation flowed quickly, sometimes in shorthand. All easily commiserated with Maggie when she described how her teenaged daughter had suddenly converted to a vegan diet. Her lovely Leah was now on a mission to educate the family on the atrocities of slaughterhouses and the dangers of clogged arteries. At dinner.

As usual, there was a new, egregious chapter in Julie's ongoing struggle with her ex-husband for child support, alimony, and dignity. Backyard gardeners all, they carefully tilled and aerated the soil of their families, jobs, and lives. Then they migrated into the family room.

Hannah held the book aloft as a call to order. "Okay, everybody," she called authoritatively, "Let's get started."

Ellen giggled. "Okay. But I do feel like a kid at one of your assemblies."

Julie, a teacher at Hannah's school, had been at more than her share of assemblies and easily joined Ellen's muffled laughter. "Right. What is it today, madam principal, *Dare to Say No*? *Bullies Be Gone*?"

Knowing they were joking didn't suppress Hannah's annoyance. It was so tiresome the way people regressed to their middle school selves and got weird regarding her role as a school principal. Sighing dramatically, she wagged her finger. "Are you children ever going to get over junior high? And anyway, do we want to talk about this book, or not?"

"Not!" Maggie sang. "There were times when this story was moving and I could really see where it was going, but I hated, absolutely *hated,* the way it ended. It spoiled the whole experience of reading the book!"

Ellen and Hannah exchanged knowing glances.

"So, what about it moved you?" Julie encouraged.

"The way she wrote their relationships, you felt like you could really see into their heads. It also seemed real, the looking back at how great, how special those first childish loves are. That stuff almost always turns out to be bullshit and I expected her to repudiate the whole theses. But, NO! It just ends, without any big, any big..." Maggie scrunched her eyes shut, scanning for the right word.

"Doesn't it feel a little creepy how she portrays those two people living together, even having a child together, but never honestly knowing each other?" Julie softly interrupted, looking at no one.

"Some wackos get away with it, though. It's an extreme example, but think of that Sanchez asshole. He had a wife and kids. The hell they must've gone through!" Ellen creased her brow into two thin lines, thinking of the bike path ordeal. Sanchez had been indicted just days after he left his DNA on a straw and a napkin at that restaurant. Initially he denied all the charges, but five months later he pled guilty and was sentenced to 75-years-to-life. His wife, two sons, suburban neighbors, and co-workers were stunned as his double life was slowly unspooled in the media. He had seemed so ordinary, so dull and unremarkable.

Maggie coughed. "Hell, yeah, you could call the whole Sanchez thing *extreme*! I hope it's a one in a billion example. Totally terrifying. I wonder if his wife *really* didn't sense anything strange about the guy."

"That's what all the articles said," offered Hannah, who, mesmerized by the case, had read every scrap of information she could unearth. Having been at that restaurant, near him, when the crucial evidence was finally obtained made the story even more personal for all of them. Hannah shook her head in agreement. "I hear you, though. You would think there would be signs that something was wrong."

"Inexplicable, totally fucked up," Maggie weighed in.

"Some people exist within entirely superficial relationships. It comes up time and time again at work." Ellen, a hospital social worker, laced her arms tightly across her chest. "There are couples who don't know the most basic stuff about each other, even after being together for decades."

"Sad." Julie said.

Hannah held the book up. "That's kind of the point of this novel, I guess."

"Don't you think lots of people do what Claire did, though, fantasize about that first big crush to distract her from her crappy marriage?" Julie asked in a near whisper.

Hesitantly, Ellen added, "Yes. I can understand her. Don't you ever wonder if you could've had more, more *something* in your life, if you'd just, I don't know," she exhaled slowly, "if you had just held on to things that matter more?"

Hannah sat up taller. "No, of course not. I made my bed and that's that. What you're saying seems to me like asking for trouble, glamorizing your regrets. People should *think* of their kids!" The other three women instantly pictured how Hannah regularly ran herself ragged "thinking" of her kids, anticipating their needs, and trying to bridge the gaps between their realities and her ambitions for them.

"At ease!" Ellen turned to Hannah, her eyes crinkling fondly. Most of the time, she loved Hannah's intensity. "None of us had this affair. This is a *book* we're talking about. I *do* think of my kids, almost constantly. All I said was that I have sympathy for Cl..."

BOOM. The nighttime hum and whir of the city surrounding them was suddenly silenced against an enormous, bomb-like explosion. Then the lights flickered, highlighting a deep, post-9/11 anxiety etched on all their faces.

Within seconds, tousled-headed Matt came shrieking, "Mom-mee, Mom-mee, Mommmeeee," down the stairs. He flew at Hannah, his streaming superhero cape affixed to his pajama top by small patches of Velcro near his shoulders. She jumped up and ran toward him, arms outstretched, as Simon charged in after their little son.

"Oh my God," Hannah cried, "what the hell was that?"

"Whoa!" Simon answered. Gently, he embraced his squirming son and hoisted him over his shoulder like a bag of garden mulch. "Easy there, buddy," he soothed, patting the child's back. "Buffalo's being hit with wind down-drafts, sort of like mini tornados. Not *mini* enough!"

Conversation was suspended as they opened the sliding doors at the far end of the room and surveyed the scene. Fierce wind had shorn a 30-inch diameter branch off a backyard silver maple and hurled it like a javelin onto the Feldman's deck. Plummeting from two stories, it slammed the weather-treated 2-by-4s with lethal force. Splinters and wood fragments were strewn about the yard in a wide chaotic swath. Weirdly twisted shards of metal lay halfway across the lawn, all that remained of the massive gas/charcoal grill and smoker that Hannah had given Simon for his last birthday. Shattered Adirondack chairs were blown into piles of sticks against the back fence. Everyone thought: thank God the branch hadn't smashed through the roof or into anyone's bedroom.

Hannah shivered, her breath coming in little gasps. Ellen put an arm around her from the left while Simon and Matt closed in on her right. Murmurs of awe and alarm gradually turned into words, as the winds quieted and the night settled back into more normal city sounds.

"Wow!" Maggie breathed. She wrapped her arms around herself and pulled her colorful vest tight across her heaving chest. "I've never seen anything like this! It was goddam amazing!"

"Lord!" Hannah ran her fingers through Matt's hair, gave Ellen a quick hug, then scooped her little son up into her arms. He was long and skinny, his legs dangling almost to her knees. She rubbed noses with him gently. "Don't worry, honey bunny, everything's going to be okay," she said softly. He giggled vigorously and rubbed noses back.

"Finally going to get something back on all those insurance premiums," Simon observed ruefully, shaking his head at the destruction of the wooden deck he had so proudly and painstakingly constructed just two years ago.

"Good stuff," concurred Ellen, whose husband, William, owned an insurance company.

After each had called or texted and been assured that their families were safe, they fortified themselves with another round of treats and added glasses of a soft, lemony chardonnay. The faux fire continued to crackle cheerily, but their mood was somber. Hannah again tucked Matt into bed and warned him against bedbugs. Simon, glass of scotch and ice in hand, retreated to his second floor office with a warm, "Good night, ladies. Drive carefully when you head out!" The *In Accord Club* settled back into their places in the family room.

Observing her worried friends, Julie asked, "Will it be too hard to pick up where we left off?"

"Do you even want to?" Maggie looked sympathetically toward Hannah. She was still in disbelief from witnessing so much devastation in such a fleeting flash.

"We're all together and we're safe. I stayed up until three last night to finish the damn thing. Please, let's try," Hannah persuaded. *She* didn't want to think about the devastation that had come so close to her home, her family.

After a collective sigh, Julie smiled. "Okay, I *liked* Claire, didn't you?"

Murmurs of agreement came from Ellen and Maggie.

Julie continued, "Didn't she feel like someone who could be here, one of us?"

"Yes," Hannah concurred, "but I have the most sympathy for the sister, Paula. How terrible to know that her brother-in-law is cheating on her sister and to be sworn to silence by him, and then to learn that her sister is cheating on her brother-in-law and to be sworn to silence on that side, too. She's really in some sort of emotional straight jacket."

Everyone nodded except Ellen. "That bothered me. I don't really think the author put in enough justification for Paula to keep her brother-in-law's running around a secret. No way would I hide something like that from *my* sister."

For a few moments, everyone sat quietly, listening for the wind or to their own thoughts. Hannah mused, "But then it would be a whole different story. If Claire is hit with the truth, she and Philip couldn't possibly just keep up their charade."

"I see it exactly like you do." Maggie added slowly. "And that's why the ending is so, so blah. No climax, no moment of truth and revelation. Just fraudulent lives, frittered away." She tossed her hands up into the air as if to throw their lives away.

Julie shook her head. "Yeah, no consequences. Aren't you bothered by that? They each betray the other, but their secret is safe with the afflicted sister as if the betrayals cancel each other out. But they don't, really. Even if you get away with it, don't you think it just diminishes everyone?"

They sat quietly again, thinking about marriage, and lies, and betrayals. The room was still.

Maggie broke the mood. "See, I thought that's all the author was saying. It was a little preachy. We don't have scarlet letters anymore, but both these characters have this guilt thing inside them and so they're not actually getting away with anything."

"That's it!" Julie concurred, biting into her brownie and licking the crumbs off her lips. "Do you think their lives could ever be free of the guilt, ever be joyful?"

Ellen coveted a bite of that brownie, too, but she held firm, except for the carbs in her glass of wine. Piously she said, "We'll never actually know. And anyway, I don't think their whole lives are necessarily wasted because of one moral lapse. Maybe they each learned something that they didn't *need* to take to the other. To me, they didn't seem all that burdened by their guilt." Remembering an article she had read recently that something in the neighborhood of forty percent of Americans cheat on their spouses over the course of their lifetime, Ellen thought of her husband, William, how secretly estranged she felt from him and how her friends might judge her if they knew her truth. There had been many soft, little misrepresentations, many she had convinced herself were not *that* bad, that weighed on her now.

Nodding, Hannah said, "All I know is, I wouldn't want to hear about it. I was glad the sister kept her trap shut." Julie gasped. Hannah added, "*Really*! If anyone discovers that Simon is…you know, *straying*, keep it to yourself. Maybe it'll go away without wrecking my life."

Now Julie sat forward, a slight flush creeping up her neck. "I know a little bit about this, you know?" She was gripping her own hands to keep them still. "I got a degree from the University of Cheating Scum Husbands. Eric thought I would never find out. But I *felt it,* even before I really did know. It's in the air between you. How you can really be in a relationship and not sense that there's something deeply wrong when one of you is lying to the other? And, Ellen, I don't know how you can call a year-long affair *one* moral lapse! But that's what happens in this book and it's just so unsatisfying. These two will take the secret of their betrayals to their graves, hypocrites forever. Doesn't it leave you feeling hollow? I cried when it was over."

Maggie and Hannah shook their heads, surprised by the breadth of Julie's admission. Ellen sympathized, "Oh, God, Jules! I'm so sorry it landed on you like that."

"Wow, I am sorry, too," Hannah offered. Julie was staring at her hands as Hannah continued, "But I don't think anyone truly understands the anatomy of anybody else's marriage, or knows what's going to be the deal breaker. So if my husband has a midlife fling, as long as he keeps it far, far away from me, I just don't want to know. I really don't want to end up divorced, period, end of sentence! And I don't think you can go forward if shit like that is out on the table."

"Do you think you can go forward if there's shit like that *under* the table?" Julie countered. Sometimes, although she would never say this out loud, it was so exasperating how Hannah knew *everything.* Hannah was a wonderful friend who would do anything for you, but she was only willing to see things her way.

"There's a world of difference between what we want out of a novel and what we want out of our lives," Ellen interjected, trying like a diligent social worker to reframe the controversy. "I like novels because you get to see characters wrestle with these issues. Which is why it's so unsatisfying when a book just pisses all its oomph away, no grand finale, no one changed for better or worse. It's too like life."

Holding the last of the stuffed mushrooms in her hand, Hannah agreed. "Life is definitely not a box of chocolates. It's got a lot in common with a litter box."

Maggie coughed. "Ick."

"Wait, I have an idea!" said Ellen. "We all liked the characters and the story right up until the end. How about we come up with a better ending? Let's rewrite the final paragraphs, or do a new epilogue, and make the story go where we each think it should. Make devious wife and spineless paramour and pathetic husband do the right thing, or a satisfying thing, or at least an interesting thing."

"You mean *us*?" Julie exclaimed. "That's kind of intimidating. Who's got time to write a better ending?"

"Agatha Christie wrote an entire murder mystery in six weeks, and Barbara Cartland dictated a romance novel in just three weeks," Ellen effused. "I read an article about them while I was waiting for my hair appointment last week. And anyway, I'm only talking about a couple of pages, maybe less! Come on, let's dust off our brain cells and see if they still work. It doesn't have to take much time. We'll set a limit. We're not trying to produce great literature. Just the bones of a more satisfying ending." She was really excited about her idea.

Nodding, Hannah grinned. "Could be fun. Not to be critics of each other's *writing* or anything, but how about making this our thing for next month, instead of reading a new novel?"

"I'm definitely no writer," Maggie was intrigued, "but it sounds interesting, different. I'll take a crack at it."

And so it was agreed. The *In Accord* selection for November would be a re-working of the ending of *Mariner's Cove* by each member of the club. Two pages or less, anything from a full narrative to an outline, or even a poem.

"And before we break up for the evening, I want to propose something," Ellen said as the women headed into the kitchen with their crumb-filled plates and empty wine glasses. "Let's all hop into my car and go to the Waterloo outlets early in November, do all our holiday shopping in one marathon day. And then have dinner somewhere really, really special." The idea appealed to all. They were busy, efficient women with little time for protracted holiday shopping. The excursion was set for Saturday, two weeks hence.

Maggie and Julie left but Ellen lingered, helping to wipe down counter tops and stack dishes. Hannah searched her cupboards for plastic containers for the leftovers. "I swear something lurks in here and eats the lids," she groused.

Grinning, Ellen quizzed her, "So, you really wouldn't want to know?"

"Huh?" Hannah sounded tired and puzzled.

"If Simon?"

"Good God, *that,* no! Not that I think Simon would, you know, but I most certainly would not want to be told. I mean, think about Jules and Eric. If he had been discreet, his affair would probably be over by now and her life wouldn't be such a mess. And her son would definitely be better off, financially at least."

Pulling on her jacket and fishing in her pocket for her car keys, Ellen replied, "Julie sounded pretty sure that there was a bomb in her marriage, even before it went off." She imagined what havoc a secret affair would wreak in her own marriage. It would be ugly. "Well, good night, Hannah. Thanks for the evening, loved the stuffed mushrooms. And I'm so sorry about your deck." She went out into the crisp night air and inhaled the spicy scents of torn hardwood, fir branches, and fresh rain.

5: Ellen

A single bulb shone dimly in the entry hallway when Ellen pulled into the narrow driveway of the tidy prairie-style house she shared with William, their sons, eighteen-year-old Cole and fourteen-year-old Jonathan, and the two stray cats that had condescended to take up residence with them a few years earlier. She could see light from Cole's bedroom flickering around his drawn window shade. He's probably on his phone or his computer or both, she thought, amazed at how much time her sons spent with their electronics. When she was in high school, girls talked for hours on the phone but not boys. Things had changed dramatically since instant electronic communication had conquered the world. Her own bedroom windows were dark. William was probably already deep in slumber, since he needed to be on the road early to drive to Cleveland, four hours away, for a meeting of insurance account managers. She had urged him to get there the night before, but considering the storm, was glad that he hadn't driven. Now that Palmer Insurance was his company, he tried to cut expenses in every way possible, and tonight was a rare time when she thanked fate for that. She hoped Jonathan was asleep although she couldn't see his window from the street. He was her night owl.

Cutting the car engine, Ellen switched off the lights and stepped out onto the crunchy gravel driveway. The night air felt cold and carried the sweet, pungent aroma of smoke from a wood fire lapping up logs in someone's nearby fireplace. Picturing the flames snapping and dancing in a darkened room, she climbed the steps to the front porch and headed for the porch swing. Romeo, the larger and bolder of the two cats, wove himself in and around her feet as she walked. It was one of his favorite dances. When she sat on the swing, he leapt into her lap with his lord-of-the-manor proprietary attitude.

"Mom?" Jonathan said quietly from out of the darkness.

Ellen's hands flew to her face, dumping Romeo from her lap while she gasped in surprise.

"Jonathan?"

"It's okay! Sorry to startle you, Mom. I was just waiting for you to get home." She could see him now, a slim shadow swaying in the ancient Amish bentwood rocker well beyond the faint light leaking out of the living room window. His long brown hair hung over his eyes.

When you can't look someone in the eye, you can't read his expression, and this was a sore point for Ellen with her younger son. "Everything okay?" she asked, feeling stupid. *Obviously not,* her brain answered itself sarcastically.

"Well, no," he paused. She held her fire. "I mean, everything's okay with me. But..."

Jonathan seemed to have lost whatever momentum brought him out to the porch to wait for her. Although they had a close and loving relationship, it was rare for him to seek her out like this, and Ellen felt an icy surge of parental alarm spread across her abdomen. Too many questions, fired too rapidly, were certain to silence him and he would disappear into himself like a deer into the dusk. So she sat still while Romeo haughtily repositioned himself, gently nipping her hands as she stroked his soft black fur.

"Something on your mind?" she finally asked, as if it was normal for Jonathan to sit in the dark for who knows how long waiting for her.

"Shit," he muttered in a voice slightly above a whisper.

Ellen cringed. She did not use f-bombs or say *shit* in the presence of either of her boys or anyone more than fifteen years her senior. She wished her son would observe the same boundary but she didn't want to drive him underground on a point of language.

"Shit," his voice rang out into the quiet night.

She took a deep breath and replied in her mildest voice, "Is that *shit* as in there's some shit happening that you want to talk about, or is that *shit* as in 'oh, shit, what am I doing here?'"

"Probably both," Jonathan answered, his own voice quiet and strained, "and if I tell you what I want to tell you, you can't ever let anyone know that I told you. *Ever.*"

Ellen's eyebrows shot up and she exhaled quickly. "Look, Jonathan, I'll honor that if I can, but if someone's in trouble, if one of your friends is, you know, into drugs or talking suicide or something…"

"Zoe's pregnant!" he blurted.

"*Oh my God,*" Ellen exclaimed. "*Fuck!* Zoe? Zoe Feldman? Does she even have a boyfriend? Jesus, Jonathan, she's *fourteen.*"

"I know how *old* she is," Jonathan responded in a wounded tone. "Jeez!"

"She hasn't told Hannah and Simon yet?" Ellen asked, recognizing the obvious as the words left her mouth.

"Nobody. She hasn't told anybody." Jonathan said, "And asked me not to rat her out, and I said I would never do that."

Jonathan and Zoe had been friends since infancy. Hannah and Ellen, already good friends from the childcare co-op they had joined with the older children, had been pregnant with them at nearly the same time. Since birth, Jonathan and Zoe had been combined as routinely as peanut butter and jelly during the joint outings and rituals that contoured their family's lives. Jonathan and Zoe were part of each other's worlds before they even walked or talked. Together they smeared face paints all over each other's small bodies, ate dieffenbachia leaves and had their stomachs pumped at Women's and Children's Hospital, invented games of magic, learned to ride Big Wheels, and print the alphabet. They were as close as siblings or even closer because they never needed to compete for parental attention and approval.

"Man," Ellen whispered. "Oh, man, poor you. That's a hell of a load to put on somebody." She paused, suddenly feeling very cold and very old. The questions began to tumble out despite her intention to hold them in check. "How far along is she? What is she planning to do? Hasn't she even told the boy?"

"I dunno, I dunno, and I *don't know*! I guess it happened at a big bonfire and party some kids had over the summer, July or August, maybe? There was a lot of beer, kegs, shots of stuff. Oh, you know. She was all pissed off at this boy she thought was her boyfriend. So then Rafael Cordero, you heard of him? The sophomore who's the star of the track team? He asked her to dance and they really hit it off. No big deal. But now she's pretty sure, I mean she hasn't had her," he stammered, not able to say the word "period" to his mother, "she hasn't, you know, that woman *thing*, since then."

"August, September, October," Ellen counted, "honey, she's just *got* to tell her folks, and the sooner, the better. She has a very narrow window…"

"She's not looking to climb out any windows, Mom. I think she doesn't want to say anything 'cause she thinks Hannah will try to make her get rid of it and she…"

"She wants to *keep* it?"

"It's her *baby*," Jonathan said with such gravitas it took Ellen's breath away. "And it's her decision. That's what they said in health class anyway. That nobody should force a woman to have an abortion."

Ellen was flooded with concern for her son, so young to be carrying the weight of Zoe's confidence. It was easy for her to picture the bonfire, the beer flowing (but not the shots), the kids laughing and smoking and swaying to music she would surely find offensive. Poor Zoe, resorting to the age-old tactic of trying to win one boy by flaunting the attention of another. And poor Jonathan, the guardian of this enormous secret and new champion of a woman's right to choose life.

"Jonathan. You're in a tough spot. How can I help you? What do you need?"

"I don't know," his voice cracked, "I just don't know."

"Hannah's been worried about Zoe," Ellen confided, bending a implicit contract between the mothers that they could talk candidly to one another about their children without fear that it would ever loop back to bite them. "Zoe was crying when I arrived for book group tonight and she looked miserable. Hannah said she's been exceptionally emotional and unhappy. I guess I could pick up from there and maybe suggest that she not just ascribe it to, you know, to Zoe's tendency to be dramatic."

"You *can't* say that she's pregnant!" Jonathan pleaded, his voice cracking again.

50

For a few minutes, they sat in silence. Desperately trying to sort through her thoughts, Ellen rubbed Romeo's head so vigorously that he started to purr in loud, short bursts: grrrr, grrrr, grrrrl, sounding like someone was trying to start a cranky chainsaw nearby. Jonathan snickered and Ellen exhaled. This was what cats were good for.

"Okay, I hear you. But she needs to see a doctor. It's not good for Zoe or for the baby." How quickly this went from an *it* to *the baby,* Ellen thought. "Honey, being pregnant is not a secret anybody gets to keep very long. Zoe's not being realistic, and I know your brain is telling you that, and I know you're worried about her. But she needs her parents to help her right now. A lot could go wrong."

Jonathan was quiet while Romeo's sonorous purr filled the air between them. Ellen shivered and sat very still, willing herself to find the right words.

"Please hear me out," she finally spoke. "I think I can get Hannah to see that Zoe's going through something without involving you but if I can't, then I need to tell her flat out. Zoe's lucky to have you as a friend, but the courageous thing to do is to take care of her when she's not thinking straight."

A rustling and a meow from the bushes told them that their other cat, Juliet, was lurking nearby, providing a small buffer from Ellen's lecture. Still, she had to squeeze her eyes closed and will herself to shut up. Her son needed her to be a mother, not a social worker. She knew that deep in her bones but she wasn't sure how to do it.

"But, but she said she would kill herself," Jonathan added.

"She also said she wants to keep the baby, and that's at odds with killing herself, don't you think?" Ellen instantly regretted adding the condescending *don't you think*. It was so easy to offend Jonathan with her parental self-righteousness.

"I don't know what to think," he spat out angrily.

Romeo roused himself in Ellen's lap, stretching to his full height, then resettling himself, his claws kneading into her thighs like tiny needles. He renewed his loud purring, so discordant with the tension hanging in the night air. Ellen's feet were numb with cold. Yet she sat very still, searching once more for the right words. Finally, tentatively, she spoke. "Okay, honey. Can you think about what I said, that Zoe needs help now, and I'll think about your predicament, and we'll talk more tomorrow? Maybe there's something we haven't thought of yet."

Silently, Jonathan stood and in the light she saw that he was wearing only a thin white t-shirt, his feet bare, his face looking gaunt and not at all just fourteen. "You must be freezing," she observed. "Can I make you something? A cup of hot tea or maybe some hot cocoa?"

"Nah, I'm going to bed." He started toward the door, then spun back toward her. "Thanks, though, thanks anyway." And in he went.

Ellen remained on the swing, scratching Romeo behind his ears and under his neck, giving him a whole body massage. It felt good to do something with her hands while the rest of her felt paralyzed. She wanted so much for this to be a bad dream. Hannah and Simon had been to hell and back when Hannah had accidentally become pregnant five years ago. Hannah did not want another baby, but Simon bitterly opposed abortion. He'd said that he would leave if she terminated the pregnancy and that he would sue for custody of Zoe and their older daughter, Beth. He promised to be an active caregiver for the new baby. He presented her with a list of all the chores he would do: taking time off from work for the pediatrician's appointments, walking the floors with the fussy baby at night, feeding and bathing and cleaning up and doing all the extra laundry. And now they have Matthew, whom they both adore, and Simon has kept his word.

Ellen imagined Zoe's pregnancy exploding within the Feldman family like a grenade. Weary sadness settled on her, and her hands stopped moving in Romeo's fur. She sat in the dark night, still and cold, waiting to see if her brain could map any kind of pathway through this terrain.

In her professional life, Ellen was the director of social work at Sisters of Charity Hospital, the oldest hospital in town. With her staff of four, her job consisted mostly of arranging for elderly patients to enter nursing homes, for accident victims to enter rehabilitation facilities, and for patients in kidney failure to commence dialysis. Crisis was so routine on the job that she barely recognized it. She managed a calm, measured approach to the pain and maddening details that accompany huge life-changing circumstances. Wives who promised to "never put their husbands in a place like that" found that they could not bathe or feed them at home after devastating strokes left their spouses paralyzed and drooling. They wept in Ellen's office while she supplied tissues and reassurance that the nearest nursing home provided wonderful rehabilitation services and that it was the right thing to do. She comforted the parents of teen accident victims who sat immobile in silent grief, afraid to take a deep breath lest they deprive their child of the one molecule of oxygen that would restore his brain function or give her back the use of her legs.

To all of her patients, Ellen described the facilities that could provide the level of care their loved one needed and patiently explained the benefits and limits of their health coverage. She listened and reassured and listened again with a semidetached efficiency that she wore like a feather-light cashmere wrap.

But no matter how well and kindly she handled the crises of strangers, when serious illness or disaster careened into her own world, Ellen always felt at first helpless, rudderless, and afraid. She loved Hannah like a sister and she loved Zoe like she were a daughter.

"Dear God, or whatever your name is," she prayed out to the universe, "dear Sweet Whatever, make this okay, somehow let this be okay."

She stood up, legs stiff and sore with the cold. Romeo meowed loudly in protest and little silvery Juliet appeared in the dim light, something limp and small hanging from her mouth. Normally, Ellen hated to be gifted with the remains of Juliet's hunts but tonight she found something comforting in the ordinariness of this small cat, presenting a dead vole to her mistress. The woman and her two cats entered the house, leaving the vole to stiffen alone on the dark steps.

6: Hannah

Hunched over his keyboard playing pinochle on the internet, Simon didn't notice as his wife of twenty years came softly up the stairs and paused in the doorway of their converted bedroom office. Something in the angle of his shoulders reminded Hannah of a turkey vulture settling in over road kill. *Too much Nat Geo*, she told herself, banishing the image. It was replaced by a warmer vision of Simon: Simon carrying Matt off to bed pretending to be his spaceship, or his camel, or his Zamboni, or whatever Matt wanted. Simon was a good father and a good man. Especially in the aftermath of Julie's sad outburst that night, she felt deeply lucky.

Matt's bedroom door was open, his yellow bus nightlight streaming a thin shimmer of light into the hall. Hannah slipped silently into his room and drew his superhero-decorated comforter back up over his small body, ever restless, even in sleep. His thick brown hair was a curly mass on his pillow and she touched it lightly, unwinding a small swirl of soft hair around her index finger. Watching him sleep, she felt a surge of maternal pride as fierce as it was irrational. To love a sleeping child is the perfect indulgence, she thought as she eased out of his room.

No light seeped out from under Zoe's bedroom door, but whether she was actually sleeping was anybody's guess. She often piled clothes up in front of her door to block the light, then spent the night listening to music on her iPod and texting her friends. Tonight, she had barely nibbled on her dinner, saying that she had eaten pizza at a friend's house after school. Hannah noticed a slight pallor on Zoe's face and briefly wondered if she was coming down with something. Their older daughter, Beth, was away on a field trip with her high school French club and would not be back until Sunday night. Hannah entered the office and stood behind Simon, rubbing his shoulders.

"Did Matt settle in okay?" she asked.

"Eventually, after *two* chapters of *The Wind in the Willows,* a promise that the windstorm was over, and a very elaborate ritual with the stuffed animals. We had to line them up according to his idea about how old they are. I wonder sometimes if he's going to be OCD when he grows up." Simon smiled, laugh lines crinkling his face and forehead. Hannah reached out and caressed a lock of his curly greying hair.

Like your father? She thought but she said, "God, I hope not. He'll go nuts in this world if he gets too obsessive or compulsive."

"I'm not really worried about it," Simon said lightly. "He's got a great life. Really bummed about the deck, though. I'll call insurance in the morning. How'd things end with your group?" he asked.

"Okay. You can come down, you know. You don't have to be holed up here like Mr. Rochester's hidden wife in *Jane Eyre*."

Simon gave a rueful laugh. "I actually was planning on coming down for a refill," he held his empty glass aloft, "but I heard some pretty intense voices and I didn't want to interrupt. And then I just got into this," he tipped his head toward his computer screen.

"Yeah, we had some issues with this book," she affirmed.

"What'd you read?"

"You wouldn't like it. It's called *Mariner's Cove*, a typical Alysen Tomas thing. Maybe less satisfying than most, or we're just getting too used to her narratives. It was about…" Hannah's voice trailed off momentarily. "Let me ask you something. Do you ever think about that girl you were involved with in high school, what was her name? Sally, Sue, or something?"

Without a second's hesitation he supplied, "Suzanna Monroe." Then he sighed deeply, involuntarily picturing the blond girl he had dated during his junior and senior years. Theirs' had been a wild ride, pockmarked by her insecurity and possessiveness. It had taken him years to venture anywhere near a committed relationship again, although he dated prodigiously. "I hadn't given her a thought in decades. Why?"

"Oh, tonight's book selection was about these two people, unexpectedly reunited at their high school reunion. They've each married someone else but off they go and have affairs, trying to recoup some of that high school pizzazz, or whatever we old dogs fantasize we had in those reckless, pretty years. And they sort of get away with lying about it, which is what really pissed everybody off."

"Ha!" Simon laughed. He swiveled around in his computer chair and taking both of Hannah's hands in his, smiled up at her. "You're the only reckless, pretty girl for me," he said and kissed her ring finger. Then he swiveled back. "I'm going to finish this game and then I'll be right in."

Class dismissed, Hannah thought, leaving the room. But at least he didn't say "You're the only reckless *old dog* for me." In their bathroom, she was pleased to see that the orchid Beth gave her a year ago had finally bloomed this evening, two of its tiny white-fisted buds now open in an intricate hood of color. She had babied this plant impatiently, waiting for it to either bloom or get ugly enough to toss out. It was stunningly beautiful, delicate, its white petals fanned out over the palest peach stamen.

She adjusted the hot water in the shower to a point just below scalding and stripped off her clothes, shuddering with relief as her bra landed on the floor. Stepping into the shower and slowly rotating in its hot stream, Hannah tried to let the tension recede from her shoulders by envisioning the tide going out. She filled her hands with coconut-scented body soap and tried to massage her own shoulders. After a few moments, she became aware that she was as stiff as a palace guard, reviewing the evening self-critically.

For her, *In Accord* book nights were normally about stimulating conversation shared with good friends. But when it was her turn to host, and despite her silent lecture to herself to stop being so compulsive, she felt compelled to serve homemade gourmet food and to clean her house until every surface gleamed. She hadn't been delayed at school…she had been home early, cleaning, but she had wanted to be perfectly ready when her friends arrived. Further, she felt foolish for saying she wouldn't want to know if Simon had an affair. From *what* contrary corner of her psyche had that emerged? Of course she would want to know! It was an inane position that, once taken, she had to defend because she had said it. Maybe spending her days around middle-schoolers was rubbing off on her. She lathered the shampoo into her scalp, vigorously trying to drive the thoughts away.

A blast of cool air startled her. Simon entered the bathroom, drawing the door closed and locking it behind him. "Could you share some of that hot water?" he asked, adding his flannel shirt to the small heap of clothes already on the floor. Hannah was surprised into rare wordlessness. Simon didn't normally like to make love when the children were home, even in the relatively insulated space of their shower. Silently, she invited him in, stepping out of the direct stream of the showerhead so he could get wet too. Simon moved in, soaped his hands, and began to wash her, beginning with the fine bones in her cheeks, then moving on to her neck and shoulders. Although his hands were large and strong, he had the deft touch of a masseur. This time, Hannah really released the tension in her muscles without needing to conjure images of tides.

When the sex was over, steam from the shower filled the bathroom, curling the seams of the wallpaper away from the walls. Tenderly, Simon dried her off, then got out, pulled on the frayed terry robe that hung on a hook behind the door, and padded back to his computer. Hannah lingered in front of the mirror, smiling at herself. Why is it so much more fun when it's not expected, she pondered. It's the same basic set of moves. She thought about *Mariner's Cove* and wondered if what Claire had really needed was to have a husband like Simon, someone who unexpectedly slips into the shower. She pulled on her warmest, softest flannel pajamas and a pair of socks, but she couldn't bear the thought of cold sheets. Plugging her hair dryer in to the outlet near the bed, Hannah turned it on high and angled it between the sheets on her side until its little burner emitted a faint, cooked odor and she had created a toasty pocket for herself. Then she slithered in between the sheets, warm and relaxed. *Delicious*, she thought, as she descended effortlessly into sleep.

It seemed only seconds later that she was climbing a ladder, its rungs slippery and mossy, up and up and up. She was high over a rocky ravine with an ocean crashing in the distance. Wind howled and shook the ladder. There were emergency vehicles and screaming voices and though she scrambled as quickly as she could she seemed unable to make any progress. Every time she stepped up a rung, it gave way and she ended up exactly in the same spot.

"Hannah, Hannah!" Simon was shaking her gently from his side of the bed, "Hannah, the phone. Answer the phone!" Opening her eyes the tiniest slit, she looked at her clock. The phone, inches from her head on her nightstand, was ringing insistently. There was no ladder she realized as sleep fled and the panic every parent feels when the phone rings in the night coursed like ice water through her veins. It was 3:30.

"Shit!" She fumbled on the nightstand and finally picked up her cell. "Hello, hello?" she croaked, her voice coated roughly with sleep.

"Oh, Mom, thank God, you're there," Beth cried.

"Honey? Of course I'm here, where else would I be? What's wrong? What's going on?" Hannah was as awake as if she'd just finished her third cup of coffee. Simon sat up and switched on the bedside lamp, a mask of alarm settling over his face.

"I'm okay, don't freak out, okay? It's just, oh God, mom, I'm sooo sorry. We got, some kids and me, we got caught…" she hesitated, sobbed and hiccupped, then continued "…drinking and now they're making us call our parents to come and get us because we can't stay on the trip."

"What?" Hannah couldn't believe her ears.

There was silence on the other end.

"What's going on?" Simon questioned from his side of the Kid Divide.

Beth sobbed into the phone. "Please come get me."

"But you're in Quebec!" Hannah objected. "Dammit to hell, Beth, you've *got* to be kidding. You were *drinking?* We're supposed to come get you, when? Now? It's the middle of the night, for God's sake. You're 600 miles away."

"I know, I know," Beth wailed so loudly that Simon could hear her, too. "It's so unfair, they're only doing this to the ones who told the truth."

All three of the Feldman's paused in the inky, enveloping darkness. The inconvenient reality stared back.

"Calm down," Hannah switched on her school principal's commanding voice. "Calm down and tell me what happened."

"Well, (hiccup) the drinking age up here is 19 and (hiccup) they don't even ask for proof and kids heard that we could get served in the bars."

"I can't believe you actually just said that to me!" Hannah interrupted. "I thought this was a supervised trip. Where were the chaperones?"

"They gave us one free night, to explore the city. They always do. And kids always go get served. I don't know why they're being so mean about it this year. But we did sign that pledge card, and you did too, remember, the one about no drugs, no alcohol, the school has the right to send you home if you break the rules?"

"Damn! Of course I remember. Beth, I just don't believe this! Are you drunk? What did you actually do?" Simon slapped himself dramatically on the forehead, groaned, and flopped back onto his pillow.

"I'm not *drunk*." Beth protested righteously. "I only had *one* beer. It was sooo expensive and I didn't have enough Canadian money, but Rachel, she had lots of money, lots of money, and she drank a lot!" Beth paused and Hannah waited, mentally reviewing every annoying thing Beth's best friend, Rachel, had ever done. It was a long list, stretching back to first grade when Rachel had cut random locks of Beth's wavy, long, brown hair right down to nubs on her scalp. Beth had the haunted, unkempt look of a street urchin for months.

"When we got back to the hotel, she was kind of staggering and I tried to get her into our room, but," Beth hesitated again. Hannah spoke not. Her lungs rose and fell against the tight muscles surrounding her rib cage.

Whimpering, Beth plowed ahead with her story. "Okay, so she threw up! Okay? She puked all over the corridor and she woke up some of the other hotel guests, and it was a big mess, with them calling the front desk and bitching about us and then the teachers got called and they were having their own party so they were really pissed off, really, really pissed off and they made me call you. Rachel's parents are on their way but they decided I had to call you, too. And there were some boys. Will Felton and Davey Johansson, they got caught, too. I am so sorry."

Hannah was well aware of the policy. She had been a member of the school district team that devised it after a group of teens got spectacularly drunk during the French Club trip five years ago. They had actually stopped traffic in Quebec doing a cheerleader routine in the road, making the Quebec evening news. The district had threatened to ban all field trips. Now, each parent was responsible for retrieving his or her own miscreant child in the event the "no banned substances" contract was violated. It was quietly violated every year, but this was the first flagrant problem since the new policy went into effect, replete with a mandatory parent/student meeting. There would be an administrative hearing. Beth would most likely be suspended. Whether or not this would go on her transcript was a nightmare for another night.

"Is Mrs. Herndon there?" Hannah asked as mortification began to well in her.

"Mom? I'm really sorry," Beth repeated miserably, fishing for absolution.

"Is Mrs. Herndon there?" Hannah repeated each word with staccato precision, each a bullet. Being the preacher's kid, the teacher's kid, the coach's kid, or the principal's kid was no picnic, she knew. Those children's behavior and performance were constantly held to a higher standard and a keener scrutiny than others'. Nonetheless, she was a principal and this incident would be a source of glee to that faction of her teachers who felt that she was too permissive, too soft on students. "Look where it's got her," they would whisper smugly, and would feel justified in their harsh responses to students with attitudes or behavior problems that made them easy targets.

"Get Mrs. Herndon now, Beth. I need to know where to pick you up," she said flatly.

Simon lay still, his eyes wide open, his face a glum mask. He had deduced the main outline of the story. His initial fear drained away, replaced by a surge of anger and frustration. He, too, felt that Hannah was too permissive and that their oldest daughter had lived a consequences-free life for far too long. Now one of them would have to drive to Quebec in the middle of the night, and the whole carefully orchestrated schedule pieced together for tomorrow, as it was for each day, would have to be reshuffled.

As one of the architects on a huge project to repurpose an old industrial building into trendy downtown condos for medical students, Simon's days were completely booked. It must fall on Hannah's plate to do the long drive. But it would fall on him to juggle at this end. There was no way for one parent to cover all the Feldman family's bases. In times of stress, Simon often conjured memories of his grandmother, an amazingly upbeat refugee from the violent anti-Semitism of 1930s Lithuania. She was always ready with a pithy Yiddish saying for whatever ailed one. About this event, she would most certainly intone, "Der mensch trakht un Gott lahkht (Man plans and God laughs)."

7: Maggie

The Brinkman family moved out of Buffalo after
Maggie's successful treatment, five years ago, for acute myeloid
leukemia. Doctors said that she was "fortunate," as her disease
was discovered early and she lived within spitting distance of
Roswell Park Cancer Institute, one of the premier cancer treatment
hospitals in the country. For her it had started with vague
symptoms that she and her friends ascribed to other, mundane
maladies. For a month or two, she felt deeply fatigued – but they
were all tired, wasn't that their normal state of being? When she
noticed that she was bruising more easily than usual, they
wondered if her diet was missing some essential nutrient. Night
sweats finally sent her to her doctor, thinking she was going into
early menopause. Then the tests came back positive for leukemia.

Maggie had waited until her friends were all together to
announce her diagnosis. They had been confused about what to
say or do. It was as if her illness had breached some implied
contract (*mothers should be spared devastating diseases while
their children are small*) and it had taken them aback. But soon
they sprang into action, accompanying her to chemo treatments,

making meals, knitting skull caps, and recording playlists to help her pass the hours.

Even with all that support, after the chemo was declared a success, she had not felt that she belonged in the home where she first confronted her version of the grim reaper, a mocking nightmarish figure that sneered at her will to live. The pace and noise and edginess of city living were overwhelming. When a car door slammed somewhere nearby, she jumped. The distant scream of a siren triggered a terrifying parade of mental images as she immediately conjured peril to her family. She pictured her husband, Brian, an assistant district attorney, caught in some weird courtroom hostage saga. Or she became terrified for her children. If they were at school, she imagined an angry boy with an arsenal strapped to his gawky body. If they were in transit, maybe a drunk blew through a traffic signal and t-boned their car.

She recognized that her hyper-vigilance was illogical and unhelpful, but she felt powerless to turn it off. Even though it meant pulling the children out of their comfortable schools and imposing a much longer commute on Brian, she pleaded for a quiet new home somewhere in the country where she could have peace in which to heal.

"I've found your dream house!" Brian jauntily announced one afternoon. He had discovered a beautifully maintained, classic American foursquare house for sale by its owner. Dating to 1899, it sat on a six-acre parcel just outside of East Aurora, 20 miles out of town. The house came with a two-story barn of the same era, a remnant of the property's days as part of a large dairy farm. Built of hand sawn oak, the barn had massive maple beams, stalls for horses, and a ten-by-twenty-foot granary on the second level. With its winding little brook, stands of firs and hardwoods, and a field that was being maintained by a neighbor (who harvested the hay in payment), the place offered the perfect safe haven for Maggie's physical and emotional recovery.

The Brinkman children, Leah and Rob, were not on board in the beginning. Their worlds had been upended by their mother's cancer, and cancer treatments, and both bitterly opposed the move. "Why can't we just get back to being *normal*?" Leah had pleaded. "It's not fair that we have to go through anything else!" That old barn, with stalls for horses, proved fortuitous. As a reward for being good sports about the move to the country, the children were promised riding lessons and – if they showed aptitude and good attitude – the chance to own their own horses within the year.

It was love at first sight when Maggie viewed the house. Charmed by the idea that it had once been part of a prosperous farm, she adored its unapologetic squareness and the regal way it owned the center of the big rectangular yard. It predated landscape companies, curvy walkways, or ornamental shrubbery. Its closets and bedrooms were small, utilitarian spaces, but the front porch gave her a lovely perch from which to watch all the creatures that lived at the margins of her new property. There was a family of foxes at a far corner by a thick stand of pines. One blue heron soared overhead every evening at six like clockwork, his huge graceful wings seemingly oversized for his taut, football-sized body. Small bands of deer grazed companionably together, hawks patrolled the daytime skies, flocks of turkeys meandered through, and she found a humane wildlife management company that was able to evict the skunk from under the porch.

In their first months there, the Brinkman children struggled to find their niche in their new rural school district, but eventually Leah found a home within a clique of theatre club kids and Rob made friends with some soccer and video-game-playing boys down the road. After a rough few months, both children settled in. For Maggie, the house's only drawback was that it added thirty minutes to her drive to or from the city. After about eight at night, she required at least one cup of caffeinated coffee in order to keep her eyes open on the drive home. The caffeine strategy was effective for getting her home but charged a stiff tariff later, as her mind raced and the wee hours dragged.

And so it was that at three in the morning following the book club meeting, Maggie was wide awake but heavy-lidded, sitting in her living room surrounded by magazines, yet too tired to actually read. She switched on the television, but its blare and banal programming seemed to mock intelligent life. Her copy of *Mariner's Cove* had been added to a small pillar of books she intended to shelve someday soon and she reached for it idly. She had been swept up by the warmth of group approval to Ellen's proposal that they each rewrite the ending, but now she was full of misgiving.

She wasn't a writer. She had been a court reporter before the cancer. She was good at puzzles and at anticipating where a particular line of questioning might lead. Scrounging around for a blank sheet of paper, she instead found a partial list of home repair projects Brian had left on the coffee table. "Clean gutters," he had penned, "replace rotten fascia on west side, get gravel for driveway." Its reverse side was blank. Maggie decided to treat *Mariner's Cove* like a puzzle, reducing it to formulas each with an inevitable ending. She wrote on the back of Brian's list:

Claire (gets divorced) + Charles (gets divorced) =

Equals what? She tried to picture an answer. Maybe equals Claire + Charles together. Happily? Miserably? What made sense? What did they deserve?

She tried another formula:

Claire (secret revealed) + Philip (secret revealed) =

She sat for a while, pondering possibilities and finally wrote "murder???"

A writer of murder mysteries might be able to make a case for homicide but did *she* think either crime deserved murder? Obviously not. Maybe instead they could go away on some faith-based couple's retreat and recommit to each other?

Maggie sighed. Claire was going to end up with Philip, her current husband; with Charles, her high school lover; with someone totally new; or alone. She would be happy or sad or a little of each. Or Philip could become a hero, save residents of a nursing home from a raging fire caused by outdated wiring, and then sell the rights to the movie, and Claire would fall in love with him for the first time and life would seem to finally begin. Maggie smiled, pleased at her Pollyanna ending. Then a new finale presented itself, unbidden: Claire would get cancer. Maggie winced and then wept, engulfed in sorrow. Could she actually write about someone having cancer? Would it bare more of her soul than she cared or dared to reveal?

Before the cancer, Maggie was open, optimistic, and friendly, and she thought that most people were basically the same. But in the days and weeks and months of treatment that followed, when her family's future hung on the results of her bone marrow biopsy, when life's capriciousness dragged her around like a child's rag doll, she observed that, actually, most people kept their real selves tightly corseted. It seemed to her like they were all in role, mouthing their scripts and hoping to avoid whatever private holocaust everyone secretly dreaded.

She came to believe that all people had something – some secret bargain with their god or goddess that kept them in fear of living their own lives fully. "Please spare me *that* and I'll promise to always do *this,* " they would think as they hit up their neighbors for the March of Dimes (*dimes! Ha*!) or put money in the Salvation Army beg boxes. "Spare my baby from SIDS and I'll raise him to be a good Catholic, no, a perfect Catholic, no, a priest!" Would that be good enough? "Don't give me MS and I'll use my strength to run the Parent/Teacher organization at school." "Don't let my husband see the credit card bill and I'll never ever buy another unnecessary designer purse. And I'll give to charity, I will, next month, when I get out of debt." She sat still in the dimly lit room, her face haggard. "Above all," she knew all too well that most women bargained, "Don't let me get breast cancer. Keep your scalpels away from my tits."

Maggie had a full remission from the leukemia but was drained in body and spirit by the powerful chemicals that saved her life. After three years, she'd begun to feel her strength return. She was taking a watercolor class and planning to do her own wallpapering in the kitchen of her new old house, when tests revealed that she had carcinoma in situ: breast cancer. Within two weeks, she was in surgery, undergoing a partial mastectomy, to be followed by a five-year course of low-dose chemotherapy. Maggie felt as though she had summoned every ounce of energy of muscle and mind to scratch and climb out of a contaminated well. She had reached its lip only to slide a thousand feet backwards into a stinking, tarry pit. She was nauseous. She resented her healthy friends. She could hardly look at her body. Her friends sent cards and asked her to call if she needed anything, but she never called them. Hannah had a preschooler and a fulltime job, Julie was struggling with a bitter divorce, and they all seemed less positive and upbeat. She didn't want anyone's sympathy, and she couldn't tolerate being told about the benefits of "keeping a positive attitude."

Only Ellen came regularly, whether Maggie felt up to seeing her or not.

And so, early one warm spring afternoon about six months after Maggie's treatment for breast cancer had begun, Ellen showed up unexpectedly.

"Why aren't you working?" asked Maggie.

"It's a beautiful day! I called in sick so I could come and see you. Come, let's go down to your barn."

Maggie rarely went there, where the swooping barn swallows, creaking boards, musty smells, and colossal spider webs made her feel like an interloper in an alien world. The concept of buying horses for Rob and Leah had crashed on the reality that horses require prodigious amounts of care and maintenance. After brief stints taking riding lessons and working at a nearby stable, both kids said, "Thanks, but no thanks" to having their own animals. But since they kept no livestock in it, the barn became a storage facility for the bulky things they weren't ready to throw out, like old chairs ("maybe someone will need this someday"), tires, and the debris from Brian's various house-rehabbing projects.

Maggie couldn't imagine why Ellen would want to go there but Ellen was determined. She had scoped it out in advance and decided that the granary, a room once used for storing oats and other grains to add to the cattle's feed, was going to be fine for her purposes. She removed an old patchwork denim quilt and a neon green sack from her car and carried them into the granary. She spread the quilt across two bales of hay, creating an inviting bench in the speckled light seeping through the slats in the door.

From the bag, she withdrew two small bottles of Chardonnay with screw-off caps. "We'd never serve this swill at a dinner party," she apologized, "but it'll help if your throat objects." Then she produced a perfectly rolled joint.

It had been almost twenty years since Maggie last inhaled. "I hear this stuff is a great help with the nausea," Ellen said, holding the joint and admiring its tight, perfectly cylindrical contour. "And if it doesn't make the nausea go away, it might make you not care as much and it will certainly boost your appetite."

"But where did you get that?" Maggie whispered in amazement.

"Cole," Ellen said matter-of-factly, referring to her son, a high school sophomore.

"Cole? You can't be serious. You're getting dope from your son?"

"Oh," Ellen snickered. "Dear, no! Cole *left* a baggy in the back pocket of his jeans when he tossed them in the wash. Sad to say, I still go through everything since the boys were toddlers leaving crayons and God-knows-what in their pockets. So, there I was, with his nice little stash in my hand. Any mother would have to confiscate it. Told him I was going to dispose of it. And that's exactly what we're doing!"

"Shit, Ellen, does Cole have a drug problem?" Maggie's daughter, Leah, and Cole were still friends from their childhood playgroup days.

Smiling broadly, Ellen replied, "I don't think so. I don't see it in any of his other behaviors. He says it's a once-in-a-while thing and he understood that I had to take it and that the parental line is that he is not to do it anymore. Frankly, I just hope he has the sense to be discreet."

"Ellen? Aren't you upset?" Maggie was incredulous.

"Nah. I think it's a mistake to make a federal case out of a kid smoking some weed. I went over the ways this is not a good thing for him... clouds his judgment, his father would freak out, yadda, yadda..."

"Will doesn't know?" Maggie interrupted.

"No! No way! Will would..." Ellen hesitated, a strained look clouding her face. "Anyway, let's see this as Cole's gift to us. If it helps with your nausea, that will be a great bonus. Obviously, I won't get more from Cole, but I have a friend at work who can be a regular source."

"Jeez," Maggie said softy. "Jeez." She shook her head and stared incredulously as Ellen produced a pack of matches printed with the colorful logo of a local restaurant. The match flared briefly and produced an acrid sulfur smell as she lit the joint, then snuffed the match in the lid of a rusty 10-gallon milk can. She drew the smoke deeply into her lungs and held her breath, her eyes watering. When she coughed, still holding her mouth shut tight, smoke escaped from the edges of her lips like steam from a boiling kettle. Exhaling and smiling broadly, she extended the joint to Maggie, turning its lit tip in toward the palm of her hand and holding the other end pinched between her thumb and index finger. Maggie reached her right hand out reflexively, a habit she had quit enjoying twenty years ago coming back as easily as skipping rope.

The two women smoked half the joint, drank the wine, and sat in a state of quiet reflection. Ellen found herself watching with acute fascination as dust motes rose and fell like microscopic swallows in the shafts of falling sunlight. She didn't know how long she had been staring when Maggie began to giggle, a girlish sound so unfamiliar that it startled them both. Suddenly, Maggie stood and raised her arms above her head and twirled in the dusty granary, her feet tracing out dance steps she learned as a girl in ballet class. Her laugh grew stronger, more centered in her belly, more undisciplined, lustily echoing off the walls in the small room.

"What?" Ellen asked. "What's funny?"

"Life!" Maggie cried. "All of it. The things that happen, the things that don't happen, how hard we try to nail it down, how fucking slippery it is. It's hysterical, don't you think?" She twirled again. "Oh, I wish I had a long, full skirt. I would look so good dancing in a skirt." She was wearing a pair of old, stained jeans, the kind that proclaim *I don't give a rat's ass how I look today*.

"You could buy a skirt," Ellen said in her practical mom voice, which made Maggie laugh more robustly. "We could," Ellen repeated reasonably. "We could drive into town right now and go to that funky little import store and buy you a pretty, flowery skirt with a nice elastic waist." It was at first insulting when her suggestion was greeted with great whoops of laughter but then she pictured the two stoned, middle aged women in the store, pawing through racks of skirts, all of them probably too tight or too teeny-bopperish.

Maggie's laughter leapt across the room, like lightning in the sky, and snapped Ellen up the way really infectious laughter sometimes can. Ellen burst into a deep-throated laugh. She rose unsteadily to her feet and swayed for a few moments. Then she found her balance and turned slowly, feeling slightly dizzy and utterly free in the warm haze of the wine and the weed. Mirroring Maggie, she raised her arms over her head and twirled slowly around the tiny room. They danced together for several minutes, grinning widely.

Suddenly tears were streaming down Maggie's cheeks. "Oh, Ellen," she cried. "Oh, God. Oh, my God." She sat heavily on the quilt and wrapped her arms around herself, sobs rising in her throat.

"What? What is it?" Ellen quickly sat close and placed a hand on Maggie's knee.

The barn creaked lightly while pigeons cooed in the high, empty loft.

"I'm so scared," Maggie finally whispered, choking back sobs.

"Tell me," Ellen invited soothingly.

"There are so many things. When you get cancer, there are things you see about life that you never let yourself notice before, things you want to do, things you find you care about, time you regret losing. How can I die now? I don't know how to think about not being."

"I know, I know," said Ellen in an attempt to soothe her. "I would be terrified. I think that's why," she hesitated, struggling for the right words.

Maggie finished her sentence, "That's why everyone abandons you?"

Ellen was startled. "Hey! I'm here."

"Yeah, but when was the last time we talked? Really talked? All people want to hear is that I'm *okay*, that my white cell count is good, that I'm keeping a positive attitude. They want to tell me that they admire me for being brave. I'm not *brave!*" Maggie spit out the word with disdain.

Pulling back from her friend, Ellen frowned.

"Do you have any idea how shitty it is to be made to feel guilty for not having the right feelings, not bouncing around like you're on the Good Attitude Trampoline? I'm telling you, Ellen, if you want to know who your friends really are, all you have to do is get cancer. Then you find out who your friends are!"

The words hung in the air, angry and heavy with accusation. Maggie covered her face with her hands and cried softly.

Ellen removed her own hand from Maggie's knee and sat utterly still, aware of a battle within herself. She was there, wasn't she? She even brought Maggie weed. She had been there for her all along. It wasn't fair to be accused of abandonment. It wasn't fair! BUT. But it was also true that she never wanted to be at this cold, raw intersection where you stood in the center of your own living, breathing, doomed body and looked death in its face. She despised being powerless, unable to defuse Maggie's rage and the terror of annihilation that lay coiled under it. So she'd brought dope hoping she and Maggie could have some fun, *lighten up, for Christ's sake.* It seemed so self-righteous, in retrospect. Where did she get off, trying to con Maggie into a better humor? Why couldn't she let Maggie have her fear, her anger, her pain? She had no business trying to take it away. Okay, she resolved, shut the hell up and listen.

Ellen put her arm around Maggie and gently pulled her close. "I *am* here," she said. "And I'm sorry if I've guilt-tripped you about anything. It sucks. This sucks."

Maggie mumbled, "Never mind," but she did not pull away. Ellen felt her friend's shoulder muscles lose some of their tension.

"I don't know what to say," Ellen continued, "I'm scared of what this means, of losing you if you really don't get better this time..."

"Oh, God, I can't go through this. I can't stand any more treatments. I can't stand to set foot in another hospital! My arm is not a fucking pincushion! Did you know that that's something *else* you can do wrong, you can be a 'hard blood draw'?" Maggie flung her arm out from the elbow and stared disdainfully at the thin blue veins throbbing beneath her translucent skin.

"Patients at the hospital have told me how lousy that is. Are you..." Ellen started to respond to Maggie's indignant question.

"I am a world-class, fucking hard *blood draw*. The nurses, they look at me and they don't say it outright but their expressions are like, 'Oh, crap, we are sorry to see her coming.' My veins are tiny and they roll away from the needles, or blow out right away, and they have to keep sticking me to get enough blood and it's a nightmare and it hurts like hell."

Ellen envisioned Maggie sitting in a hospital lab, her arm stretched out on a yellow wooden slat, her face tense, a hunter-green vinyl ribbon wrapped tightly around her bicep, forcing the blood to pool in her veins so she could give some of it away. "I'd hate that," she said from the depths of her being.

Maggie searched Ellen's face then, looking her over as frankly as if she were jewelry for sale. She could faintly smell the sweet botanical perfume of the products Ellen used to keep her hair shiny and straight. She saw tiny crow's feet etched at the corners of wide, hazel eyes that were completely open. Ellen's face was sad and sorrowful, her eyebrows knit together so tight that they puckered her forehead, but her full lips were slack. She was wordless, yet her expression spoke of a loving openness that

Maggie hadn't felt since the early days of her first battle with cancer, when the word *leukemia* had swept the friends all away.

"You really are here," Maggie said.

"Yes," Ellen answered, "for what it's worth. But, I honestly don't know what it's like for you. All I know is you seem angry most of the time and that's something I hide from. I'm sorry."

"I'm sorry, too. I miss just being one of the girls, you know? I hate how cancer singles you out, gives you this extra load and you either have to minimize how heavy it is or pretend carrying it hasn't changed you. But it does change you, it reaches into every corner of your life."

"I don't want to lose you, changed or not changed." Ellen said simply. "You do what you need to about being a cancer victim. I'm with you."

"God, I wish," Maggie said and then her voice trailed off. She was fingering her wedding ring nervously.

Ellen noticed but sat still, determined not to take over the conversation.

"The really big problem is Brian." Maggie sighed. "We disrupted everybody and moved out here so I could heal in the peaceful country, and then I ended up sick again. He's just not dealing with it."

"Not dealing with it *how?*" Ellen invited.

"This could be the dope talking, but I think he's pissed that I'm sick again. He won't even use the word *cancer*. He really gets mad if I hint that I'm down or scared."

"Whoa, that sucks."

"No kidding."

Again they sat and listened to the barn sounds, the insects buzzing, birds chirping, building creaking. Human silence wrapped them both in their own reflections. Ellen found herself breathing deep yoga breaths as she removed, brick by brick, the walls she had erected to protect herself from feeling powerless. After all, she *was* powerless. It was that simple.

At the same time, Maggie was allowing her perception of being stranded alone on an iceberg to melt away. She wasn't *really* lost and she wasn't *really* freezing. A flood of joy rose in her throat, as unbidden and surprising as her earlier flood of grief had been. She started to wrap her arms around Ellen but at that moment, Ellen rose from the hay bale they were sitting on and pulled off her sandal. Maggie slipped unceremoniously to the floor as Ellen whipped the sandal at a small brown mouse that was scurrying across the floor.

"Damn!" Ellen cried, "Missed him, how could I miss him?" He disappeared into a crack in the floor boards.

"Awwwh, I'm glad you missed. He wasn't hurting anything." Maggie reached for the hand Ellen offered and scrambled to her feet. "I'm okay, I'm okay!"

"Good." Ellen shook her shoulders. "Mice! I hate the way they snoop around, noses twitching. They chew everything and poop all over the place. Ick! We had a cabin at Chautauqua when I was a kid and that mouse smell always made me gag!" Animated, she paced the room using her foot to disturb every clump of hay that might conceal a mouse. Dry straw gave up its sweetly musty odor amid little puffs of dust. But the mice had fled.

"Aren't you the great hunter? I thought you opposed killing things for the joy of it!" Maggie laughed. Ellen stopped pacing and looked at herself, one foot bare, indignation pouring out of her.

"My God, you're right, what am I doing? It's a *barn*. There's probably thousands of mice in here. I just freaked a little."

"Yes you did," Maggie teased. "But, hey, I'm suddenly crazy hungry! Did you remember to pack any goodies to go with the wine and…"

"On it!" Ellen opened the neon green bag and extracted brownies, sharp cheddar cheese cubes, and apple slices. She placed them carefully on a Santa-themed paper plate. "Here you go. Sorry about the plate. It's all I could find."

"What a feast! I'm starved! Famished! And is there more of that weed?" Maggie's mood was many shades lighter and brighter.

Ellen reached back into her bag. "A little."

They took a few more hits on the joint and talked freely of Maggie's cancer treatments, the nurses she liked, the ones she found to be severe or detached, and the dietary restrictions she struggled to observe. Then they moved, sometimes laughing, sometimes crying, through the litany of things they held in common: children in high school, in-laws with chameleon-like expectations, strange dreams. But one arena Maggie was wholly unwilling to reenter was the way her husband felt and acted about her disease.

After that afternoon, Ellen supplied Maggie with a quarter ounce of marijuana every month. On the days when Maggie felt sick or depressed or particularly angry, she would slip down to the granary and light up. She kept a sketchpad and a diary hidden behind a few bales of hay. Sometimes she needed to inhale only a single deep hit to find her center again. Sometimes, she smoked the entire joint.

She lived in mild trepidation that her husband or children would discover her secret. In idle moments, she sometimes visualized how they might react. Brian would be aghast, lecturing about her lawlessness and pointing out the potential for her to get arrested and their lives to be dismembered. He would also fret that she was a terrible example for the children. But she would counter that their children's values were already formed and she and Brian could do little now except enjoy the show.

Leah would feign disdain, seeing her mother as patently "too old for this kind of shit," although sometimes Maggie wondered if she detected a hint of that distinctive pot bouquet on Leah's clothes as they turned up in the family laundry basket. Her daughter was doing well in school and Maggie liked Leah's friends, so she made an informed decision to not rock any boats unnecessarily. Robbie might express some dismay, protective as he was, but he would be won over quickly by her explanation that it helped with the nausea. She could point out that this behavior was considered legal in California and many other states. Brian would be nonplussed by that argument. "It's illegal in New York, end of discussion," he would say. "I'm an assistant district attorney and if you get arrested having drugs in my house, everything goes to hell." *Well! It's my house, too,* Maggie thought defiantly.

On this night, so late it was nearly dawn, Maggie felt that she would never get to sleep on her own and that she could not function during the day if she didn't snare a few hours of rest somehow. She pulled on her old coat and barn boots and went down to the granary. She had smoked part of a slim joint a day ago and she finished the rest of it with a few drags. Then she made her way back to the house by the fading light of the moon and left Robbie and Leah a note, giving them breakfast suggestions, asking them to please not wake her before school, and drawing little arrows to the dollars and coins she left on the counter for their lunches. She stripped off her clothes in the laundry room and slid them under a pile of damp towels she would wash later in the day, hoping no one would detect the strong odor of weed. Then she took a quick shower, using Leah's melon-scented body wash to dissolve away all evidence of her "little secret." Finally, she crawled into her side of the bed, finding the familiar indentation of her body on the soft mattress, and surrendered to the sweet peace of sleep.

8: Julie

Pulsing, flashing lights from a police cruiser exploded into the calm of Julie's bedroom. She had neglected to close the blinds when she collapsed into bed after book club. As she stretched open her numb fists, myriad tiny needles seemed to pierce every cell in her fingers and palms. "Damn it," she muttered, realizing that she had clenched her fists the whole night through.

Her alarm was set for 5:15, but Julie, finally focusing, saw that it was already 5:08, so she hauled herself to a sitting position and pawed around on the nightstand for her glasses. She padded into the bathroom where she had laid out her running gear the night before. Exchanging the soft, waffle weave t-shirt she slept in for a skin-hugging, moisture-wicking turtleneck and cold, silky running tights, she entertained her usual morning inner dialogue: "Do I really have to do this today? Yup, but I ran yesterday and it's going to be cold! Take tomorrow off, then." Julie was paradoxically motivated by an utter lack of faith in herself, fearing that if she deviated from her exercise regime she would fall off the wagon like an alcoholic at an open bar.

Lack of faith was embedded in her psyche, a family heirloom her mother had bequeathed to her. Words ("Should you be eating that? You're getting chubby!"). Deeds (forgetting to pick her up after a grade school concert). Gestures (hugging her brother, but not her) had been a winning trifecta in crushing Julie's chances of capitalizing on her pleasing looks and sharp brain. But as an adult, with good friends and professional help, Julie had been carving out the right to assert herself. Although her parents lived only a few miles away in a tony section of Amherst, she had stopped running to see them whenever they demanded and started really running instead.

After checking to see that Stephan was still asleep, she slipped out her front door, a thick and well-padded asexual figure in space age garments, a black balaclava warming her face. The reflective tape stitched along the outside seams of her black running pants made her look like a moving neon sculpture when she was caught in the lights of a passing car emerging through the darkness. She jogged briskly to the end of her block.

In this period before dawn, especially in the autumn months, the neighborhood was lovely in its peacefulness and well-tended simplicity. It reminded her of Christmas card art depicting some English village of a century ago. "Peace on Earth," the card would herald. Not that she had ever seen an English village or actually knew if they were peaceful. Julie's passport, acquired eleven years ago in hopeful anticipation of a trip to France, lay at the bottom of her junk drawer, expired and unstamped. She had been to the Canadian provinces of Ontario, Quebec, and Nova Scotia, and on camping trips in the United States east of the

Rockies, but that was the extent of her travels. The trip to France had been postponed indefinitely, as had her ambition to see the Van Gogh Museum in Amsterdam.

"Not had an adventuresome life," she thought wistfully, which is why *In Accord* was so important to her. Through it, she had been transported to the Chinese countryside, French provinces, Louisiana bayous, even the freeways of California. And she had met wonderful individuals – resourceful women, revolutionaries, dreamers, people who acted on passion and were sometimes impulsive. Not like Julie. Julie was careful. "But," she appended her self-critique, "I'm learning."

When she reached Elmwood, one of the major arteries into the city, she scanned the street both ways before committing to a right turn. A bus rolled by, sheathed in colorful advertising for the zoo, its bright interior lights illuminating the weary faces of commuters heading into the city, its shrieking brakes piercing the dawn's quiet. Another bus lurched by, going out of the city, its sides painted with a winsome ad for Women and Children's Hospital. That ad always conjured memories of the horrible night when her only child, Stephan, then a normal, reckless ten-year-old, had ridden his bike into the path of a car on Ashland Avenue. The young driver never even saw him until he bounced onto her hood, caromed off her windshield, and landed on the curb "like a sack of potatoes" as one witness crudely observed.

Julie had been grocery shopping, so husband Eric was the one summoned to the emergency room. Later, she would obsess

during the dark, still hours of the night over what she had been
doing at the precise moment of impact. Had she been choosing a
bottle of ketchup? Deciding between cans of vegetable and lentil
soup? How can a person be doing something utterly banal at the
very second her child is in the middle of catastrophe? It seemed a
simple enough prayer: the earth should stand still when your child
could be dying.

"Stephen was hit by a car while riding his bike. Meet us at
Children's," Eric had scrawled in nearly indecipherable script on
the back of an envelope he'd taped to the door where Julie
couldn't miss it when she came home laden with groceries. She
had no memory of driving the mile to join him in the emergency
room at Women and Children's Hospital. She remembered waiting
for what seemed like eons, thoughts and feelings suspended in
disbelief, until at last a doctor came out and informed them that
their son would need extensive rehabilitation but would recover.

Julie resigned her job as music teacher at a suburban
school in order to keep Stephan current with his studies and
chauffeur him to a seemingly endless round of rehab appointments
and doctor's visits. When, finally, Stephan returned to school, she
found a sliver of time to follow her intuition that something was
out of whack between her and Eric. A few furtive clicks on his
laptop computer, which he had accidentally left open on his secret
Facebook page, revealed a stunning history of deception and
several affairs. As she scrolled through pages and pages of
messages and photos of him with various "friends," she saw that

he was drawn like a magnet to thin, young women with long blond hair. Raised to understand that she was a chubby disappointment, Julie found his deception loathsome and devastating. Her book club friends saw her through, even offering – maybe facetiously – to form a posse and run the bastard down with their Accords. With her marriage in shambles, she gratefully accepted a new job at Hannah's school.

Middle-schoolers were a breed apart, she quickly discovered, with their childish needs and their adult aspirations in constant juxtaposition. Just last week a tiny twelve-year-old who often tarted herself up like a sex-crazed rock goddess collapsed in tears in Julie's lap after she failed to win the part of little Gretel in the school's upcoming musical, *The Sound of Music*. Julie would've understood this reaction had she been casting *The Rocky Horror Picture Show*. Not that *Rocky Horror* would ever fly with the school board or the parent advisory committee.

Now a high school senior, Stephen had a slight limp, a few scars, and a wide grin. He and Julie had an easy, close relationship as a result of hours and hours in the car together while she drove him to appointments all over Buffalo during his recovery, listening to oldies rock stations and singing along to Paul Simon, Led Zeppelin, and even Jimi Hendrix. Towering over her now, he liked to pat her on the head and remind *her* to be careful, to always look both ways.

Slap – slap – slap, her running shoes hit the sidewalk, slap – clop – slap. She ran by a little restaurant that used a sea-and-surf motif to carve out its identity on the Elmwood strip. Sailboats adorned its awning while fishermen's netting served as window treatments. An aquarium scene worthy of *The Little Mermaid* was rendered in stained glass on its front door. *Mariner's Cove* popped into Julie's mind. How would she rewrite the ending? She had sympathy for Claire's feelings but scorn for her actions. And yet, she asked herself, what *would* I do if my first serious boyfriend had called me out of the blue while I was still married to Eric?

As a twenty-year-old, she had been crazy about that first boy, Dorr Szymanski. Crazy. There's no place she wouldn't have gone, no change in herself she wouldn't have attempted to hold his attention. But when a new girl drew his eyes elsewhere, he told Julie to *get over it! Just move on! No big deal!* Julie ran harder, her arms pumping rhythmically, as if she could grind the memories of Eric and Dorr into the pavement, render them dust. Maybe she should rewrite her ending to *Mariner's Cove* so all the Evil Ex's got what's coming to them, she thought. It was a chance to exact some revenge and stay out of jail while doing it. She smiled and slowed, turning onto Ellen's street.

Halfway down the block, Julie caught sight of Ellen in a bright purple running jacket, balancing on her toes on her porch steps, stretching her calves.

"Morning," Ellen called cheerily.

"Morning," Julie answered as she reached the steps and bent to scratch Romeo behind the ears. "Hi, big fellow. You're looking tremendous, for a basketball."

"Hey! That's my dear sweet old cat you're dissing." Ellen protested mildly as she scooped Romeo up and set him inside the house. "I, for one, envy him."

"You envy your cat?" Julie asked as the two women began to jog up the street.

"Yeah! All he does is eat, shed, lick himself, and sleep. He's round as a sausage and everybody thinks he's adorable. I don't get why fat is cute on pets and ugly on us."

Julie laughed. "We're insane!"

Ellen noticed Julie's running gear. "That a new jacket?"

"Yup. This baby's wind-proof, waterproof, moisture-wicking, and good to ten degrees. It'll hold up to the worst that our winters have to throw at me, or that's the pitch anyway." Julie grinned.

"You're really committed to the running thing." Ellen observed approvingly.

"I am! I've lost ten pounds and I haven't felt this good since years before Eric and I split up. I'm thinking that's long enough, you know?"

Ellen looked quizzical.

"Oh, I was just so, so frozen. Now I really don't care what he says. Can you imagine how nice it is to know that I won't ever trust one word out of his mouth? And I'm ready to, to…" Julie faltered.

"Date?" Ellen finished her sentence.

"Good Lord, no!" Julie cried. "Can't you see I'm still too fat for that?"

Ellen gasped. "Too fat for…"

"Oh, you know," Julie ducked her head and devoted herself to a slight adjustment on the cuff of her left sleeve. When Ellen continued to stare at her, Julie sighed. "Never mind," she murmured.

"No, talk to me, Jules. Too fat for what?" Ellen persisted. Furtively, she glanced at her cherished friend and saw the softly rounded contours of a normal middle-aged woman. Crossing the street, they ran in silence for a moment. Then Julie pinched a small chunk of her soft belly and explained. "I'm like a thick old book that's been shelved for years. If you open it even just a little, it will fall apart."

Ellen raised her eyebrows and stifled a laugh. A throaty old pickup truck rumbled by as she rolled the book image around in her head.

Defensively Julie cried, "Smirk if you must but I'm too fat for everything, or for *anything*. Don't you understand that when you've been out of circulation so long, it's impossible to just waddle back in?" Again, she patted her belly.

"Oh, gosh, I'm sorry! I wasn't laughing at you. By the way, you most certainly are not fat, and you do not waddle.

You're not going to fall apart if you go out with someone although I do suppose it's kind of scary to imagine the whole..."

Julie interrupted hotly. "Jeez! Did you even listen to me?"

Breaking her stride, Ellen threw her hands up in the air. "Sorry, sorry!" she cried. "I truly didn't mean to offend you. It just sounded like you wanted to get back into circulation and date, that's all. No big thing."

"Ah, but it is a *big* thing! Can't you see that it's a very big thing?" Julie corrected her, aware of sounding aggrieved but unable to tone it down. They ran in step for a dozen yards, accompanied by the rhythmic beat of their shoes on the pavement and the sounds of street traffic as the city awoke. Then she continued, "'Date' is a miserable, pinched little word. *Date!*" She isolated it and spat it out. "A number on a calendar, that's a date. Not the whole complicated, fraught thing that happens when you start seeing a man. And who would want to date me, anyway? And who would I want to date? I've been alone so long I just can't imagine doing all that compromising."

Surprised by Julie's admission, Ellen did a double-take. "Oh come on! There's no reason for you to stay holed up in your apartment. Stephen's a senior. It's time for you to get out. And by the way," Ellen panted, "you might not have to compromise as much as you think, just find your right person." She was picking up their pace and chopping her words into single syllables. They entered the long pathway through Delaware Park. Dawn painted the sky in shimmering streaks of silver and peach. High cumulus clouds clustered like ethereal sheep above the tall maples. It was going to be a simply lovely day.

The concept of dating danced in Julie's thoughts. A year ago there had been a man whom she could have dated. A mutual friend introduced them at an arts fundraiser and he held her hand decidedly longer than necessary while they were being introduced. Nathan was a cellist with the Buffalo Philharmonic Orchestra. His hands were large, strong, and beautiful with long slim fingers and impeccably groomed nails. Those hands! Julie was intimidated by the mere thought of them, the idea of touching them and even more, of allowing them to touch her. Looking at herself in the full mirror in her bedroom, she saw too much flesh, lumpy flesh that no one could possibly find attractive. Apologizing profusely, she cancelled two dates with him, and he never called back for a third.

"Morning ladies, glorious day!" the booming voice of an oncoming runner broke into her thoughts. Several other denizens of early morning were out now, walking their dogs or jogging on the wide path. The regulars on this circuit greeted one another companionably, exchanging encouragement in the sympathetic code of this brotherhood and sisterhood of predawn exercisers.

Waving back and nodding, Julie and Ellen reached a split in the path and slowed their pace. "Sorry," said Julie, "I am touchy this morning. I think *Mariner's Cove* got under my skin. Why do some people go off and have affairs when others can't even find one decent partner? Anyway, see you tomorrow?" She turned to double back home.

"Sure, tomorrow." Ellen waved, then ran another mile on her own before heading back.

9: Hannah

By 4:45 in the murky predawn, Hannah was in her car, fortified with directions she printed off Google to avoid the outrageous international roaming charges she would incur if she used her phone's navigator in Canada, a book on tape (*Motivation and Meditation: A Manager's Marriage*), an oversized travel mug of extra strong black coffee, bottled water, and two granola bars. She also wrote a long note to Ellen:

> *Good morning. Didn't want to call you this early, or risk you not checking email, so going the old-fashioned route of pen and paper. Problem! Beth was caught drinking on the French Club trip and I have to pick her up ASAP in Quebec (though nothing's all that ASAP from 556 miles). Simon's busy with Matt. Please, could you pick Zoe up at 5:30 after her dance class (and give her dinner)? If you can't, it's no big deal; she'll just have to skip dance today. But if you can do it, Simon will swing by and get her after Matt's gymnastics class. Please text Simon when you get this and let him know. Thanks tons & tons, Love, H.*

Romeo and Juliet posed like gargoyles on the steps as Hannah turned into Ellen's driveway. "Why are you guys out so early?" she asked, then remembered that Will was likely already on the road to an early meeting in Cleveland. Kneeling, she scratched Romeo on that delicate patch of cat real estate between jaw and ear and enjoyed his rumbling, ecstatic purr. He arched his neck and leaned into her fingers while Juliet paced nervously nearby. When Hannah extended an upturned hand to her, shy Juliet backed away. "As you like it," Hannah muttered, standing and sliding the envelope containing her note between the screen door and the solid oak front door where Ellen would be sure to notice it when she retrieved her morning paper. Glancing at the sky, Hannah noted that it was going to be a postcard-perfect day. At least there was that to look forward to. She eased her car back onto the street and made her way toward the eastbound Thruway for the first long leg of her journey.

At six in the morning, she telephoned her assistant principal, Scott, to explain that she was heading to Quebec today.

"You're goin' *where?* Why?" He mumbled in a sleepy, gravelly voice.

"I'm sorry, Scott. Beth is on a field trip with the French Club, and last night she hit the bars in Quebec with some of the other kids and now I have to go get her. Board policy, remember?" She sighed and continued, "It was going to be a light day but now I need you to catch one meeting in the morning, a Special Ed committee thing with some pissed-off parents. They're mad as hell about the committee's recommendation that their kid be labeled *special needs* so he can get a math tutor, which the kid really needs. Sue can fill you in."

"Quebec is 600 freaking miles away, Hannah. Are you crazy?"

"556 miles, so sayeth Google," Hannah corrected miserably. "But I had a hand in writing the policy, Scott. I *have* to go get her."

"Wait, wait…what did she do?" Scott was still half-asleep.

"She went out *drinking*." Hannah repeated, wondering how many times and to how many people she would have to repeat this.

"She's so damn lucky she's not my kid," Scott grumbled. "I'd kill her."

An unexpected smile crossed Hannah's face. When her children were small, they had briefly loved a series of little paperback books with title characters named after human traits such as "Mr. Happy" or "Mr. Grumpy." Since their first meeting, Hannah had thought of Scott as her own "Mr. Bluster," spouting threats that were sometimes quite effective in his role as the school's rules enforcer. "I don't know whose kid she should be today," she said, "but I have to get her. I'll have my cell phone on, though God only knows how the service will be once I get up into the north country."

"Wow, I'm actually sorry for you. Take it slow, watch out for deer," Scott advised, "and don't worry about things at school. It's covered."

"Thanks." She clicked off and squared her shoulders into the long drive ahead.

10: Ellen

Back from her run, showered and sweet from her lavender body wash, Ellen was glaring into her bedroom closet when she heard the newspaper land with a clunk on the porch. Ignoring it, she focused on finding something clean, comfortable, ironed, and appropriate for today's weather that she could tolerate having next to her skin for nine hours. Not one single item in her wardrobe really appealed. A management meeting in the morning required that she dress formally. Finally, she pulled on a sleeveless cream-colored shell and a steel-blue pinstriped suit and surveyed the effect. Too severe, she critiqued, and added a chunky necklace of alternating silver beads and blue quartz stones shaped like shark's teeth. The necklace had been an extravagant surprise birthday gift from Cole and Jonathan and she loved it just for being from them, as well as genuinely appreciating its jazzy artistry. She smiled at herself and went downstairs to enjoy her morning coffee and read the newspaper, starting with the obituaries.

Spotting Hannah's handwriting on the envelope as it fluttered to the floor when she opened the front door, Ellen wrinkled her brow inquisitively. "Weird," she thought, "why would Hannah write to me when she can just text or call me on my cell?" Then the memory of her conversation with Jonathan blasted her like beach sand on a windy day and she *knew* what the note had to be about. Hannah must've learned about Zoe's pregnancy after book club ended last night and she had probably been up at two or three in the morning, unable to sleep or haunted by her dreams. Ellen pictured her friend sitting at her home computer just inside a small circle of light, tapping out an anguished note, and she felt an empathic churning in her stomach. She extracted the letter from its envelope and quickly absorbed its message. "No, oh no!" she said out loud, bringing Cole running from the kitchen.

"What? What's the matter, Mom?" he asked, his tall, lanky frame filling the doorway. He held a glass of orange juice in one hand and a piece of buttered toast in the other, its crumbs spilling down the front of his shirt.

"Oh, hi, Cole, good morning," she smiled at him and tried to recover her calm. The sheer height of him always took her by surprise. It was as if her memory card didn't have enough space to stay current with her sons' relentless march toward adulthood. Her mental images of them defaulted to some point years earlier when they were gangly boys with missing teeth or unruly hair or a t-shirt pulled on inside out. "Nothing's wrong," she said lightly, then corrected herself. "Well, not nothing. Well, crap! Let me ask you, could you pick Jonathan up at 5:30? He'll be finishing wrestling practice and I have to get Zoe."

Cole's eyes narrowed. He was already a creature of habit, his father's son, and he didn't like to rearrange his routine. "Why do you have to get Zoe?"

Ellen held up the note. "Hannah can't, Simon can't."

"So why not Beth?"

"She's the reason Hannah can't. Beth was caught drinking last night on the Quebec trip, you know, with the French Club, and now Hannah's driving up there to pick her up."

Cole's smile was huge. "That's rich, Mom, really rich!" He started to chortle. "The Perfect Miss Beth Feldman went out drrrrinking in Quebec? And got caught? Oh, life is too good." His laughter erupted in short bursts.

"Cole, you're being, you're being," Ellen struggled to chide him but started to giggle instead, guiltily at first and then in uncontrolled spasms. Once it started, laughter they couldn't suppress cascaded out of them, one setting off the other until tears ran down their cheeks. Finally Ellen got control and held it. "Oh, God, we're mean," she declared, wiping her eyes.

"Yeah, yeah. But Beth's so – well, let me put it this way: this couldn't have happened to a more deserving person." Cole and Beth had been close friends prior to high school, but their paths then sharply diverged. Cole was a stoner ("former stoner," he reassured his mother) who did the minimum necessary to placate his parents and school officialdom. Beth was a classic overachiever: president of the student council, president of Students against Drunk Driving, member of the debate team and the French club, editor of the student paper, teacher's pet extraordinaire. Her fundraising activities made Ellen weary while Cole responded to all her accolades with scorn. To suck up to authority as Beth did so relentlessly violated his definition of self-respect. The one thing he would give her an award for was being a champion brown nose. He rolled his eyes at his mother and shook his head. "Sure, I'll pick up Jon, no problem."

"Somebody talking about me?" Jonathan loped downstairs, his long hair still dripping from the shower, his backpack already slung heavily across his shoulders.

"I'm going to pick you up after practice, buddy, so be ready," Cole said in his father-knows-best voice that so infuriated his younger brother. "And let's get a move on this morning. I don't want to be late."

"I'm ready. I've been ready," Jon shot back sullenly.

Ellen wished Jonathan was less thin-skinned when it came to his older brother. She was about to tell him about having Zoe over for dinner when he reached the door.

"But you haven't had anything for breakfast!" she protested instead. "The Zoe situation" was not a conversation to have on the run.

"I'll get something at school," he mumbled, letting the door slam shut behind him.

"'S'up with him?" Cole tilted his head toward the slammed door. He hadn't finished his toast and some of the butter lay in yellow pools on the crust.

Ellen shrugged. "You know your brother." It was only morning and she was already tired. The prospect of picking Zoe up, giving her dinner, and pretending not to know about her being pregnant, when her own mother didn't yet know, was daunting and depressing.

11: Zoe

In the semidarkness of her bedroom, still populated by the herds of stuffed animals that are so adored by pre-adolescent girls, Zoe groaned softly. She hadn't even rolled on her side, hadn't even lifted her head off her pillow, and already she was nauseous. This wasn't fair! She had eaten an apple and forced down a glass of milk before bed, hoping the combination would settle her stomach despite the food tasting like sawdust. No luck. Slipping quietly into the bathroom, she turned on the shower so its noisy splashing would drown out the sounds of her retching. How long could she keep this secret from her eagle-eyed mother, she wondered miserably.

Three weeks earlier, Zoe had been granted internet research privileges on the computers in her school's library. Since all sexuality oriented web browsing was strictly prohibited, she lied to Ms. Kren, the librarian, claiming to need information on pregnancy to fulfill a sociology assignment. There, under Ms. Kren's watchful, worried eyes, she was aghast to discover that pregnant women typically gain thirty to seventy pounds and lose the strength (and flatness) in their abdominal muscles, often ending up with stretch marks. The photos of round bellies with silvery vines etched across them were *disgusting.* She read "nausea and vomiting may start as early as a week into the pregnancy. There is no explanation as to why pregnant women feel this; however, snacking on saltine crackers seems to give some kind of relief."

Actually, Zoe could find no relief. Even the information that "early pregnancy symptoms generally can be felt once implantation occurs (8 – 10 days after having sex) and will lessen after the first trimester" left her reeling. *Implantation.* Is that what happened to her – she'd become implanted, like a vegetable garden? There was something unreal, gross, and biologic, jarringly close to earth and farmers and seeds, in this concept. Mortified, Zoe fought the urge to throw up right there in the library, all over the shiny little black keyboard. Surreptitiously doing the math, she figured she had one more week of being sick in the morning and then…then, what? The article's final words: "After your precious baby arrives, you will forget the bouts of nausea and the discomfort you are now experiencing" echoed in her mind. "Your precious baby!" Oh, what the hell was she going to do? Before she could follow that question toward any possible conclusion, the bell rang. Zoe exited the website, deleted her search history, stuffed her notebook into her backpack and moved to her next class, *Spanish II,* where she eked out a barely passing grade on a mid-semester exam.

Now, on the morning following the *In Accord Club* gathering at her house, Zoe finished retching, took a long, hot shower and dressed for school. She was a dancer with a slim, taut figure, muscled thighs and calves, and beautiful posture. Standing in front of the mirror, she smiled to see that her body did not yet betray her. With Beth away on a field trip, she enjoyed extra time in the bathroom and was pleased with the results. It would be delicious next year if Beth went far, far away to a university. She could hear Matt singing along to a commercial downstairs and the low sounds of her father's voice as he helped her little brother get ready for preschool.

Finally, Zoe joined her family in the kitchen, her eyes darting around for her mother. Instead, her father grinned at her and rolled his eyes.

"Mom's not here," he said, responding to her quizzical look. "We got a call from Beth last night." He quietly explained the Quebec debacle, glancing toward Matt to warn Zoe not to ask explicit or embarrassing questions. "So Ellen's agreed to pick you up after dance," he finished.

"The hell!" she exclaimed, ignoring his silent plea for restraint. "Beth got drunk in Quebec and now Mom's got to go get her? This is gonna be all over school. What an asshole. That's soooo like her. She doesn't care about anybody but herself."

"Aathole! Aathole!" Matt lisped in the sing-song voice he copied from a catchy cereal commercial.

"Shush, Matt, that isn't nice, we don't use that language," Simon reprimanded. Stung by his father's angry voice, the little boy instantly started crying.

"Thanks a bunch, Zoe. You don't have to look very far to find selfish, do you?" Simon growled.

Tears streamed down her flushed cheeks as Zoe fled the kitchen, raging silently to herself. How typical that Beth would do something stupid, but she, Zoe, would end up in trouble! She retreated into the bathroom and bolted the door. Her make-up was already smearing, black rivulets flowing down from her eyes and branching out across her cheeks. She desperately wanted to stop crying, but she couldn't make herself suck it all back in.

12: Hannah

Although it was only 10:30 in the morning, Hannah felt as
though she had been driving her entire life. She had long since
abandoned the sanctimonious *Meditation and Motivation,* could no
longer pull in a strong consistent signal for public radio, and was
switching between oldies stations and the strange chatter of local
radio talk shows. It amazed her the things people continued to be
loudly, passionately ignorant about: who controls the wealth in
this country; are people really allowed to exercise their free speech
protections when they offend their neighbors with their political
signs? And hadn't that been settled 200-plus years ago? While
radio surfing, she had also been mentally conversing with Beth,
but she couldn't get her half of the script to come out okay. Beth
was a born litigator and would argue, in eloquent and dignified
prose, that this situation was inherently unfair, that she had done
nothing, *nothing,* deserving of the severity of this response. "It's
like they're deploying a Cruise missile to destroy a mouse for
doing what mice do," she'd complain.

"But you're *President* of Students Against Drunk
Driving," Hannah would rebut, exasperated.

"But I wasn't *driving*," Beth would counter in level, reasonable tones, "nor was I drunk. I was helping a friend. "

"Who, by the way, *was* drunk…ridiculously, disgustingly drunk," Hannah would add, remembering the vivid description of the staggering, vomiting girl provided by the hysterical Mrs. Herndon the night before. Beth's "one beer" story was suspect, too. Maybe she had only *purchased* one beer.

Hannah's imaginary conversation tapered off as a huge flock of Canada geese arched overhead in a ragged v-formation. She rolled down her window to listen to them honking to each other as they calibrated the nuances of their course toward a warmer winter home. She wondered what they were communicating. Did they remember which farmers left the most corn in the fields after harvest? Where the richest, best stocked ponds and lakes were? Where the nastiest dogs lived? Just outside Watertown, in far north-central New York State, Hannah pulled into a rest stop. She stretched her aching back, filled up her gas tank and grabbed some fresh coffee. She hoped it was fresh, anyway. With 300 miles yet to go (and a return trip), she would need serious help to survive this day.

13: Cole

Standing in the lunch line in the high school cafeteria, Ellen's oldest son, Cole, was weighing his choices: greasy pizza, greasy tacos, greasy chicken nuggets. Or he could just fill up on peanut butter cookies. They were the one wonderful food produced in this cafeteria. His lunch period was late, 1:00 pm, and he was famished. As he reached out for the cookies, someone jostled his arm and he nearly lost control of his tray. He wheeled around, prepared to snarl and terrify, only to find Kelly Masten laughing up at him, her hair tossed carelessly back, her dark eyes flashing, the contour of her breasts unmistakable under her tight red t-shirt. His heart leapt and raced. They had been dating for four months and he was still butter on a hot burner in her presence. He tried valiantly to appear miffed and dignified.

"Dammit!" he said, "you almost made me drop my tray."

"Oh, chill," she chided flippantly, "you didn't drop it." Her voice dropped. "I got the code into the yearbook office. Meet me. "

"When?"

"Now." Heading toward the door, she disappeared into a gaggle of students.

Cole bought three cookies, tucked two of them into his backpack and nibbled on the third. Folding himself uncomfortably onto the bench seat of one of the greenish laminate tables nearest the door, he waited for the cafeteria monitor to be distracted. Soon, with the inevitability of snow in February, three freshmen boys started to argue. One stood suddenly, his fist raised to throw a punch. With an uncanny knack for predicting this kind of thing, the cafeteria monitor was in the midst of the boys before the raised fist could connect with the other boy's jaw. Cole slipped out a side door, silently thanking the young delinquents. He was in the yearbook office in seconds.

Kelly seized his hands and drew him close for a quick kiss. Every cell in his body buzzed awake. Cole was mentally blocking off a "not here, not now, are you kidding?" voice in his head when Kelly pulled slightly away. "I've found one!" she sang. "It's perfect for us; we can both get in, we can be together. It's got engineering for you and international business for me…"

"Whoa, whoa, whoa!" Cole interrupted. "What are you talking about?"

"College, dumbass! I've found a place we can both go to. There's still time to apply and we can be together next year." Kelly's flushed and happy face quickly registered her disappointment as Cole looked puzzled.

"Don't you want to go away to school together?" she asked in a voice now quiet and unsure and just a little accusatory.

"I dunno," he mumbled, "I never thought about it."

"Well, I have and there's a perfect school. What's wrong, why are you looking so weird?" Kelly's stammered.

"Kelly, I just don't know, I mean, picking a college, it's... I mean, we've been together four months, it's really great, but next year is a long ways away." Cole had dropped her hands and taken a small step back. He knew that his father held some very firm ideas about where he should go to college. Also, he was happily taking their relationship a day at a time and hadn't given a thought to Kelly as part of his college planning.

"Don't you even want to know where? You're not even interested, are you? Why won't you even *think* about it?" Kelly cried. "I can't believe you! I thought you really cared! I guess *I'm* the dumbass." In a whir of grabbing and organizing, she swooped up her backpack and purse while she spoke, tears welling in the corners of her eyes. She pushed around him.

"Kelly, wait, don't go!" Cole pleaded belatedly, reaching out to hold her arm.

With the full force of her body, she jerked away, "Don't touch me!"

"You just surprised the hell out of me. Can't we talk about this?"

Kelly shook her head furiously. "Forget it," she snapped, letting herself out into the hall.

As the door clicked shut, Cole stood and stared out the window. Kelly's last words rang in his ears while his jumbled feelings bounced around in his head. The high school's soccer field was visible from the window and he could see a group of students from a gym class clustered around a student who was down on the ground, clutching his shin and writhing dramatically. Cole recognized the boy, one of Jonathan's classmates. *Sophomores*, he thought. They don't know how good they have it, all the time in the world to make their decisions. He wasn't even sure he wanted to go to college next year, much less go *away*, although everyone around him seemed to think this was as inevitable as his next birthday. He wondered what school Kelly had found and wished he had been at least slightly prepared for this discussion. Right now, he would happily spend every waking second in her presence (and every sleeping second as well, but her parents were a bit of a barrier to that). But next year? Cole felt like he was driving in thick fog at midnight.

14: Hannah and Beth

Quebec glittered in the afternoon sun as Hannah finally reached the city. It took considerable effort to drive and navigate at the same time and, after several false turns, she finally found the hotel where she was to pick up her daughter.

One by one, the other young violators who had signed the Field Trip Rules & Responsibilities Contract had been towed away by their furious, exhausted parents, finally leaving Beth by herself to gnaw alone on the indignities and injustice of it all. Backpack at her feet, she was slumped on a floral settee in a corner of the Chateau Mont St. Lawrence lobby when Hannah first spotted her. From across the marbled hall, she looked innocent, young, and utterly forlorn. The eloquent speech about stepping up to responsibility, which Hannah had been mentally rehearsing and honing to a bullet-proof state for 500 miles, instantly dissolved in the tangle of the mother's heartstrings. *My poor baby*, she thought.

Beth spied her and leapt to her feet, throwing off her lethargy in an instant. "Where were you?" she cried. "I've been sitting here alone *forever*. I'm sorry, I really am, that you had to drive all this way, but this is so unfair, Mom, so, so unfair! I was just taking care of Rachel, that's all, I swear."

While Beth paused to catch her breath, Hannah groped for words. Beth continued before Hannah found her footing. "I could have lied and said I wasn't drinking, but I told the truth and now I'm being punished. Well, guess what? Almost every single kid on this trip had at least as much to drink as I did. Most had twice as much. Don't they get that when you punish someone for telling the truth, that person learns to lie? This is so incredibly stupid!"

Suddenly, tears streamed down her face and she fell into Hannah's arms like an aggrieved five-year-old. Hannah could do nothing but hold her daughter, stroking her hair comfortingly although Beth was slightly taller than she. It *was* a little ridiculous, Hannah reluctantly agreed. And now she was faced with the dilemma of upholding school policy, something for which she had professional responsibility, versus responding from her own heart to her daughter's distress.

"It's okay, honey," she murmured softly.

"It's *not* okay!" Beth had refueled on her mother's shoulder and was ready for another lap. "They *better not* think they're going to suspend me! Where is the concept of the crime fitting the punishment? Okay, I see why they're pissed at Rachel. She did puke everywhere, and that was gross, so gross! Oh my God, Mom. It made me want to just *die,* but I really wasn't drunk. These teachers are utterly ridiculous. They just don't know how to be reasonable."

"Hey!" Hannah's anger constricted her throat. If there was anyone she knew well, it was teachers, and most of them worked themselves to the bone to educate and care for their students. "Don't blame the teachers. You knew the rules. There's nothing in there about it being okay to drink *a little bit*. Just what do you think '*zero* tolerance' means, anyway?"

Beth was stunned into momentary silence. "You're going to side with them?"

"Let's see," Hannah retorted, furious that her daughter showed no remorse. "I get a call at three in the morning requiring me to rearrange my family's life so I can drive all day to pick you up because you and Rachel, in clear violation of the rules set for this trip, went out drinking. Do you think it matters whether or not anyone else was drinking? Let me tell you something, baby, that doesn't matter one bit!" Hannah's voice was steely. "You did the crime, you knew the punishment. Don't try to push this off on the teachers, or on me, for that matter."

Recognizing her mother's refusal to supply the oxygen needed to fuel her rant, Beth collapsed on the settee and started to cry instead. "God, I'm sorry, I'm sorry! I can't go back to school, Mom. I can't face everyone. This is so humiliating," she sobbed.

Arguing was futile when Beth was this righteously committed to her position, so Hannah held her breath. Instead, she handed her daughter a clean tissue and sat quietly on the bouncy little floral print, exhaustion overtaking her like a third glass of wine. The prospect of doubling back, 556 miles, down the St. Lawrence Seaway in the frenetic Canadian traffic, through

Montreal, then endlessly west on the New York State Thruway in the dark, filled her with dread.

"We're not going home tonight," she realized out loud. "No way can I face that drive again yet. Let's find ourselves a new hotel. I'll nap a little and we'll have dinner somewhere in the city. We'll deal with this all soon enough, Beth. There's nothing to be done now, and it's really not the end of the world."

Hannah and Beth soon found themselves a cozy room on the third floor of a small, delightful inn in the four-century-old walled city rising on terraces of land shelved up from the St. Lawrence River. After curling up on their tiny beds and drifting into deep but brief naps, they wandered the crowded cobblestone streets exploring quaint little shops until they found a bistro both liked. Once they had settled comfortably into their seats, their server, in a charming French accent, inquired, "What can I bring you ladies from the bar?" and Beth unsuccessfully fought her desire to smirk. Her mood brightened as the evening wore on, while Hannah couldn't help but be enchanted by the unexpected pleasure of finding herself in a new, slightly exotic world. Holding her phone up everywhere, she took dozens of images of the city and the turreted, brick and copper-green Chateau Frontenac, a gravity- defying luxury hotel. "I'm going to show these to your father," she said. "Maybe someday we'll come back here ourselves to celebrate an anniversary or something."

15: Ellen, Zoe, Cole, and Jon

The hospital was unusually quiet for a Friday afternoon, and Ellen was grateful for the chance to finish her paperwork. She often dragged a stack home, vowing to finish it first thing Saturday morning, or (for sure) by Sunday night. Often, though, it sat on a corner of the dining room table, untouched, until she dragged it back with her on Monday morning. It was liberating to be really caught up. Ellen got to the parking lot to meet Zoe at exactly 5:30.

Late afternoon shadows cast long striations across the pavement. At 5:35 Zoe emerged from The Nelson Sisters' School of Dance, hauling her gear bag, book bag, and purse, a pink flush covering her face, wisps of sweaty hair sticking to her forehead. As Ellen watched, Zoe scanned the rows of vehicles until she recognized Ellen's Accord and remembered who was picking her up. They waved at each other and Zoe waltzed over to the car. Ellen was amazed at how impeccably lovely Zoe looked, her internal transformation still completely obscured by her dancer-perfect, fourteen-year-old body, long swinging hair, and sweet upturned nose.

"Hop in," Ellen invited, smiling outwardly. She had been dreading this ride all day, wondering how Zoe would look and what she might say to her. When she tried to imagine herself confronting the issue directly, she couldn't find words to say to Zoe that didn't compromise Jon. She had cared for Zoe like a daughter when Zoe was a baby but that easy intimacy faded as the teen years unfolded. Zoe was probably ten years old the last time Ellen had felt completely at ease with her. At twelve, Zoe started her period and became a moody, introspective, hypersensitive young woman.

Zoe slid into the passenger seat, tossing her things into the back. "Hiya and thanks," she said breathlessly. "Sorry I'm breathing so hard. Miss Judy really put us through a workout today and I'm wiped. Glad it's a weekend. I'm so sorry you had to pick me up, though. Have you heard from Mom?"

"Yeah, she got to Quebec City okay. We talked a little bit ago. They're going to spend the night somewhere near Quebec and drive home tomorrow." When Hannah had called, her focus was on Beth and how angry and embarrassed she was by her eldest daughter's lack of judgment and remorse. There seemed to be no decent way for Ellen to draw her attention to Zoe. Not that she would want to do that over the phone, anyway. Ellen had decided to wait, to see how this evening progressed, and to tell Hannah what she knew in person sometime over the weekend.

"Stupid Beth. How could she do that? I guess even the perfect princess can fall off her throne," Zoe's voice contained more than a hint of triumph.

"I have an older sister, too," Ellen commiserated, remembering how hard it was to always place second, no matter what you did or do. Zoe waited for more details but Ellen cautiously pulled onto the street and headed home, giving her full attention to the evening traffic. They rode in companionable quiet, pulling into the driveway just moments after Cole and Jonathan.

"Hey, Zoo Keeper, what's happening?" Cole greeted Zoe affectionately, using a name he had coined back when she was just toddling around and he was a five-year-old dynamo. Zoe had liked having Cole as an honorary older brother, but, like everything else in her world, that had changed when she entered high school. "Zoo Keeper" was now an embarrassingly juvenile moniker and having Cole treat her like a baby was almost unbearable. "You're a crazy animal!" she flung back her old retort, hoping Cole wouldn't push her into more conversation.

Chicken chili, simmering in the crock pot all day, filled the house with mouth-watering smells. A bag of premixed salad and a loaf of crusty Italian bread completed the table, and they were all seated within five minutes. Cole, starving after his three-cookie lunch and one-slice-toast breakfast, fell upon his food like a desperate, abandoned puppy. Zoe took small portions of everything and began to twirl her spoon in her chili and push her food around her plate, pretending to get morsels on her fork. Ellen observed her and was trying to think of something more appetizing to offer her when Jonathan asked, "So where's dad?"

"Still on the road," Ellen replied. "He'll be home later tonight."

"Guess you two don't have a hot date planned for later, huh?" Cole asked through huge bites of bread.

"Not tonight, not tonight." Ellen smiled at Cole. "But speaking of plans, what are you guys doing this weekend?"

Jon shrugged.

"I guess I'm going to the football game," Cole replied.

"With Kelly?" Ellen wondered out loud.

"Nah."

"No? What's the matter?" Ellen liked Kelly and it was an exceedingly rare weekend night that Cole didn't spend with her.

"I'm just, we're just, people don't have to spend every second together, you know. I'm going to the game with Jared and Nate." Cole's tone gave away more than he intended.

Jon tuned in like Cole was the weather channel during a blizzard. "Something messing with the lovebirds?" he inquired levelly, laser-eyes on his brother.

"Shut up," Cole snapped.

"Shhh!" Ellen arched her eyebrows. She hated "shut up," the way kids are mean to each other, so quick to find the jugular.

Cole turned to Zoe. "Rafael will be meeting us at the game. You should come. Didn't you two have something going?"

The color drained out of Zoe's face as she struggled to maintain her composure. "What do you mean?" she murmured.

Cole shrugged dismissively. "Nothing, no big deal."

Zoe turned accusingly to Jonathan. "Did you go and spread it all over school? Did you? Did you?"

"Spread what?" Cole asked innocently as Jonathan, in the middle of swallowing a full mouthful of chicken chili, flushed and shook his head no.

"I didn't say nothing, chill, Zoe! Chill!" Jon mumbled through his mouthful but Cole was focusing his whole attention on the fourteen-year-old girl.

"Spread what?" he asked again. Then, more softly as he saw Zoe's trembling lip, "Zoo Keeper, what's the matter?"

The room was suddenly as quiet as midnight, Ellen holding her breath, Zoe in wordless agony, Jonathan trying to swallow his chili, which suddenly felt like a mouthful of straw.

"Dammit, Cole, dammit!" Jon finally swallowed and snarled at his older brother. "Can't you tell when to get your face out of other people's business?"

"Boys!" Ellen raised her hands to protest the tenor of the conversation when Cole connected the dots between the rumors he had heard and Zoe's strangled expression.

"Holy shit, Zoe, you, you're not pregnant, are you?" he said, stretching pre-eg-in-nant into four syllables.

"Oh my God," she cried, tipping over her chair as she jumped up and raced up the stairs to Jon's bedroom.

"Jesus Christ!" Cole swore. His words drowned out his mother's soft "Zoe, honey…" which were nearly lost under

Jonathan's plea, "Mom, please, please, do something!" Ellen was already on her feet, sprinting anxiously up the stairs after Zoe.

16: Revelations

Muffled sobs escaped from Jonathan's bedroom as Ellen hesitated in the hallway. She raised her hand to knock then let her arm drop and simply pushed the door open. Once in Jon's room, she stepped over damp towels and a cereal bowl with dried milk crusted in the bottom. Plaid boxer shorts and unmatched socks lay strewn across the floor. Abandoned pennies, crumpled school papers and empty candy bar wrappers competed for floor space. A calendar picturing NHL hockey players hung from a nail in the wall, three months out of date, while a huge, placid-looking gorilla surveyed the room from a poster over the bed. Ellen sat gingerly on the bed beside Zoe, who was bunched into a ball, sobbing. She stroked the girl's heaving back, saying nothing for a few minutes. When the room grew quiet and still, Ellen whispered, "Zoe, honey…what's going on?"

"Ooooh, Ellen," Zoe wailed, pulling away.

"Is it true what Cole said? Is that true? Are you pregnant?"

Shaking her head, she whispered, "Yes."

"Oh my." Ellen was quiet for a moment while Zoe sobbed again. Then she asked, "When? How far are you?"

"I think it was August," Zoe confirmed the date Jon had already confided.

"So you're possibly three months along? Wow. And nobody knows? That must be pretty hard for you."

"It really sucks," the pregnant child concurred.

What Ellen desperately wanted to do at that moment was to grab Zoe's shoulders, shake her, and yell, "Are you nuts? Are you out of your goddam mind?" Instead she gently asked, "What do you mean?" Once, in a rare instance of teen recklessness, Ellen dove off a speedboat into the middle of deep, frigid Sherkston's Quarry, just a few miles north of Buffalo in Ontario, Canada. The boy driving the boat then shot laughingly away, leaving Ellen terrified that she didn't have the strength to swim to shore. She felt like that now, scrambling inside herself to find her footing, to swim to the safety of a dry shore somewhere. She did *not* want to have this conversation with Hannah's daughter, but at the same time the social worker in her *had* to make it safe for Zoe to talk.

"I'm so sick, Ellen. All I want to do is throw up and sleep."

"Classic pregnancy symptoms," Ellen affirmed. "But you haven't told anybody? Have you taken a pregnancy test? Are you sure? Does the boy…"

"Oh, God, no! I haven't told anybody, well, I told Jon but he can keep his mouth shut. Nobody else."

"So," Ellen's almost purred She didn't want to spook Zoe into silence. "When were you going to talk about this with your mom and dad?"

"Oh God!" Zoe renewed her sobbing, pulling herself into a tight ball. "Don't tell my parents, please, Ellen. Don't, they will kill me, oh God!"

Ellen slumped forward and held her head. "They need to know. You can't keep this from them much longer, no matter what."

"I can't face them, I can't," Zoe pleaded.

"It's not going to be easy," Ellen agreed, "but you must. It's not possible for me to know this huge thing and *not* tell your mom. She's my best friend. And you need their help and support. Dealing with this isn't something to do alone." Pausing, she imagined Hannah and Simon's devastation upon hearing that their fourteen-year-old daughter is pregnant. A fleeting sense of relief washed over her that she had only sons. "Zoe, remember this, your parents love you. You need them. You have a strong family."

"What do you know about my family?" Zoe cried. "It's a big fake! We're not some happy, one for all, all for one family. They should've stopped when they got Beth. She's the only kid in the family they *really* want. Matt's just a stupid, stray puppy they drag around. And I'm just always, always, *always* wrong!" She sang "always, always, always," in a series of ascending notes while blobs of teary mascara splattered onto Jon's old bedspread. Ellen offered the nearby box of tissues.

Memories of being fourteen and knowing herself to be ugly and unlovable, an all-around mistake, came into sharp focus from the deep archives of Ellen's memory. Successful older sisters were a scourge, for sure. Matt was more than an inconvenient puppy, she knew, but Beth *was* the chosen one in the Feldman family. Hannah had once confided her belief that Beth was "the most special child on earth." Ellen had to control her impulse to spit when she heard it. Their argument nearly destroyed their friendship when Ellen countered, hotly, that all good mothers feel that way about all their children. She massaged her temples.

"When your dad gets here, I'll tell him that you have something to say and then I'll take Matt for a walk. It doesn't seem possible to you now, I know, but you *will* be okay. The sooner you get this out into the open to your parents, the sooner it can get better." Ellen left the room.

Jon was doubled over himself on the bottom step, giving Romeo the massage of his lifetime. "Please go hang out with Zoe," she said, "until Simon gets here. It shouldn't be long." Jon climbed slowly, reluctantly, up the stairs.

Cole was hesitating at the back door, keys in hand.

"Things okay?" he asked with strained indifference.

"No," Ellen replied indignantly. "Things are not okay! Zoe is pregnant. And did I hear you imply that the father is your friend?"

"Crap, Mom, don't call him *the father*. They just fooled around, that's all, no big deal. It's fucked up if she's pregnant."

"Jesus, Cole, *Jesus*! What can you possibly mean when you say *no big deal*? It's a very big deal and if he impregnated Zoe then *father* is technically the correct term."

"She's not going to keep it?" Cole sputtered, incredulous.

"She doesn't seem to be trying to get an abortion. God, Cole, she's only fourteen. What was he thinking?" Ellen gripped the back of a kitchen chair to steady herself.

"Well, mum, he probably wasn't exactly *thinking*." Cole noticed her white-knuckled hands on the chair. "You going to be okay?" he asked gently.

"I'm kind of stunned," she observed. "It stops me cold in my tracks to hear you say that it's no big deal."

"I didn't mean, you know, if she has a kid, that's no big deal, but sex, well. You know, it's just not all that..." stammering uncharacteristically, Cole stepped back into the kitchen and leaned against the counter. He looked at his mother quizzically. She was the mother who didn't flip out about a little weed in the pocket of your jeans in the laundry, who didn't go crazy about the lyrics to rock songs, the language you used with your buddies, the movies you wanted to see. She seemed liberal about sex, too, although now that he thought about it, this was one subject she hadn't really come clean on. "I can't believe you're surprised. Lots of kids have sex. Not everybody, but lots. It's not all that big a deal."

"You and Kelly?" Ellen's eyes narrowed involuntarily.

"Well, what do you think? I use protection, though. Jeez, mom, not that it's your business at this point," Cole said levelly.

Now Ellen looked straight at her son and thought: *so this is what you get* when you tell your kids to be honest and to feel good about their bodies. This is how it works out if you avoid shaming them and encourage them to be independent thinkers. Do I really get to be surprised? Or am I just surprised to be reminded that there's a cost to everything?

"I'm going out." Cole announced, sensing his mother drifting off. She shook her head as he turned away.

As arranged, Simon came to pick Zoe up on his way home from Matt's gymnastics class. When he reached the driveway, he was puzzled to see Ellen standing on the porch, wearing a light jacket, as if she were eager to go somewhere.

"Am I late?" he asked, trying not to sound irritated as he got out of his SUV. This was why he hated to ask favors, especially of Hannah's friends. There was always a hitch.

"Oh, no," Ellen assured him. "I just want to take a little walk with Matt while you go inside. Zoe needs to tell you something."

That can't be good, Simon thought to himself, recalling Zoe's irrationally tearful outburst in the morning. But he poked his head back into the vehicle and said to Matt, "Hey, sport, Auntie Ellen wants you to give her some exercise. Can you get out?"

"Help me look for Romeo and Juliet, okay, Matt? They haven't had their dinner," she added as the sturdy little boy climbed out of his car seat.

Matt loved Romeo, whom he had resolutely renamed "Mee-oh." He took Ellen's hand as they disappeared behind the house. Simon entered the front door and found Zoe curled up on the couch in the living room, the anguish in her puffy, blotchy face driving huge icicles straight into his heart.

17: Alone

At 8:30, Simon pulled out of Ellen's driveway with Zoe hunkered down beside him and Matt waving gaily from his car seat in the back. Watching from her kitchen window as their taillights receded down the street, Ellen was struck by a profound emptiness in her own house. Cole went out immediately after dinner. Jon left when Simon arrived. Will wasn't home yet and even the cats were nowhere to be seen. Only the refrigerator hummed companionably. Ellen stood in front of it for a few minutes, finally reaching for a Labatt's Blue. Then she put the cold can back, unopened, and rummaged around under the counter until she found her bottle of Southern Comfort. A splash of vermouth, a few chunks of ice, and she was ready for…what? The drink went down fast, gone before she had finished scrubbing out the crock pot. She vowed to nurse the second one slowly. Where was William? Why hadn't he at least called? She dialed his cell phone and immediately heard it ringing back at her from the pocket of his jacket, hanging by the back door. "Damn," she muttered as she hung up. William maintained his initial dislike for mobile phones, claiming that carrying one made him feel like a dog on a leash.

There were no lights on in the living room. Feeling restless, jumpy and aimless, Ellen gathered a small pile of old magazines to recycle, then set them down on a side table to ferment for another month. She sat in the semidarkness cast by the streetlights, noting how her years of collected stuff threw dim shadows on the walls. She would've loved to call Hannah for a long talk. Who else could she call? Not Maggie; Maggie would be busy with her family. Not Julie. They were dear friends, but she couldn't call Maggie or Julie to sort through her feelings about Hannah's kid. Those weren't her beans to spill. She went back into the kitchen, made a pot of tea, and retrieved the box of dark chocolate chunk cookies that she had stashed behind the kids' old insulated lunch bags. Back in the living room, she clicked on the television and limited herself to just two of the cookies (*low carbs be damned!*) while she scrolled through seventy channels before clicking it off in disgust. Where was Will? It really was getting late. Her eyes wandered to the dusty cluster of her wedding pictures on the wall.

Ellen and William started dating when they were juniors in high school. She'd been introverted and insecure, fearing that she could never measure up to the path blazed by her older sister. William was cocky and funny. He made all their decisions. They had fit each other like old slippers. By their senior year, they were having furtive, unprotected sex. Ellen lived in constant fear of getting pregnant. Timidly, she made her way to a clinic advertised on a city bus. She hid her stash of birth control pills in a tampon box behind her shoes in the back of her closet. Her mother was pleased by Ellen's sudden interest in keeping her own room clean and the pills were never discovered.

To save money, she and William attended local colleges and lived at home with their parents. They married two weeks after graduation and moved into a cramped apartment near campus. After several months of unsuccessful job searching, William went to work in his father's insurance business.

While Ellen's friends struggled to find commitment in their relationships and jobs that offered any kind of economic security, her life had been a steady, safe trajectory up the steps of the middle class. Soon, she and William stopped swapping dreams about moving to new, exotic places and instead bought a modest prairie-style house with a nice porch on a long, narrow, city lot between Elmwood and Delaware Avenues. Ellen landed a social work position at the Sisters of Charity Hospital. She was not unhappy as she went off birth control and waited anxiously, every month, to become pregnant. When that didn't happen after a year, a year-and-a-half, two years, the quest to get pregnant began to settle over everything else in her life like a cold, wet fog. Scheduling sex according to her basal body temperature turned the heat between them down so low that Ellen wore socks to bed even on hot summer nights.

Working sixty-hour weeks allowed William's star to rise quickly in his father's business. Perhaps it also helped to be the boss's son, but he poured himself into the work so industriously that he avoided even the whiff of nepotism. To advance his career, his father urged him to buy a membership at a particular golf club, join the Rotary club, and sing in the men's chorus at their church. Male bastions all, they suited William as seamlessly as his double-breasted blazers. He didn't even mind that Ellen soon declined to attend church with him.

Ellen imagined adopting a baby and scheduled a home study. She took up yoga and jogging and learned to make pottery. The home study was approved. She and Will were put on a waiting list to adopt. Would they consider an older child, a child of another race, or a child with a disability? "It's up to you," Will shrugged. At that, Ellen found herself letting go, floating away from her life with him. And then, unexpectedly, Cole was conceived. He was a revolutionary army of one – his arrival overwhelming every other distraction in their company. He was premature, born with heart problems that required delicate surgery during his first month. After the surgery, when their new infant son gripped their index fingers with his tiny hands, Will and Ellen united to see him live and to be parents who deserved this miracle child.

Ellen recalled all this now, sitting in her dark living room surrounded by the photos and mementos of the life she and Will had constructed. I have been a good mother and here I have a good life, she thought. Why am I so antsy, so restless?

Lurching to her feet, unwilling to be home alone another second, Ellen slipped on a denim jacket and let herself out into the brisk evening air. The full moon cast strong shadows, turning her familiar neighborhood into an eerie noir movie set. A walk would have suited her well, but a middle-aged woman alone at night in the neighborhood had been mugged a few months earlier and reignited memories of the bike path rapist. So now Ellen stood on the sidewalk in front of her home, as uncertain of where to go as she was certain that she could not go back inside. The chill air filled her lungs as she drew in deep breaths, reminding herself to "feel your feet on the ground." This was something a colleague had once told her, useful advice she could still count on to help her stop her anxious self-induced spirals, if she happened to recall it.

The light of the moon glinted off the windshield of her car, beckoning her. A half hour later, Ellen eased into the parking lot of the Riverview Inn, a tavern that she and Will frequented occasionally in the years before children, but never since. Its interior had been extensively renovated and now featured a small stage at the end of a large, dark, comfortable lounge. A black and red poster advertising the Jones Quartet leaned against a worn guitar case at center stage. Ellen squinted at the band members. Three men, not young, and a twenty-something woman with extraordinarily long hair and jeans that were tighter than skin were positioning mikes, tuning guitars, arranging drums, and chatting with each other. Ellen hesitated. Did she want to sit alone at the bar or alone at a table? Where would she be most inconspicuous? She decided to pretend that she had come to listen to the band and pulled out a captain's chair at a table near the wall, about a third of the way back from the band. A waitress appeared and took her order for a Manhattan on the rocks. Ellen called the waitress back, sheepishly, and added, "I would also appreciate a glass of water and some pretzels, if you don't mind." She drummed her fingers on the table while she waited for her drink.

Suddenly, the band leapt into action, playing three old rock numbers that transported Ellen back to her high school gym and the urgent dancing she and her friends did there. The sound was many decibels above her comfort level and the young woman was disconcertingly intimate with the microphone, but Ellen found herself tapping her feet and swaying in her chair. After the pressures of the last twenty-four hours, it was a pleasure to be somewhere too loud to think. The music ended abruptly and the bearded, bespectacled bear who played lead guitar stepped forward to the mike.

"G'evening, ladies and gents," he began in a hoarse voice, "and welcome to the Riverside. We're the Jones Quartet, in case you can't read, and we're real pleased to be here tonight. I want to introduce my band. I'm Sam Jones and this here is my daughter, Samantha, the one with the purrty voice. The *only* one with a voice," he added ironically. "On bass guitar, those of you who know the local scene will recognize Ezekiel Winters and, out of retirement after many years, how many is it, Ty, my man, twenty? Our drummer tonight is Tyler Moynihan." The crowd (the place had filled in during the last half hour) clapped enthusiastically while Ellen gasped. Tyler Moynihan? Ty Moynihan!

Twenty-plus years crumbled away as she flashed back to Chemistry 101, the most difficult course of her college career, and her last course in the sciences. Ellen had squeaked out a C due to the superhuman efforts of her lab partner, Tyler Moynihan. A whiz in the sciences, he was also a drummer with a 35 mm camera always dangling from his neck so he could shoot pictures of his friends, as well as crowds at concerts, landmark buildings being wantonly demolished, blighted ghetto landscapes, and scenes of barges on Lake Erie. Ty had an eclectic thirst for photos, which he then developed in his own tiny darkroom. He was funny and warm and generous with his time.

When Will was busy (which was often), Ellen hung out with Ty and his band, smoking weed, eating pizza, posing for pictures, talking about how fucked up the world was, and inventing herself as a more liberated free-thinker than she truly was. For most of a year, she and Ty danced around the edges of a strong, silent sexual chemistry, since Ellen was (diamond ring on finger) engaged to William. Then, after one particularly debauched evening, they shared a long hungry kiss ending in a tumble onto Ty's bed. When his hands slid under her bra and cupped her breasts, Ellen shivered, hesitated, then pushed him away, staggered up, and went home. Mortified, she refused to talk about it later, other than to tell him it was a mistake she wanted to forget. Ty called her a craven coward and bitterly taunted her to look him up if she ever decided to "grow up." That had been their last conversation, their last contact. The anniversary of that final conversation, even after all these years, was still an agonizingly slow day for her.

Now there he was, in jeans and black t-shirt, a full head of curly graying hair, needing a shave but otherwise looking decidedly *good*. He had grown into his face, his jaw a little squarer, laugh lines radiating jaggedly out from his eyes and his smile as generous as in her memory. A wave of delighted recognition washed over her, startling her with its intensity. Mostly in shadow herself, she stared unabashedly at him as the band resumed playing. Arrayed in front of him were several intricately carved African djembe and conga drums of various sizes as well as cymbals, a Jaw Harp, a rusty cowbell, and a tambourine. His hands flew from one instrument to the next, while his head worked the air, his eyes half-closed, his lips occasionally mouthing the lyrics pretty Samantha was pouring breathily into the microphone. Tyler Moynihan embodied joy.

"Want another one?" the waitress asked for the second time. "While you check out the cute guys in our band?" Ellen looked up at the grinning girl.

"I'm fine," she said, startled back to reality. "In fact, I'll take my check now." She was glad the lounge was dark enough to conceal the schoolgirl blush that fanned over her cheeks and neck. Given that the lounge wasn't that full, the waitress took an inordinately long time to furnish her bill, and the band was winding down its first set by the time it arrived. *How hard can it be to add up one drink?* Ellen thought, agitated and increasingly nervous that she'd be discovered. She left a small tip and nearly made it to her car when Ty's sonorous voice rang out across the parking lot.

"El? Ellen, wait up!" He came loping down the line of cars. She could see by the strong light of the full moon that his t-shirt was wringing wet. He'll catch his death of cold, she thought.

"Tyler Moynihan," she turned to face him, voice light, forcing a happy smile. "It *is* you! How are you?"

"Amazed," he said, as he encircled her in a warm hug and then quickly pushed away. "But I'm freezing. Come back in, we're on break. Talk to me. Shit. I saw you leaving. I can't believe you were sneaking out without even saying hello!"

"I didn't think you'd remember me," she lied. "But if you're on break, sure, I'll come back in for a few minutes."

"Good, great," Ty smiled broadly. "You look amazing, El."

She remembered that she hadn't bothered to brush her hair before driving away and silently thanked the forgiving light of the full moon for all it concealed as they walked back toward the bar, gravel crunching under their feet. "So, you're still drumming." she observed. "You were wonderful."

"Aaugh," he coughed derisively. "Actually, we sucked. Samantha thinks she's gonna get discovered and be the next American Idol and she overdoes everything. But Sam's a good friend and they needed a drummer and I thought *what the hell*? I'm not doing anything. It's actually been kind of fun."

"It looks it, and your band definitely does not *suck*," Ellen declared, suddenly feeling shy.

As they made their way back to her table, the waitress reappeared, a wide grin on her face. Ellen felt a surge of briny dislike for this thin, young woman. "Get her another of whatever she was having," Ty ordered, tilting his head toward Ellen, "and I'll have a pitcher of water and a pint of whatever's on tap."

"You got it," the girl said sweetly.

Now Tyler looked at her frankly, a smile playing around his eyes. "So what's up, El? What have you done with the last twenty, or is it twenty-four, years? Are you out bar hopping all by your lonesome? You never struck me as one to go off on your own."

"Yeah, this is unusual, and you sure ask a lot of questions!" Ellen said, laughingly ducking his questions. "I hardly know where to start. Tell me what's up with you. "

At that, he sat back in his chair, laced his hands across his chest, and smiled appreciatively. "Okay. I left town after graduation, worked down south about fifteen years, came back to take care of my dad after mom passed. He's gone now, too, and I actually live in the old family place and work for the town. I'm a building inspector, code violations and shit like that. I work with Sam, the guy on the lead guitar. Divorced. I got one kid, a sweet girl I don't see except in the summer. She lives in North Carolina with her mom, my ex." He took a deep breath and pushed his beer at her as if moving a chess piece. "Your turn."

"So sorry to hear about your parents," Ellen remembered how welcome the Moynihans had made her feel on those many occasions when she had stopped by Ty's house.

"Yeah, sucks." Sorrow drew down the contours of Tyler's face. "You never get used to it, but at least I no longer expect to see my dad at the house when I get home. It's been months since I had that thought that I'll have to tell him something or talk to him about something as soon as I walk in. I guess I'm getting over it." He forced a smile. "So, you gonna tell me what's up with you?"

"Um," Ellen hesitated. "I never left Buffalo, actually. I'm a social worker at Sister's Hospital. Two great sons, Cole and Jonathan, both in high school. Two cats…" She trailed off.

Silence hung between them for a few moments and then Ty said, "So, you going to make me ask about you and Billy? Or was it *Willie* he preferred?"

Ellen smiled as she flashed on a clip from a vintage movie where the handsome actor slips off his wedding band at the propitious moment and slides seamlessly into a double life. She imagined Claire, of *Mariner's Cove,* sitting here, opposite Ty, feeling vital. But when she spoke, her words came with a thin sigh. "*Will*. He goes by William or Will. We're still married."

Ty echoed her sigh and sat in silence for a full minute, looking at Ellen through quizzical eyes. "Wow, still married. Okay, where is he, then?"

"I imagine he's home now," she said, flustered. "He worked in Cleveland today and I just didn't feel like being home alone tonight. It was a horrible day. I just needed to get out of the house." She bit her lower lip to hold back the unwanted tears that stung her eyes.

Ty leaned toward her. His smile faded. "Sorry," he said. He took a slow pull on his beer and held her gaze in his. "Let me ask you, are you *happily* married, El?"

Startled, she dropped his gaze and busied herself with drying off the beads of moisture that were condensing on the outside of her drink. "Wow, that's quite a question! I guess I would say we're *thoroughly* married."

Leaning his head back, Ty laughed out loud. "*Thoroughly* married," he mimicked, not unkindly. "Never heard that before. Okay. It's a rush to see you, after all these years and I'm kind of high right now, an hour of drumming does weird shit to your brain." He drained his water and continued. "I would like to have a cup of coffee with you, anyway, thoroughly married or whatever. My dad used to say you can never have too many friends. You're an old friend and I would like to catch up. Break is almost over and I gotta get back up there. Will you have coffee with me?"

"Ah, that would be... that would be nice," Ellen fumbled.

"Nice." He drew the word out slowly. "You're a social worker, you must have a card with your number."

"Don't inspectors have cards, too?" she gently retorted as she fished a business card out of her wallet.

"Oh, I got cards, all right, but I don't believe you'd really call me." Ty's voice was teasing and light but Ellen was stunned by his directness.

"God, Ty. You don't beat around the bush!" she exclaimed.

"Not anymore," Ty shook his head. He picked up her card, stuffed it in his back pocket and smiled broadly. "It's truly very cool to see you. I'll call you next week." Then he sauntered toward the stage without waiting for her reply.

Ellen tried to pay for her drink but the waitress told her Tyler had covered it. Walk-running to her car, she drove home with her heart racing. Her normal life was settled and predictable. Since William had joined the insurance business, they joked about being "risk averse" but it wasn't a real joke. The batteries in their smoke detectors were fresh, their health care proxies were signed and clearly marked in the filing cabinet, and they never vacationed where they might be exposed to water-borne diseases, terrorists, or complicated currencies. Ellen fervently hoped that everyone in her family was either asleep or busy when she got home. She desperately wanted to be alone, to sift through her feelings away from her family's prying questions or inquisitive eyes.

18: Hello

Turning onto her street, Ellen was alarmed to see her house awash in light. William's and Cole's cars were in the driveway, the porch light ablaze, the front door open, and all the upstairs bedroom lights twinkling through the curtains. Even Juliet was out, pacing like a nervous sprite on the wide porch railing. Instantly, Ellen feared that something terrible had happened to Jon. She pulled in, cut the engine, and was relieved when her younger son bolted out of the house, hopping over the porch railing in his dash toward her.

"Mom!" he barked. "Where have you been?"

"Out," she said, her fear quickly displaced by irritation. Why was he practically shouting at her? Then William and Cole sauntered down the steps, looking like twins except that one was twenty-six years older than the other.

"Where have you been?" Will echoed, clutching a can of beer in his right hand. He still wore his business clothes, a dark blue suit, yellow button-down shirt and a blue and yellow-striped tie loosened at the neck.

"Out," Ellen repeated softly. It was unsettling to be on the receiving end of her family's apparent worry. "What's the matter?"

"What have you been doing, Ellen?" William asked tersely. "You didn't leave a note. Didn't tell anybody anything. The house was actually locked when Jon got home. It's after 11. What the hell!"

"Hey!" she protested a little more assertively, "None of you ever bothers to leave me any notes! The house was sooo empty tonight, and I didn't want to be here by myself so I went out. I tried to call you but you left your cell phone home." Ellen felt unjustly indicted as well as faintly guilty. "So everybody's okay here? You had *me* worried with all the lights on and even the cats out pacing."

"Yeah, Mom, we're cool here," Cole said with a warm smile. "Just, jeez, if you're going to do that again, leave a note or something, okay? It's a little weird." He turned and went inside with Jon following closely on his heels.

Ellen watched them mount the steps. The boys' worry seemed overly melodramatic and she wondered if William said something to arouse their insecurity. How he had changed, she thought, countering his scrutiny of her as he stood, arms crossed almost accusingly over his chest, looking at her. He had added twenty pounds to his girth in the past few years, and when he was weary, his loose jowls sagged in his round face. Ellen noticed how his hair and his paunch were in inverse symmetry: as the one receded, the other protruded.

The moon was huge and high in the sky, grinning down on them like a child's drawing. Its strong light cast short shadowy caricatures of the humans facing off on the sidewalk.

"What?" she said, over-pronouncing the *t* at the end of her question.

"What?" he repeated. "Don't you have anything else to say?"

There may have been a wounded undercurrent to his tone, but Ellen heard only veiled accusation. "Like what?" she said, staring into his eyes, again clipping the *t*. "I already said, I was *out*. If it's important for you to know where, I took myself to the Riverview Inn, listened to a terrible band, had a drink, and here I am. No big deal." Hearing the sarcasm in her own voice, Ellen felt nauseous. Why had she said the Jones Quartet was terrible when she actually enjoyed them? Why not tell William that she had seen Ty? What did it mean that her insides were churning as she glared at her angry, exhausted husband whose crime seemed to be an excess of concern? William glared for a moment longer. "Fine," he said. His voice was now hard and gritty, full of no feeling anywhere close to *fine*. "Great. Just beautiful." He pivoted with military precision and stalked into the house.

If she remained like a statue frozen to the sidewalk and simply let him go, Ellen knew how the next several weeks would play out. William hated emotional confrontations and retreated into a distant, icy, silent cocoon. The last time they had slammed into this wall (maybe two years ago, she couldn't remember exactly), they had coexisted like actors who detested one another off camera. In the presence of their sons, they conversed civilly about family issues (*Yes, Cole could stay out late for a concert on Friday night. Yes, Jon could have extra money to order a yearbook*). Otherwise, Will treated her as if she were invisible, less than a memory. He slept on the old sofa in his basement office/workbench area, retrieving his clothes from their bedroom when she wasn't home. Determined to wait him out, Ellen scrubbed and deep cleaned her house the way people do before putting their home on the market.

After a week of standoff, William began to speak to her again in the simple commerce of families. *Good morning, do you need anything from the store? I'll be late tonight.* Several days later, he moved back into their bedroom, although he slept with his back to her. They both avoided physical touch, which, for Ellen, meant sleeping on the outermost lip of the mattress. Then one night, after several glasses of wine at one of his mandatory company functions, they came home and performed cursory sex. By silent agreement, the freeze ended, its underlying issues relegated to an unlit corner of their marriage.

Anything but endure that again, Ellen thought. Pulling herself back into the moment, she entered her house and scouted room to room until she found her husband, settling in at his computer in the cold, cob-webbed basement. She had hoped she was not too late to salvage some version of a marriage relationship, but seeing his back stiff to her, she blurted out, "Do you even want to be in this marriage?"

He sat very still as the clock ticked behind them for a full, long minute. His breathing was a little labored. Ellen imagined herself exploding into a million shards, but she stood her ground and resisted the impulse to try and un-ring the bell.

"Do *you?*" his terse reply, finally.

"I hate it when you answer a question with a question."

"You hate a lot of things."

"I do! You know what I hate?" she erupted. "I hate this! I hate being subjected to your silent treatment when I haven't done anything wrong."

Will pushed back from the computer and turned to her, arms crossed, glaring. "Ellen, why would I bother to talk to you when you have already decided that I am the asshole here?"

Ellen gasped. "I wouldn't have to decide anything myself if you would show up for a discussion. But you don't! Your defense is that you don't *need* a defense, that everything you do is hunky dory. And then you come down here and freeze me out."

"Listen! I am goddam exhausted. You worried the shit out of me and the boys and then you came home and got pissy because we were worried. What the hell was that?"

"I'm sorry! It was a terrible day and I felt like you were attacking me."

"Why would you think that?" he asked coolly.

"You acted like I didn't have the right not to be here. Like I have to have permission to leave the house. I felt so alone here tonight. I didn't want to be alone."

"Oh, for Christ's sake! Why in hell can't you be satisfied here? What don't you have that you could possibly want?" William glared at her, the veins in his forehead and neck throbbing so violently she could almost hear them.

Ellen stared back, debating whether it was worth the risk of answering. If she spoke her truth and he didn't care, what would she do? Feeling reckless, she pursued it. "I want the same thing the meanest, poorest person in the world wants; the same thing everyone wants: I want to be loved. I don't want to be just some functional unit around here, something that makes life go smoothly for everyone else. I want you to love me, to want to be with me, to *want* to listen to me." Ellen sat on the dirty workbench and concentrated on hardening the muscles in her face to derail her tears. If she focused on holding her eyes open, she could sometimes succeed.

"Shit, Ellen. What do you think it is that happens here? When I was growing up, love was what you *did,* not what you said. Why do you think I come back every night to this family? But, I'm no horny teenager. I'm not going to follow you around with my tongue hanging out. You are a million miles away most of the time and I have no goddam idea what's going on with you."

Renegade tears escaped down her cheeks as Ellen whispered. "So *ask* me! Let me know that you notice! I feel like you don't care what's going on, so long as I don't inconvenience anyone. Goddam it. I don't want to be crying. I don't want any fucking sympathy."

"Don't worry about sympathy. I'm shit out of that. So what, *exactly*, do you want? Flowers?" he asked. Her tears were working on him. His question was sincere, his lips slackening as his face slightly relaxed.

"What do I want?" she repeated. Ah, she wanted to be heartbreakingly beautiful and utterly irresistible, the heroine in an epic nineteenth century novel. She wanted her life to have worth and meaning, depth and passion. She wanted her friends to be happy and healthy and possessed of smart, lovely children just a tad less accomplished than her own. She wanted a perfect marriage in which she and her husband anticipated each other's needs and gladly fulfilled them. Extraordinary perfection in all things, that's what she wanted. The spilled cornucopia of wants seemed a little funny and a lot pathetic. Breathe, she reminded herself, inhaling so deeply that it hurt.

"I want more of a life as a couple. The boys are almost grown up and we don't have anything that we enjoy doing together. I want us to fix that. I want a whole bunch of ridiculous other things, too, but they're probably just a mid-life spasm. You know, or maybe you don't? Did Jon or Cole tell you that Zoe's pregnant?" She paused for breath and then added, softly, "I want that not to be true."

Will whistled softly. The *In Accord* families had celebrated and sorrowed together through so many years and occasions that they were bonded like cousins. "Zoe's pregnant? Holy mother of Jesus, you got to be kidding! How are Hannah and Simon?"

"Hannah doesn't know, unless Simon called her in Quebec and told her. It's been a hideous day, Will, a long, long day. Come upstairs. Have a drink of something – tea, vodka, tea and vodka, I don't care, but please, let's talk."

Managing a half-smile, he started after her unsteadily. Ellen wondered how much he had already had to drink. He would be asleep soon, she knew, and they would not truly talk.

19: Hannah, Friday Night

Both the mattress and the pillow in the little Quebec hotel were firm and unforgiving, so, like a stone skipped across a pond, Hannah bounced off the outer edges of sleep on into the night. Dropping off easily, she startled awake at midnight, visualizing Beth's high school record stained by this drinking incident. Angrily willing herself to let go of it, she drifted back into an uneasy fog. At 1:05, she was awake again, sweating and asking herself how the stupid rule infraction might affect Beth's chances of getting into a good university. "High time to learn life's lessons and it serves her right besides," she thought grimly, forcing her eyes shut again, and berating herself for not thinking to pack a sleeping pill. At 2:15, she awoke to the pleasant fantasy of Beth turning the whole episode into a positive by weaving it into her admissions essay as an example of a personal growth experience. That's insane, she quickly realized, and anyway, was it going to be a personal growth experience? Why was she, Hannah, obsessing about this now anyway?

All she craved was to sleep, to sleep and to get home. She tried to relax slowly and methodically, first focusing on letting go of the tension in her feet, then her calves, then her knees. Then she was thinking about her family again, worrying about how surly Zoe had been lately, about how little time she'd had for Matt, and feeling a sludgy mix of guilt and resentment which she thought ridiculous even while she couldn't set it down. At a very primitive level of her being, Hannah harbored the conviction that everything was her fault, the result of some inadequacy in her mothering, some critical moment when she had failed to impart the right lesson. Cozied up beside that conviction was a second, mocking belief that it was tiresome narcissism to entertain the idea that she had the power to control anything. She hunted for a mantra that would ease her mind, but she couldn't hold one long enough to detach from all the noise in her head. Beth snuffled lightly in the next bed.

At 4:30, Hannah startled awake, unbearably hot. She bolted upright and heaved the stiff polyester quilt onto the floor. "Shit!" she muttered. By the dim corridor light seeping under their door, she groped her way to the scarred mahogany desk and switched on the desk lamp, keeping one eye on Beth for signs of wakefulness. But Beth was enjoying the deep, effortless sleep of the young and the guiltless. Opening the drawer, Hannah found the obligatory two sheets of hotel stationary. "Might take my mind off this whole mess if I start my chapter of *Mariner's Cove,*" she thought.

During her rise to the rank of middle school principal, Hannah had drafted dozens of proposals seeking funds for various educational purposes. She liked the discipline of grant writing and used it whenever she wanted her words to achieve some objective quickly. First, state your purpose; then, convincingly explain the need; finally, describe your brilliant, economical solution.

She wrote "Purpose" under the hotel's address and stared at it blankly. "Need," she scribbled, then "Solution." After staring for a few more minutes, she doodled a pansy, a bee, and a butterfly with intricate scrolling on its wings. She underlined need three times. "Shit!" she whispered in frustration as no further thoughts or storylines materialized. In a fancy script, she wrote "need" several ways while pondering whose need she was addressing. What did *Mariner's Cove's* Claire truly need? What did she need from *Mariner's Cove?* What was missing? Distraction, moral absolution, fun? Can you get them all in one book? And what on earth did Ellen need so badly that she had cajoled her friends into rewriting the ending of someone else's book? How absurd!

Hannah ran her fingers through her hair and rubbed her temples. The words and curlicue butterflies on the page began to dart around like insects in a puddle. Her eyelids felt leaden. Without thinking, she folded her arms over the pages and laid her forehead across them as sleep finally wrapped its arms around her.

20: The Saturday Run

Ellen was skilled at compartmentalizing important feelings and events. It was part of her career training, a part she particularly embraced. At 10:15 in the morning, a patient could be crying in her office about a devastating diagnosis. Forty-five minutes later, a different patient could be bitching bitterly about the frustrations of dealing with insurance companies. Leaning slightly forward, eyes steady and attentive, Ellen could seem equally engaged in both conversations.

This talent carried over into her personal life as well, particularly with William. She deliberately conveyed an impression to most of her friends and acquaintances that she was happily married. Only to Hannah did she fully expose and examine her pain. But Hannah was not available, so by Saturday morning, Ellen had erected a mental moat around the good feelings stimulated by running into Ty, as well as the ugly, distressing clash she had with William the night before. Her focus was on the things she wanted or needed to do in the moment, including taking her regular run in the park.

There's a street-festival quality to every sunny Saturday morning in Delaware Park, even when temperatures hover in the

40s. A well-groomed, sprawling, eighteen-hole municipal golf course. A venerated yet antiquated zoo with charming gothic red brick buildings. A few basketball and tennis courts, soccer fields, swings, and slides all vie for space on the rolling little hills of the park designed by Frederick Law Olmstead for Buffalo's 1901 Pan Am Exposition. Encircling the whole of it, a six-foot wide, 1.8 mile track is usually thick with a colorful stew of walkers, amblers, joggers, and serious runners of all ages, races, shapes, and degrees of athleticism. Ellen had been running this track for several years, two laps on weekday mornings, five on Saturday.

Checking the odometer strapped to her wrist, she sniffed happily to see that she had already clocked 6.4 miles. Since she ran this course every Saturday except when she was running a race somewhere else, Ellen knew exactly what distance she had run, but she savored a sweet little surge of pleasure upon *seeing* the evidence digitized on her wrist. Partway into her fourth lap, salty rivulets of sweat stung her eyes and ran down her neck, dampening the old cotton t-shirt she especially loved to wear on Saturdays. It was the first shirt she ever won, a prize for simply completing a 5-K Thanksgiving race seven years earlier. The wind off the lake whipped at her hair, standing her bangs up around her headband like a weed-whacked edge. Spotting Julie trotting east along the path to meet her near the soccer fields, Ellen waved.

"I'm hot!" Ellen complained as they drew close. "I'm seriously overdressed." She was wearing thick black runner's tights, a pink neoprene turtleneck under the old t-shirt, and a silvery jacket constructed to keep out wind and sleet. She'd reached that lovely plateau in her run where the muscles of her legs were no longer whining, her feet and knees had stopped protesting the pounding they were being given, her heart and lungs were heeding the oxygen demands of her mitochondria, and she was in a completely comfortable rhythm with herself.

Julie, jogging for only a few minutes, felt every cell in every muscle recoil against the demands of pavement, air, muscle, and will. Outfitted in the same warm clothes she had worn yesterday morning, she laughed. "You're crazy!" Her hot and labored breath was visible in the crisp air. The steady breeze off the lake penetrated her tights and jacket with icy efficacy. Were she alone, she would have trotted back to her car in defeat, so she was grateful for Ellen's distracting company. Only fools run in cold weather, she thought, fools and friends. Reversing course, she fell into step with Ellen.

"Didn't you stretch?" Ellen asked sharply, noticing Julie's off-center gait.

"Oww, you don't miss a thing!" Julie exclaimed. "I got such a late start that I was afraid I'd miss you, so I skipped the stretching."

"Not recommended," Ellen commented dryly. Then, seeing Julie's strained face, she asked, "What's going on?"

Julie rolled her eyes. "Stephan's got his test for his driver's license next week so he wanted to practice parallel parking. So, being the good mom, I took him out to practice and he was taking corners like he was in a crazy Bruce Willis movie! I told him it wasn't a video game and he needed to *watch out* and *slow down,* and then we had an all-out fight. You know how teenagers know everything, right? It was like he was *trying* to have an accident. I was scared to death. And this kind of stuff doesn't usually come up with Stephan and me."

They both shuddered, thinking of Stephan's real accident several years ago.

"That's tough," Ellen commiserated. "My dad was the one who taught me to drive, and you just didn't screw around when he told you to do something. What about Eric?" Picturing Julie's ex-husband, Ellen added, "Can't he help with stuff like this?"

A hard wind gust slammed across the parkway alongside the park, rattling the light posts in their concrete moorings and momentarily sucking the air out of their lungs. Dried leaves swirled crazily at their feet. Julie huffed. "He's *supposed* to. It's in the divorce decree, liberal visitation as part of the custody arrangement. But, does this make any sense to you? He says he doesn't *get* Stephan. He says the boy's too sensitive and that's, of course, because I've sissified him."

"Sissified! No way, that's ridiculous."

They moved over to make room for a group of geriatric power-walkers, their fists pumping and their grey hair flying.

Julie continued, "Every now and then they do something together like get pizza or go to a Sabres game and Stephan always comes home upset or mad about something." She ran in silence for a minute, then continued, "You know what I mean? It's more work to fix it than if I just let it slide, don't push them together. Like when we were married, it was harder to get him to do his share of anything than it was to just do it myself. You know? If I'd ask him to pick up his own wet towels off the bathroom floor, he'd pout for days and whine that I reminded him of his mother."

"That sucks!" Ellen sympathized again. William left his wet towels in piles on the bathroom floor, too, and like Julie, she picked them up and resented it. She snorted again.

"What?" Julie asked.

"Husbands!" Ellen grimaced and picked up their pace.

"Get out. *You* have a lovely marriage," Julie retorted in a faintly accusatory tone. It was maddening to hear the carping and criticizing of women whose husbands were loyal, decent, regular providers. That was all she had wanted.

Ellen shot her a quick glance. Memories of last night's confrontation sloshed over her mental moat. "I don't know if there's any such thing as a truly good marriage!" A blanket of guilty awareness dropped on her, and she pushed thoughts of Ty Moynihan to the back of her brain. She *did* have an enduring marriage, after all, if she would just accept its imperfections and inequalities. These seemed to be the price of not being alone and she wished she were the type of evolved, secure woman who could accept the costs graciously. Instead, she was always angling to renegotiate the terms when what she really had was a fixed rate. "I'm sorry," she mumbled. "I don't really have much to complain about, although I could complain all afternoon if you would let me. I probably drive William as crazy as he drives me."

"I'm listening." Julie extended a peace offering. She knew it was self-righteous to censor her married friends for saying whatever was on their minds, and she understood as well as anyone that marriage is an always-shifting puzzle.

"Thanks." Ellen offered softly. "It's okay, really." She didn't feel like burdening Julie, or like hearing herself admit to all the raw, cutting details of her sharp-edged marriage.

They ran on in unison, past the empty, manicured bocce courts and the crowded, shabby basketball courts. The path took them by the outer ring of the zoo. American bison snuffled on the other side of the high wrought-iron fence, their pungent scent hanging heavily over the paths and parkland. After a lap together, Julie decided to try another lap on her own. Ellen was done. They parted with plans to meet the next morning for *In Accord's* other standing date, Sunday brunch.

Julie pushed herself to run alone at an easy, steady pace. Unbidden, a lyric fragment from an old Taj Mahal blues song looped through her mind: "Baby, I was built for comfort, not for speed." Faster, leaner runners passed by, some looking like they were actually built for speed. It didn't matter; she wasn't on the clock. She had warmed up and her legs and lungs were in sync. Running, by drawing her attention so intimately into her own physical universe, cleared her head and gave her a cushion from the daily frustrations of a high-maintenance teenage son, a critical mother, and a vindictive ex-husband. Despite all those things, she was feeling good, really good.

Padding over the rise at the southwest corner of Ring Road, she stopped suddenly at the rear of a small group being held at bay by an angry brindled dog the size of a small adult black bear. He was standing in the middle of the running path, barking furiously, runny red gums bared around brown-stained incisors. Short hairs stood erect in a ridge along his massive, muscular back. Four other runners had screeched to a halt in front of Julie, a human version of an expressway pile-up on a slippery morning. A similar cluster formed on the other side of the dog as the clockwise runners also halted in their tracks.

"Whose damn dog is that?" an extremely tall, thin woman in neon purple tights shrilled.

"Pit bull!" one of the runners answered.

"Nah, it's a mixed breed. Mastiff, lab, maybe a little pit..." came a calm voice from the back of the pack.

"Who cares what *kind* of dog it is? Where's its fucking owner?" the tall woman anxiously demanded.

Julie grimaced. It made her uncomfortable to see people losing their cool, and their manners, so quickly, though her adrenaline was rising, too.

"Maybe it escaped. It don't got a leash and I don't see nobody coming 'round after it," said another onlooker.

"What do we do?" Julie stammered, beginning to feel panic. Her fear of dogs was one reason she avoided running alone.

"Anybody got a cell?" a reasonable masculine voice asked. Although his back was to her and it had been at least a year since they last spoke, Julie easily recognized Nathan's deep, distinctive accent. He was the last man she almost dated and she had often regretted her cowardice in turning him away.

All of the women in the cluster clawed at their pockets, producing an array of silvery or purple-clad phones.

"Don't *all* call!" Nathan spoke with exasperated authority. "You..." he nodded toward the nearest woman. "Call 911. They'll send someone from animal control. We just need to stay calm. This guy's not going to go after the whole group of us."

"What's in your jacket?" someone asked.

Nathan turned so Julie could see that he had stuffed a very small, tan and black, shivering, squirming dog into the front of his jacket, like a kangaroo's joey. "This is my dog," he said apologetically. "I think he's what caught the attention of the big fellow." His miniature pincher looked like a quick appetizer for the angry bear-dog in the road. It stood its ground, barking its staccato protest, as the phone call to animal control was made. "They'll send someone right away," she reassured the uneasy group.

"Nathan!" Julie stammered, feeling both awkward and delighted to see him.

He looked over to see who had called his name, then stepped toward Julie, smiling broadly. "Hey!" he said, "I'd never have guessed you were a runner."

"Good God, not hardly." Julie panted, clutching her side. "I'm a total newbie."

"Well, good for you!" Nathan said, securely holding the little twitching dog inside his jacket. "I'm kind of a newbie at this whole park thing myself. A friend talked me into rescuing this excuse for a dog and now, here I am, rescuing it again."

"Kermit! Kermit!" a small boy came running from the direction of the basketball courts, leash and empty collar in hand, his high voice thick with worry. The bear-dog turned off his bark as if the boy had pushed its mute button, wheeled away from the assembly of terrified runners, and trotted toward the boy, stubby tail wagging joyously.

"What the hell, would you look at that!" the purple tights shrilled again. "That little boy has no business bringing a dog bigger than he is here, especially since he's got no clue how to control it. Someone should stay for the animal control guy and point them out."

"You've got to be kidding!" Nathan answered her angrily.

"What*ever*," she said. With her back to him, she bent over, straight-legged, knees locked, and laid her silk-gloved palms flat on the ground, every muscle and dimple in her ass unmistakable as she wiggled and stretched her legs and buttocks beneath her expensive tights. Most of the rest of the group broke up, grumbling, and resumed their runs or walks, a tad colder.

"Well, I'm sure not going to make life miserable for some poor kid and his dog," Julie declared to the woman's backside, smiling at Nathan. "That's an adorable puppy you have there. What do you call it?"

"His name is Captain. He'd wiggled away and I was just grabbing him when that monster dog appeared. I sort of wonder if that other dog thought I was calling him."

Julie shivered. "I've always been terrified of big dogs. Oh, well, all's well that ends well, right?" The words sounded so lame when they hit the air that she wished she could issue a recall. She flushed.

"So you think things ended well?" Nathan asked with mild sarcasm before she could slink away.

"Oh, dear!" A crimson map inched up her neck and onto her face, a blush too red to pass off as simply runner's flush. "I, I didn't mean that!"

"I've been wondering about you," Nathan ignored her ruddy face and smiled. "How've you been, really?"

Whether it was adrenaline from the dog fright or serotonin from the long run, something loosened Julie's normally reticent manner. "I'm okay, more or less, if you don't count issues with my teenage son, my ex-husband, or my job, or cranky plumbing in my old house." She paused, "And the fact that I keep kind, attractive men like you at arm's length."

Horns blared from the parkway, providing her with a welcome interruption. She met his eyes, appreciating his reassuring smile, and charged on. "I've always been sorry we didn't get that dinner or that movie or time just to get to know each other."

"Is there anything stopping you now?"

She smiled self-consciously. "Well, no. Nothing."

Nathan beamed. "Great! How about tonight?" Captain was squirming and struggling to get down.

Julie looked toward the zoo, worry lines fanning out from the corners of her eyes, as she mentally scanned her calendar (empty), imagined telling her son that she had a date (scary), and wondered what she might wear (disastrous). But the serotonin was still working its magic. "Okay!" she agreed, surprising herself. "Pick me up at seven?"

21: At the Feldmans', Saturday

Back at the hotel in Quebec, Hannah was sound asleep, head still resting on her arms at the desk in the small room she shared with Beth.

"Mom! Mom? What's going on?" Beth shook her mother's shoulder gently. "It's ten o'clock. I thought you wanted to be on the road now. You okay?" Hannah raised her stiff neck off her numb, tingly arms and squinted at her daughter. Beth was showered, her hair freshly done, makeup carefully applied, back pack zippered neatly and leaning against the wall near the door of their hotel room. She looked radiant.

"Oh, damn!" Hannah mumbled, sitting up gingerly. "It's ten? Why didn't you wake me? Damn, it's late!"

In a flurry, Hannah showered in the tiny stall with a showerhead that could be angled no higher than her breasts. She decided to forego washing her hair for yet another day. Curly hair can be a godsend, she thought, running her fingers through it appreciatively. She yanked on yesterday's jeans, snagged a warm croissant from the hotel's continental breakfast offerings, filled her travel coffee mug with black caffeinated brew, and claimed her place in the left lane on Highway 20 barreling south along the St.

Lawrence. It was a lovely day, cool and clear with glorious remnants of autumn reflected in the golden aspens sparkling on distant hills.

In Montreal, they stopped for food and fuel and gaped at the stunning skyline. To most Buffalonians, Canada is a gigantic space occupied by maple trees, compulsively neat flowerbeds, bears, frozen tundra, beer drinkers, and hockey fanatics. The soaring, ultra modern architecture of this sparkling Canadian city temporarily pulled Hannah and Beth out of their parallel reveries.

"Mom, look at it!" Beth excitedly pointed to a spiraling, glassy building. "What happens here? Why is Montreal so awesome?"

Hannah groped for an intelligent reply, scanning the archives of her brain and discovering that her Montreal file was utterly empty.

"I don't really know, Beth," she admitted.

"Oh, I thought you knew everything."

"Not *everything*," Hannah replied with exasperation.

Beth dozed off south of Montreal. Once back in their own country, she awoke and was exaggeratedly polite, listening without comment to her mother's CDs of Broadway musicals, Bruce Springsteen, and the Beatles. Hannah continued to fly down the interstate from Watertown to Syracuse, then sped toward Buffalo on the I-90, stopping for greasy pizza, to fuel up, and to walk out a spasm in her lower back. Eleven hours after leaving Quebec, they pulled into their Crescent Avenue driveway.

171

The Feldman house was built in the early 1900s on a deep, narrow lot with a garage at the end of an eighty-foot-long driveway that delicately threaded between their house and their neighbor's on the right. Hannah pulled forward cautiously to avoid scraping her side view mirror on the clapboard siding of the house.

Beth had dropped off to sleep again just west of Rochester, her head slumped forward on her chest like a rag doll. She stirred only slightly at the whirring clang as the garage door chains slowly dragged it toward the ceiling. Pulling in beside Simon's SUV, Hannah relaxed her shoulders, let go of the wheel, and listened as the thrumming of her tires continued to echo in her brain. Then a train's whistle cut through the air and she smiled, happy to hear the familiar sounds of her old, friendly city. "We're home," she announced to her sleeping daughter. She was imagining the long, hot shower she was going to be taking in just a few sweet minutes.

Climbing the back porch steps toward the kitchen, an acrid whiff of burned microwave popcorn reached her. Opening the door, she was dismayed to see a half-empty jug of milk open on the counter near a loaf of bread that was spilling its slices like playing cards from a magician's deck. Peanut butter was smeared on a knife balanced on top of an uncapped jelly jar. A partially gnawed apple was browning up nicely nearby. Cups, glasses, and cereal bowls were stacked, unrinsed, in the sink. A soup can stood in a circle of spilled red goop, drying into its own cement on the tiled counter.

"Jesus Christ!" Hannah walked through the house, searching for her husband. "This is disgusting!"

She found him. Their son, dressed in superman pajama bottoms and a dirty blue t-shirt, lay sprawled across Simon's chest on the couch in the family room. The child's red superman cape was draped over his body like a thin blanket. The Feldman males were fast asleep. Slack-jawed, her unshaven husband snored loudly. Toy action figures and their tiny arsenals were strewn about the floor while a child-friendly DVD perched on the edge of the coffee table.

"Simon! Simon! What the hell?" Hannah whispered as she reached down and shook his shoulder, trying not to awaken their son. The look in his bleary eyes – spent, haunted, and, yes, old – stopped her tirade before it she could fully launch it. "Simon, what's wrong? What's going on here? Where's Zoe?"

Simon rose to his feet unsteadily, carefully nestling Matt back into the pillows on the couch. The slightly sweet scent of whiskey clung to him heavily.

"In her room," he sighed.

At that moment, Beth came clomping noisily into the house, dumping her backpack by the stairs. She was expecting a warm reception and sympathetic audience with her father.

"Crap!" she exclaimed dramatically as she sized up the kitchen. "What happened here? This place looks like sh... crap!" She made her way to the family room where her parents were awkwardly faced off. Her shrill, critical voice dragged Simon into the moment. "Hush!" he directed. "Don't wake your baby brother."

"God! Sorry," Beth complained. "What's the matter? What's going on?"

Roused by the voices and creaky sounds echoing through the old house when Hannah and Beth came in, Zoe descended from the second floor, her eyes swollen nearly shut in her puffy face.

Seeing her, Beth gasped. "Whoa! Look at you! Who died?"

"Shut up!" Zoe snapped at her sister. "Just shut up."

"Zoe?" Hannah turned to her middle child.

"Beth," Simon commanded, "Put your brother to bed. Now." He passed Matt's sleeping body into Beth's arms, his eyes stern. Beth did as she was told. He turned to Zoe. "Tell her."

Zoe opened her mouth but nothing came out. Then, in what seemed like slow motion, she faced Hannah. "I'm, I'm, oh, Mom, I'm so sorry, I'm p… p… pregnant," she whispered.

"You're what?" Hannah asked, disbelieving. "Pregnant? Zoe, you're *fourteen*, how can you be pregnant? Are you *sure?*"

Zoe stood silent, hands on the back of a chair for support, eyes brimming. She looked fourteen: thin, not fully grown, the expression on her face flitting between girl and woman as she stared at her mother's feet.

Suddenly, there was not enough oxygen in the room and Hannah's legs became weak. She dissolved onto the floor, wrapped her arms around her shins and hugged herself into a self-contained ball, head on knees. She held herself still, pulling air as deeply into her lungs as she could. Oh, to turn the clock back 24, no, 48 hours, no two months, maybe four. How long had she been without so much as a single clue? When pregnant middle-school girls loitered in the halls by the bathrooms, she was the first to suspect. This wasn't possible. My daughter. How could that be possible?

Seeing her mother collapsed on the floor, Zoe dissolved into tears and darted up the stairs, her sobs diminishing as she cloistered herself in her room. Beth, having overheard enough to know the basics of the situation, and to know she wasn't welcome to say anything now, began slamming cupboard doors and glass bowls around in the kitchen.

Simon sat heavily on the chair nearest Hannah. He had been desperate to talk with her since learning the crushing news last night. All day, he had mentally played various snippets of conversation they could have. In one version, Zoe had always been their bad seed: willful, difficult, self-absorbed. Then he blamed himself that Zoe was pregnant: the poor middle child was forced to seek male attention elsewhere because her dad was too busy to give it. Then, it was Hannah's permissive attitude and failure to set any limits or impose any consequences on either daughter's conduct that produced all their difficult behaviors. And finally, he pictured that he and Hannah would pull together, somehow discover the right thing to do. Whatever that was. But now Hannah was balled up on the floor in front of him, and he had nothing left to say, numb from his endless rehearsing. Meanwhile, Hannah sat in silence, as self-contained as a granite sculpture.

"Hannah," after several minutes that seemed like an eternity, he spoke, more sharply than he had intended.

She raised her arm, palm upturned, as if to ward off a blow. He clenched his teeth. "Zoe told me last night. I thought it could wait until you got home. I'll go check on Matt." He padded off. He didn't have the words to comfort her or even reach her.

Hannah remained tightly coiled, hair covering her face, knuckles white. She was desperate to silence the screams in her head. She felt unreal, stuck in some kind of frozen mud. There was nowhere to go. Gradually and almost involuntarily, her eyes began to record the worn patterns in the carpet, the vines and leaves and small woodland creatures worked into the stained, aged Persian rug left to her by her grandmother. Everything in her home was as she had left it and yet everything was different. She raised her head and tuned in to the loud sounds in her skull: her blood rushing, whoosh – whoosh – whoosh past the amplifiers in her ears; the vertebrae in her neck clicking softly; her lungs struggling to pull the air down deep enough. Zoe. Pregnant. Fourteen. GOD DAMN!

Releasing her knees, she put her hands down on the rug, steadying herself. A clock ticked somewhere, a toilet flushed, a car roared away into the night. Half-consciously, she hoisted herself to her feet and, zombie-like, climbed the stairs. She pushed her own internal chaos aside as a primordial motherly instinct compelled her toward her daughter. Without knocking, she walked into Zoe's room and sat on the bed beside her child. Zoe's long dark unwashed hair hung in strings down her back. She was fingering the threadbare, floppy ears of the stuffed bunny that had gone everywhere with her in her toddlerhood. Its name was changed from "Peter" to "Pinkie" when Zoe had invented an imaginary friend who lived with them and imposed a reign of pink on everything. Hannah flashed on those years, yearning for simple days when imaginary friends gave stuffed animals new names and a big crisis would be to accidentally leave one in a supermarket shopping cart. To her tired eyes, Zoe looked waifish and sad, sitting on her bed stroking the mottled old thing.

Touching the stuffed animal gently, Hannah said, "I remember when you got this." Zoe looked down. "It was your first Hanukkah. Grammy Irene gave it to you and you loved it from the moment you laid eyes on it. "

"Grammy Irene," Zoe repeated.

"Yes."

"I miss her."

"Me, too." Tears were stinging Hannah's eyes as she thought of her mother, gone six years.

"But you're glad she's not here for this," Zoe whispered.

"I'm never, *ever* glad she's not here," Hannah corrected as a tear escaped down her cheek.

"Oh, Mom!" Zoe flung herself into her mother's lap and wept freely, the levee breached, her anguish pouring forth in great gulping gasps. Hannah stroked her child's head gently and dug deep into her own reserves for patience to let Zoe exhaust herself.

After twenty minutes, her heaving and sobbing slowed. Then, gently prodded, she told the story of the beer party, the hurtful disinterested boyfriend, sex she wasn't sure even counted, "it was over so quick I hardly felt it." Shame. Denial that it even happened. Never heard of the morning-after pill. Just prayed she would never have to tell her mother: "I was too afraid." Now she had missed at least two periods. The boy? She couldn't bring herself to name him, not yet but she would, tomorrow. Jon Palmer knew, and Cole, and Ellen, as of last night. No one else, especially not the boy. She was sick, puking, exhausted, and felt awful, awful, awful. Nothing worked, not crackers or ginger ale, eating or not eating, exercising did nothing. The days just kept marching onward. She knew she was too young to have a baby but she would *have to* keep it; she had seen pictures of new babies on advertisements plastered on the city busses and it wasn't right to get rid of them. Hannah was stunned. When had her wild baby girl formed these opinions?

"Oh, Mom," Zoe shuddered at last, "please don't be mad."

Involuntarily Hannah sighed, marveling that someone who could sob out that whole wrenching tale could finish with "Please don't be mad."

"How do you expect me to feel?" she asked sternly.

"I dunno," Zoe looked down and asked meekly, "Do you still love me?"

Hannah's exhaustion almost overtook her, but she reached over to Zoe and gave her a soft hug. "I will always love you, Zoe." The words sounded right to her ears, but Hannah continued to feel hollow. "There will be lots to talk about in the morning but now, we all need sleep."

Twisting a strand of her hair around her index finger and staring at the floor, Zoe said, "I'm hungry."

"Well, go make yourself a sandwich."

"Eeeeyewwww."

"What?"

"Could you make me something, Mom? I don't want to go downstairs again."

"Zoe, you have got to be kidding! If you're hungry, go make yourself something to eat." Hannah realized that her relationship with her daughter was going to change, had already changed, and there would be no turning back of clocks.

"Never mind, I'm not *that* hungry." Zoe clutched Pinkie to her chest and flopped back on her bed, staring glumly straight ahead.

Leaving her daughter's room, Hannah slapped her open palm against the wall outside the room, making a little smack. She left her hand on the wall and rested her head on it, collecting herself to go downstairs. She wasn't normally given to punching walls but she yearned for some way to spend her pent-up energy.

Scrubbing the kitchen would normally have done it but when she got downstairs, Beth had already cleaned every surface to a sparkling and antiseptic state. Beth! What luxury it would be to only have to deal with a daughter who had a beer and took care of a sick friend in Quebec.

Hair disheveled, face haggard, Simon was slumped in his chair in the living room with a large scotch and ice in hand. He appeared to be studying wispy cobwebs in one corner of the ceiling.

"Shit!" Hannah announced, sitting opposite him. Then, "damn it."

"Yeah," Simon met her eyes, ceremoniously, lifted his glass and took another sip. "I'm so sorry, Hannie. I had a lot to say earlier in the day but now all that's left is *I'm sorry*."

An air of immobility hung in the room like old rayon drapes, absorbing the light and the life. Each waited for the other to say more, afraid to spark a fire that would illuminate their stockpiled resentments. They still had fun together, still had common interests and politics, but on matters of child rearing, there were profound differences and Hannah's decisions had mostly prevailed. Nothing had ever brought their dissimilarities into sharper focus than the previous twenty-four hours.

Night noises whirred in the background as they sat, each with swirling thoughts about the consequences of their differences. Draining his glass in one long gulp, Simon rose and poured himself another Cutty Sark. He had made it nearly back to his chair when he hesitated, staring at his wife. He had never seen her look so small, so defeated. He turned back to the liquor cabinet, reaching around the everyday bottles for the ones they saved for special guests. For Hannah, he poured a small tumbler of Chivas Regal, aged 25 years. Their eyes locked as he slid it into her hand wordlessly. She tipped her glass toward him in mute appreciation and took a huge gulp, feeling the smooth liquid fire race down the back of her throat. They sat in silent solidarity until the liquor did its work and they made their way to bed.

22: At the Feldmans', Sunday Morning

On this particular Sunday morning, the clock's urgent chimes couldn't compel Hannah out of bed. Pulling the sheet over her face, she fell back into a restless stupor. When she opened her eyes again, Matt's sweet, grubby face was barely five inches away from her nose, his little fists full of plastic action heroes armed and ready. "C'mon, Mommy," he invited. "Play with my guys with me." His pajama bottoms had been abandoned somewhere and his small knobby knees protruded from his superhero boxers like new saplings. Hannah wiggled over in bed toward Simon's slumbering torso and patted the sheet beside her, inviting her little one in. She accepted one of his tiny plastic men, surprisingly fierce-looking given its diminutive facial features, and made a growling sound as she stabbed it at the air. Giggling and retaliating with shooting sounds, Matt threw himself into the game.

"I'm gettin' the bad guys!" he cried. "Shoot 'em til they all dead! Pop! Pow! Pop – p – p – pop!" He punched at the air near his mother's plastic warrior.

Groaning piteously, Simon rolled over, raised himself on one elbow, and peered through bleary eyes over Hannah's body.

"Hi, Daddy, bang, bang!"

Simon grunted. His eyes now coming into focus, a wide smile spread across his face as he admired the boundless energy of his little boy. "Earthquake!" he cried, flopping his arms up and down and shaking so energetically that the bed bounced. Matt squealed with high-pitched laughter as Hannah pulled a pillow over her ears and whimpered. Her mind re-wound the events and news of yesterday while Simon continued to writhe and Matt continued to laugh. *Boys*, she thought, glowering at her young son and her middle-aged spouse. She slid gingerly out of the bed. "Okay, I'm getting up."

The answering machine was blinking insistently in the kitchen so she reluctantly pressed "play." There were two messages for her from Ellen, one simply conveying "Hey, I'm here if you want to talk," and the second offering a ride to brunch this morning. Facing her friends filled her with dread and, she was surprised to note, shame. As if *she* had failed. And then the deep, ugly feeling she'd been suppressing surfaced: she *had*. She'd failed. Nope, she definitely wasn't up to brunch today.

23: Sunday Brunch

Ellen shot out of bed early Sunday morning, frantic to do something practical. She weeded through the week's accrual of mail, tossing junk and setting aside the bills to pay, put a load of whites in the washer, set the oven to self-clean, cleaned the litter box, and made a shopping list.

Normally, Ellen had trouble recalling her dreams, but last night's dream was vivid. In it, she and Ty were somewhere on vacation having a heated and disjointed post-coital argument about where to go next, Hawaii or England? When Ty accused her of being unable to think about any place except England, she suddenly felt overwhelmed with guilt, not for being with Ty, but for going on vacation without leaving a note for her husband and her boys. She gasped awake, worrying if she had just had an extraordinary orgasm or had just dreamed about one. It took several long moments to locate herself in her own bed beside her husband, heart still racing.

Friday night's encounter with Ty buzzed on the outskirts of her thoughts like a couple of bees in a garden. She desperately wanted to talk about it with Hannah, sort through her jumbled feelings in the presence of her friend's safe and sane ears. Instead, her thoughts turned to Zoe. A woman's right to choose? What bullshit! Zoe was no woman. Regardless of how the crisis of Zoe's pregnancy was resolved, Hannah would pay a price for her daughter's (and some random boy's) mistake and, if history were any sort of predictor, it would be steep. Zoe's life was literally fucked, too, she sadly conceded, thinking of how much harder it will be for her to have the kind of life everyone expected for her, the life she must certainly have envisioned for herself. At last the hour arrived when Ellen could quit trying to distract herself, head to the brunch and, hopefully, to time with Hannah.

The air was unseasonably cold and biting. Sharp winds tore at the dried leaves still clinging to the trees and hurled them in great clusters in the air. Seeing that out her window, Ellen layered on a silk undershirt, a cotton turtleneck and a beige nubby sweater, battling the annoyance she always felt as winter made its first icy stabs into the region. She dug out her thin leather gloves, stiff after a summer in a drawer, and a warm wool jacket, and left a note on the counter for her sleeping family. "Out to brunch with book club. Then grocery shopping. Please change the loads. FOLD them! See you later. Love, Mom."

Reaching the restaurant early, Ellen cycled twice through the parking lot, searching in vain for Hannah's Accord. Bacon and cinnamon and roasted coffee essences from the restaurant's huge exhaust fans co-mingled with the outside smells of autumn. Inside, on a long table covered in white linen and adorned with tall slender vases of yellow mums and crimson gladioli, the breakfast food was piled high: pyramids of blueberry and chocolate chip muffins, cheese Danishes, huge bowls of fresh fruit salad, bagels and waffles and English muffins you could toast yourself, syrups and salsas, butter and butter substitute. She was the first book club member to arrive so Ellen asked for a table for four and a pot of coffee. "Yes, caffeinated, *please*."

As Ellen was settling in, Maggie arrived in a splash of color. She was toting a massive red leather purse and wore two scarves, a skinny shimmery aubergine and a paisley swirl of dark greens and yellows, draped around the shoulders of her black leather jacket. "I hate fall!" she greeted Ellen, kissing her warmly. "It's so cold! Do you know if everyone's coming? Oh! There's Julie now." She waved.

Flushed and happy, Julie sang out, "Hey, ladies! How is everyone this morning?"

"I'm just fine. Where's Hannah?" Maggie asked.

"She drove to Quebec on Friday to retrieve Beth from a school field trip. I think they got home late yesterday so she might be sleeping in. I don't really know." Ellen sighed.

"*Quebec!* Damn, that's an ass-kicking drive. What did Beth do?" Maggie grimaced as she settled into her chair.

Ellen quickly summarized what she knew of the field trip kerfuffle.

Julie shook her head. "Poor Hannah, doesn't it seem it's always something with those girls?"

Nearby, diners rattled their silverware and asked for coffee refills. At the next table, a small boy whined about the strawberry syrup. *Blueberry* he plaintively informed his flustered mother. *No, no, no*, she could not just scrape the strawberry off. His complaints escalated.

"Shall we move our table?" Julie suggested, signaling to their waitress without waiting for assent from the others.

"Good idea, but let me say, Jules, that was pretty assertive," Maggie observed.

"Yeah," Ellen concurred. "What's up? You look…"

"Happy," Julie finished for her. "I am happy. So, ummm, just so you know, I had a date!"

"What?" Maggie clutched her chest in mock horror. "You did what?"

The waitress helped them move to a booth far from the four-year-old, who was now verging on a meltdown even though his mother had ordered a new short stack with blueberry syrup.

"Well, well, well," Ellen teased as they took their seats. "Wasn't it just maybe twenty-four hours ago that you said you hated the word, the very idea of, *date*?"

Too excited to pull off looking believably sheepish, Julie grinned and raised her hands in the air. "I know, I know! After you left me at the park, I ran into this guy I should've started dating last year, his name is Nathan, and things just snowballed and we ended up going out to dinner last night and it was," she paused to take a deep, elated breath, "amazing. Can I be amazed or am I too old for that?"

"Shit, Honey!" Maggie blurted out. "You're too old for nothing. You deserve to have fun. Tell us about it."

In exacting detail, Julie recreated her evening with Nathan. A fabulous dinner at a cozy, upscale restaurant on Bryant Street. Warm and easy conversation from the first bite of the antipasti salad to the last bite of Pappardelle alla Lepre. "Yes, I ate rabbit. It was amazing!" Born in London, he loved being a transplant to Buffalo, the unpretentiousness of its people, the ease of getting anywhere, even the fantastic change of seasons. She found him to be both gentle and masculine, traits she hadn't dared hope could co-exist in one adult man. They strolled down Elmwood and indulged in divine lemon cheesecake at a wonderful Italian cafe. No surprise that they both loved Bach and Beethoven, but how many people still adored the work of Lukas Foss, a conductor/composer with Buffalo ties...

You've lost me at the composers, Ellen thought. She fought to keep her attention on her friend but Ty and her all-too-vivid dream kept intruding into her thoughts. She needed Hannah's steadying hand. Taking a huge gulp of coffee, she gamely said to Julie, "This is such great news. What happens now?"

"Don't know," Julie's brow wrinkled as the worry she could never suppress for long crept across her face. "When Eric finds out I had a date, don't you think there will be drama? He's been waiting for the chance to prove that I'm an unfit mother so he can get custody and stop paying child support."

"Good lord, did I hear you right? I'm still willing to hunt him down and kick his sorry ass," Maggie half joked. "Crap, Julie, Stephan's almost 18. What will he say?"

"Oh, Stephan's ready for me to, as he says, get a life. Of course, he says it nicely but still, I don't think he'll have any problems with it."

The waitress came, the food was finally ordered, and Maggie fished some handwritten pages from her purse and slapped them on the table. "Not to completely change the subject, but, well, I guess I am changing the subject. Either of you start writing your chapter of *Mariner's Cove*?" she inquired. "This is a bitch, Ellen, a real bitch!"

Julie flinched.

"Sorry," Maggie said without conviction.

"Why do women ever use that word?" Julie wondered.

"It's a good, strong word! I like how it just rolls off your tongue. Like spitting! *Bitch!*"

"But you don't spit and neither do I! That word degrades women."

"It's just a word, Julie! Anyway, I'm talking about *writing,* not about women. I'm the last person who would bash women," Maggie declared.

Maggie'll never back down, Ellen thought.

"So," Julie was in a rare assertive mode, too, "when was the last time you used *bitch* to describe a man? It is a little hateful; you just have to admit that."

"Okay!" Maggie threw both hands up in surrender. "Let's get back to this whole crazy business of rewriting the ending to someone else's book. I mean, really!" She looked imploringly toward Ellen.

Ellen sighed. "I thought it would be fun, but for heaven's sakes, don't do it if you don't want to!" Impulsively, she drew some money out of her wallet and pushed it towards the center of the table. "I'm sorry, I really am. I just can't stay for breakfast today. Please pay my share. I've got to go. "

Maggie frowned. Julie spoke. "Whoa, Ellen, is something wrong?"

"No, *no*, I'm sorry. I'm just antsy, I can't sit still." Standing, Ellen looked at the worried and slightly offended faces of her friends. She sighed apologetically. "I, I don't know what else to say. I'm sorry. I just need to get moving."

"Are we still on for our excursion to the Outlets?" Julie queried. Maggie's eyes were narrowed but she said nothing.

"Sure," Ellen nodded, "Of course. See you Saturday, 9 sharp." Leaving as quickly as possible, she stopped at the nearest coffee shop and bought three cups of coffee, a half dozen bagels and a dozen donuts. In twenty minutes she was on Hannah's porch, take-out breakfast in hand. She rang the bell and shifted from foot to foot, waiting in the cold.

After a long pause, Hannah cracked open the door. "Hi," she said half-heartedly. Her hand automatically reached out to receive the gift bag Ellen thrust toward her. "You didn't have to do this!" Hesitantly, she peered into the bag, then backed into her foyer with a quiet, "Come in, come in."

"I won't stay long," Ellen replied hurriedly. "I just thought you might like some breakfast and I wanted to see if you're okay."

Hannah shrugged. "Well, you see I'm okay, then. Made it back from Quebec. Freaking long trip. I'm wiped out." She looked away, as if something riveting was happening over Ellen's right shoulder.

"Ten hours, isn't it?" Ellen stammered, confused. Quebec? What about Zoe; was it possible Hannah didn't yet know about her younger daughter's pregnancy?

"Yeah, it took us eleven hours. It was backed up at the border." Hannah was pale, wearing an old blue plaid flannel shirt that must have been a Simon cast-off and baggy moss green leggings with a huge run over one knee. Her hair hadn't seen a brush yet this morning. Even the usual enhancement of her sable eyeliner was missing.

"You must be exhausted," Ellen tried to commiserate, taking a tiny step toward the kitchen.

"Yeah, I am. That's why I couldn't go to brunch or even call. I can't, I just can't…" Hannah's voice caught, strangled in the back of her throat. She didn't yield an inch of floor however, so Ellen stepped back, regretting that she had imposed herself.

"Okay, it's okay," Ellen murmured, wanting to reach out to Hannah, hug her and let her cry on her shoulder. Instead, she felt a cold, uncharacteristic gulf between them that forced her to stand stiffly and offer no comfort. "I shouldn't have barged in. I was just so worried about you and Zoe."

Zoe's name slipped off her tongue before she had time to engage her self-editing gear. She instantly regretted it.

Hannah turned white. "I just cannot talk yet, Ellen, you've got to understand," she pleaded wearily.

"I do understand. I'm so sorry I just showed up like this. Call me sometime," Ellen said softly as she turned and walked out the door.

She stumbled numbly down the street. Back in her car, Ellen drove a few blocks and then pulled over so she could compose herself or at least dab off the hot, salty tears streaming down her cheeks.

After Hannah clicked the old oak door shut behind Ellen, she slumped onto the bottom step of the stairs in her foyer, holding the bag of bagels, and gritting her teeth. "Shit, shit, *shit*!" she stammered under her breath, shaking her head.

"What's going on? Was someone here?" Simon trailed a slight, stale smell of whiskey as he came down the stairs.

"You need coffee!" Hannah handed him one of the cups Ellen had delivered. "This is from Ellen. I swear she is going to drive me crazy. She was here just now."

"Where is she?"

"I didn't invite her to stay."

"You're kidding!" Simon was astounded and, his voice belied, pleased.

"I *never* thought I would say this, but there are some places where girlfriends just don't belong. This is *our* problem and I can't deal with Ellen's shit about it right now."

"I never thought I would hear you say that. And I say, alleluia!" Simon's desire for privacy from the "book cartel" was only sort of a joke between them. He raised the cup to his nose and sniffed appreciatively. "This, however, *is* fine coffee."

24: Julie's Coffee, Sunday Night

Dropping his bound report on the kitchen table, Stephan smiled broadly. "I pulled it off, Mom, look at that!"

Julie extracted the report from his envelope and whooped. Straight A's, even in physics. "Oh, honey! I'm so proud of you!" The accident, the surgeries, the rehab, the divorce; her son had weathered them all with a grace she found astounding. Her marriage may have been a huge, horrible mistake, but Stephan was no mistake. He was and is the one perfect thing in her life.

Later in the evening, examining the crowded kitchen shelf she had dedicated to teas and coffees, Julie contemplated her choices. It was after 11 and she didn't want to jettison her chances of falling asleep but she craved coffee. Before her was a glass canister of fair trade coffee beans, shade grown, rain forest friendly, glistening darkly, but the brew they produced made her heart race. Beside them, in a gaily decorated bag, were the vanilla- and maple-flavored decaffeinated coffee beans that her sister-in-law had given her for Christmas last year. A little late to pull out the grinder, she thought. Behind the whole beans, she saw the eight-ounce, vacuum-sealed bag of already ground decaf Colombian she'd ordered from a catalog of earth-friendly products. But when her order arrived and she scrutinized the invoice, with its added taxes and shipping costs, the beans felt too extravagant for personal use so she stored them for a special occasion. *Okay,* she thought as she reached for that package, *I'm special enough.*

For the past year, Julie had been making weekly visits to a therapist. With the wounds of her divorce stubbornly refusing to heal, and her one stabilizing force, Stephan, nearly out of the nest, Julie quietly recognized that she couldn't get to the place that she wanted to be on her own. The therapist had instructed her to start writing a journal. Each day, she was to complete two sentences: one beginning with "I feel..." and the other, "I fear..." After filling in whatever came first to her mind, she was to contemplate her answers for a few minutes, then take no more than twenty minutes to write a letter to herself. Writing about herself wasn't a skill that came naturally, but she tried to follow the expensive professional advice and enticed herself to stick with it by choosing an attractive journal for the daily assignment, a dark blue leather bound book with finely textured linen pages. No faux profound or syrupy quotations streamed across the bottom of the pages and no adorable baby animals graced its cover.

At her desk, journal open, she took a sip of the delicious overpriced decaf and reviewed yesterday's entries. "I feel scared" she had written, and "I'm afraid to mess up." Most of her entries were like this, short and unfriendly.

I feel dull. and *I fear being boring.*

I feel fat. and *I'm afraid to look in the mirror.*

The letters to herself were tough to compose.

Dear Julie, she would begin and then stare at the page for fifteen minutes. *Get OVER it.*

Dear Julie, You are not doing yourself any favors by focusing on your big fat thighs. Who do you think cares? Who do you think even looks at you? The world has bigger fish to fry. Get off your ass!

It pained her to review her bruising self-critiques.

Sitting very still, rereading her words, Julie was suddenly flooded with different words for today's entry. The dinner with Nathan on Saturday night had been electrifying. After years of not really talking to any men, except to mechanics about car problems and to lawyers about forcing her ex-husband to ante up his child support, Julie was astounded that she and Nathan had talked so easily, so intimately.

Without thinking, she began to write. *I am scared witless and excited.* She took a deep breath and penned, *I feel afraid of everything.* She sucked on the end of her ballpoint for a minute, and then changed the period at the end of the "I feel" sentence to a colon. *I feel afraid of everything: of being too timid, of being too bold, of taking chances, of not taking chances, of falling in love, of getting hurt, of letting my life wither away like something left too long in the vegetable crisper.*

Drifting back to her date with Nathan, she entered a dreamy reverie. Agonizing about what to wear that night, she had settled on a soft camel wool jacket, a sage silk camisole, a dazzling necklace with silver, opal, and topaz beads, and a pair of slimming black jeans. When she met him at her door, he looked at her appreciatively, his smile wide, his dark eyes flashing. Slowly, she was shedding the extra pounds that years of depression had helped her to accumulate and daring to imagine that she could be attractive. His eyes suggested that she was succeeding.

Ten minutes ticked by, then fifteen. Finally, timidly, she brought her attention back to her journal and wrote, *Dear Julie, you don't have to get a life. You have a life. Go ahead and live it.* Her twenty minutes were up.

25: Maggie's Coffee, Monday Morning

On cold fall nights, Maggie replayed one theme over and over in her head: her dread of the coming winter. She often hummed to herself, looking for dark words to match her darker mood. *Deck yourself in winter hues, fa-la-la-la-la, la-la-la-la. Now's the time to sing the blues, fa-la-la-la-la, la-la-la-la. Don we now our grey apparel, fa-la-la-la-la, la-laaaa, oh fuck it.* While she lay awake, she mentally compiled, and then alphabetized, a list of things she wouldn't be able to do for the next six months: nibble warm tomatoes fresh off the vine, go outside without changing into boots, come in without leaving a muddy puddle on the floor, enjoy the chorus of the morning songbirds, wear her comfortable sandals. Winter reminded her of dead things – dark days, grey landscapes, desiccated flowerbeds, all of nature's bounty asleep. Everything asleep except herself. Sleep was a garter snake in her perennials, a slippery thing she glimpsed but could rarely catch with her bare hands. As winter advanced on her bunker, she took almost nightly treks to the barn to get stoned so she could sleep. On the Sunday night following the book club's brunch, Maggie managed to fall sleep on her own but awoke at 2, shivering and awash in a general sadness. Groggy, she made her pilgrimage to the granary, smoked half a slim joint, and slipped back into bed. She was pleased to think that she had not disturbed Brian as she finally drifted into a deep, unknowing fog.

Her mind was miles from her body when she felt a rough shaking of the bed and heard Brian's angry voice. "Maggie! What the hell is this?" he was demanding, dragging her reluctantly toward wakefulness. He was holding a glassine bag containing twelve neatly rolled joints.

"Ahhh," Maggie couldn't summon coherence through her baffled senses. "Where?"

"We're out of coffee. I was looking for the coffee, and goddamn if I don't find marijuana, *here*, in my own goddamned kitchen. My first instinct was to blame Leah or Rob, of course, but guess what? They said *no*, this belongs to their mother. They said you've been smoking weed down in the granary for years! Christ, Maggie! Are you out of your goddam mind?" Brian, dressed in the austere garb of an assistant district attorney, hair neatly trimmed and combed, dark suit, club tie, face freshly shaved, was dangling the bag away from his body as if it contained dog shit.

Normally Maggie hid her stash in the barn, but last week when Ellen dropped by with some fresh joints, Rob had been home sick from school. Maggie hurriedly squirreled the weed away in an old speckled casserole, tucked back on a shelf in her pantry. It was such a fine hiding place that she was not concerned about anyone stumbling across it. The casserole itself was so old that she worried about leaching lead paint into food so she never used it now, not for baking, not for serving, and certainly not for storing the damn coffee her husband was rifling around, looking for.

Staring at the glassine bag with its neat marijuana contents incontestable, she stammered, "Ummm, that's just something, something to help me with the cancer."

Her husband fumed. "You don't have cancer."

"I wish, Brian! I'll always have cancer or the shadow of it. Cancer haunts me!"

"That doesn't have to be true." Brian's eyes were blazing with his absolute conviction that they had beaten her disease. "That's a lousy attitude. You have to get that idea out of your head."

"Easy for you," Maggie countered, appreciating how perfectly he had knotted his tie. A lovely noose, she thought.

The twin creases between his eyebrows deepened and a slight flush crept across his face. "You are not thinking straight! *Dope* is not something that helps with cancer. If anything, this crap will *add* lung cancer to your list of problems. I shouldn't have to remind you, but I *am* an assistant district attorney. What happens to my career or to my children if you ever get caught with this? Dammit, Maggie, have you given any consideration to your family?"

Sitting up now on the edge of the bed and staring at the floor, Maggie felt drained. She noticed that the burnt umber toenail polish on her right big toe was chipped and that a thick patina of dust lay like grey shag carpet under her dresser. She had always hated hiding her marijuana from Brian yet she knew, as surely as she knew the color of her children's eyes that he would never, ever understand. She thought about pointing out that sex had been much more exciting since she started smoking pot, and then she sighed. "I need to use the bathroom. There's a fresh bag of coffee in the fridge, on the right side, second shelf from the top, probably behind the honeydew melon. I bought it yesterday. Please brew some and we'll talk when I get downstairs."

Brian stomped off, his feet pounding with extra force on each stair as he descended. He didn't stop in the kitchen. She heard his car door slam and listened to its engine growing fainter as he drove away.

"Guess I'll make my own," Maggie murmured to herself.

26: Ellen's Coffee, Monday Afternoon

Later that afternoon, Ellen rear-ended a blue Toyota Corolla. She was on her way to meet Ty for coffee in a nearby strip mall when BAM! Her first accident in twenty years, Ellen could not explain, even to herself, how it happened. *Baby, You Look Fine Tonight* was playing on the radio as she drove dreamily down the familiar boulevard. Then she hit the car stopped in front of her at the red light. She had been slowing down as she noticed the light slide from amber to red. Somehow, though, she didn't see the Corolla. The other driver, a hefty young man about her son Cole's age, was so rattled that he had trouble fishing his brand new license out of his wallet or reciting his home phone number. Damage to her car was minimal and she told the boy she would pay out of pocket to repair his dented bumper, whatever it cost, wanting with every cell in her body to avoid the humiliation of explaining to anyone at her husband's insurance company how she caused an accident. In broad daylight. On dry pavement.

The coffee shop, bookended by a mattress outlet and a beauty salon, looked drab from the street, yet customers flocked to it in a continuous stream, drawn to its potent coffee, buttery scones and chocolate brownies baked on site. When Ty invited her to meet him, Ellen told herself that it was a simple cup of coffee with an old college friend, but her heart was unconvinced as it skipped around in her chest.

Despite her little fender bender, she arrived slightly early and saw that Ty was already waiting at a small table near the rear of the shop. He wore a black oxford shirt, blue jeans, and an expensive, exquisitely tailored grey tweed jacket. *Gorgeous*, she thought reluctantly, her eyes riveted on his well-dressed figure. The Ty of her youth had rolled out of bed and pulled on the nearest pair of grungy jeans and most nondescript t-shirt imaginable, sometimes even reclaiming one from his pile of dirty laundry. Picturing her own taupe silk jacket, hanging neatly in her closet beside her flattering black rayon pans, Ellen rued her morning's choice of comfort apparel. She was wearing the kind of outfit Cole, her style-conscious son, derisively called her "teacher clothes," a one-size-fits-most jacket in a tapestry pattern that would also work well as upholstery material, a gored denim skirt, and an LL Bean turtleneck sweater the color of honey.

"Great to see you," Ty stood with a wide, warm smile as she approached. They leaned and pecked at the air near one another's cheeks. After ordering coffee (decaf for her) and scones, they sat facing each other in the café's soft light.

Ellen, flushed and fidgeting, spoke quickly. "I'm sorry but I'm a little rattled. I just rear-ended a kid on my way over here."

"You did what?"

"Rear-ended some kid out driving alone for the very first time on his brand new license. Probably traumatized him! So, sooo embarrassing and I have no excuse. I just wasn't paying attention."

Ty's look was bemused. "Since you're here, I assume everyone's okay?"

"Oh yeah, damage was minimal, except to my ego."

"And how much damage did your ego sustain?"

"Oh, it's banged up pretty good! I think of myself as, you know, someone who's responsible, on top of things. This doesn't fit my resume."

The coffee shop door jangled as an elderly couple tried to maneuver their way in. Gingerly, the wispy-haired old man pushed a walker ahead of his feet as if this were his first foray into public with the bulky contraption. The woman, her white hair in a severe bun, bore a worried, solicitous expression, clucking over every inch of his progress. She was slightly bent-over herself, but there was a solidarity about them that was both sobering and comforting.

Ty looked at her frankly. "So, what were you saying? Is a fender-bender off-limits for you?"

"These days, I feel sort of crazy," Ellen admitted. "My colleague's on vacation which doubles my load and my closest friend is having a family crisis, so my attention might not be all it should be, but *yes,* ordinarily, I don't have fender-benders." Her voice trailed off as she stared at her hands, aware of how raggedy her nails looked. "And yet, the whole world seems out-of kilter, kind of frenzied."

"It really is," Ty agreed affably, smiling with his whole face. "It is too fast for me."

"How so?" She spoke in her lightest voice, happy to redirect the conversation back into his court while wondering if things could really move too fast for him.

Laughing, Ty answered her unspoken thought. "Oh, yeah, things can move too fast for this old rocker. For a while, I worked with a guy in Georgia who actually believed that *sleeping* was a waste of time and that we could get so much more accomplished if we would train ourselves to get by on four hours a night." He held up the four fingers of his right hand.

"Four hours. That's ridiculous." Ellen agreed.

Ty added, "Yeah, I was a walking zombie, and I ended up hating the guy, so I quit."

"Well, that sounds like it sucked. Sometimes, though, I don't get much more than four. Sleep is a hot topic among my friends; we're all running on fumes. We talk all the time about sleep: sleep aids, herbal or prescribed meds, legal and illegal drugs," she paused, wondering if she was sharing too much, then hurried on, "herbal teas, sleep studies, sleep apnea, C-pap machines, does yoga help? Of course, we still talk about our kids and, well, I guess we talk a lot about our diets. Everyone's always trying to lose weight and, oh man!" she gasped. "Sorry, I'm rambling!"

Reaching to touch her hand, a smile playing on his face, Ty said, "Ha. Take a breath, El."

She did. She took a taste of her scone and noticed the wildlife photographs by local artists that adorned the walls. "Seeing you is weird, Ty. It's been like twenty-four years and yet it doesn't seem like more than," she snapped her fingers, "a few moments. The past seems so compressed."

Ty nodded. "Yeah, time doesn't carry its weight the way I used to imagine that it would."

Ellen looked away, remembering how they parted, and wondering if it was on his mind, too.

His shrug was nonchalant. "It's my theory that that's why people love photography. It lets everyone have something to hold on to, keep the past close, or prove they have it."

A grin played on her face as Ellen remembered, "Even back then, you were always taking photos."

Ty smiled. "Everywhere I look, I still see things that would make an amazing photo. It's a huge part of my life. I've actually starting selling photographs to some magazines."

"How fabulous! Is it a kick to see your stuff in print?" Ellen asked.

"It is," Ty couldn't stifle his grin. "A hundred years or so ago, if you weren't rich, you were pretty much shit out of luck if you wanted your image preserved, and now everybody's got a camera in their pocket. But it's a thrill, with those millions of photographers out there, to see my own name in print."

"I would like to see the magazines sometime, although it's possible to imagine some advantages to a time before there were cameras everywhere! Why do we need them built into all our devices? Folks record every burp and bump."

"They can't resist!" Ty's tone was playful. "When I was cleaning out my dad's place, I came across boxes and boxes of photos I took back in our college days. There were some great shots in there, including several really sweet ones of you."

Ellen suddenly felt hot with embarrassment.

"So, I thought it would be fun to do a 'Then and Now' photo update on the old gang. You know, my friends, the guys from my band, the folks who ran the record co-op, the starving students' food pantry, you remember them?"

She laughed. In college, she and several friends had briefly run a food pantry for broke, hungry college kids. They stocked it with soups and dried beans and rice and other foods that could fill a belly on the cheap. "Sure, how could I forget those days? I still make a to-die-for black bean and rice casserole I learned back then, although I use gourmet rice now, and high-end, organic salsa. Um, but what do you mean, a 'Then and Now' update? I'm not sure I want to be updated!"

"I have a possible buyer, a magazine that does a photo spread every month. They're interested in doing a piece on what happened to the slackers and I guess that's the wave we sort of caught. So I wondered…"

"No!" she gasped laughingly. "Ty, seriously? Photos? Good grief!"

Ty opened his mouth to reply as Ellen's cell phone jangled in her purse. It was Cole's unique ringtone. "My son," she explained, answering her phone.

"Mom, where are you?" Cole asked. Before she could answer, he continued, "Don't get upset, nothing's really wrong. It's just that my car won't start. I might have left the door open a little all day and now the battery's dead. There's no way I can pick up Jon. Can you get him?"

Ellen hesitated.

"Mom?"

Ellen still hesitated.

"Hello, Mom? Is there something wrong with your phone?"

"Darnit, Cole! This is really inconvenient. Of course, I will pick up Jonathan."

She apologized as she gathered her purse and took a last, fortifying gulp of coffee. "That's actually irritating," she admitted, "and I'm really sorry to cut this short. You probably got the gist of it."

"Go," he said kindly.

27: Simon's Coffee, Wednesday Morning

By 7:30 on Wednesday morning, Simon was in the kitchen, getting breakfast for himself and Matt. He had Matt's plastic superhero set of bowl, plate, and cup on the table and was debating whether to scramble an egg or pop a frozen waffle in the toaster oven. The coffee was dripping in noisy spurts and sputters in the old coffeemaker, little whiffs of steam escaping through the vents in the top.

"Ugh, that smells gross," Zoe gagged, entering the kitchen and pointing to the brewing coffee. "How can you even drink that, Dad?"

"Sorry, honey. Your mom used to hate the smell of coffee when she was carrying you; it will pass. I need my cup of joe in the morning and I'm not going to quit because you're pregnant," Simon said levelly.

28: Vitamins

A peach cotton lab coat swung loosely from Dr. Judith Conner's square shoulders as she led Hannah and Zoe toward a consultation room off a long beige hallway in her maze-like clinic. Strands of her light brown hair escaped in a wild frenzy from the French braid winding down the back of her head. At five-ten, she was an imposing presence.

Hannah wondered if the unruffled doctor ever suffered misery as a result of her own family's errors of omission and commission. Did she even have children? Hannah hadn't noticed a wedding ring or any family photos in the doctor's coolly professional office during her prenatal checkups five years ago, while pregnant with Matt. Back then, Dr. Conner had been unfailingly patient and sensitive. Week after week, Hannah raised questions about being an older mother (she was thirty-eight) and fears that, because she had not intended to have a third child, this baby would be damaged. Would it sense that it was unwanted? Would a hearty red Shiraz she had drunk before she knew she was pregnant exact a price, causing the child's cognitive synapses to randomly misfire? Would mother and child fail to attach and the child end up hating her?

The doctor listened thoughtfully and explained away each of Hannah's specific fears until at last Matt was born, a resoundingly normal infant. "I can't promise that he won't end up hating you, though," Dr. Conner said half-jokingly.

"Well, what do you suggest for that, doctor?" Hannah asked with a hint of playfulness.

Dr. Connor grew serious. "That depends on what happens now, on whether you give him plenty of room to be his own person, roots he can trust, unconditional love, and high enough expectations so he has some reason to use whatever potential he was born with."

Hannah had memorized that advice, thinking it contained all the wisdom of the dozen or so baby books she had been given but would never actually find time to read. So now, sitting in the exam room with her pregnant little girl, she pondered, where had she, or she and Simon, failed Zoe? Because surely having your fourteen-year-old turn up pregnant was a sign of parental failure, a neon billboard announcing that your family is fundamentally screwed up.

Parents reap what they sow Hannah had once believed firmly, from her perch as a middle school principal. It was always *so* obvious why a particular kid was acting out in a particularly sculpted way. Mouthy kids had parents who didn't listen to them or discipline them. Bullies had been bullied. Delinquents had parents who engaged in modest little hit-and-runs, who lied to callers on the phone, celebrated cheating at the grocer's, or just altogether ignored them, good or bad. The little girls who were cutting themselves or starving themselves often felt that they couldn't live up to their parents' high expectations and couldn't even talk about it. So what had Zoe been? What deep, unmet need was she fulfilling?

"So as clearly as I can tell without a sonogram," Dr. Conner was looking at Zoe, "you appear to be eleven or twelve weeks pregnant." Hannah jerked herself back into the small, airless room that held her daughter, her doctor, and words that hit her like a truck. In her eyes, Zoe looked stricken, small, more like an eight-year-old than a sexually active teenager. A thick, cold fog of silence hung in the room. Hannah felt too heavy to move her lips or give life to any thoughts.

Dr. Conner sat quietly, waiting for some cue from the mother or the daughter. None came. Finally, she said, "I don't know what options you're considering. We don't provide abortions at this office but there's a small window of time left..."

"Abortion! No!" Zoe's verbal skills were restored, shrilly. "No way, no way! You can't make me, Mom, you can't! It's not right."

"What's not right is you being pregnant," Hannah said softy.

"I didn't mean to get pregnant, *Jesus*, Mom! Okay, I get it. This is a big mistake, my mistake. You can all hate me for it, but I'm not doing an abortion." Zoe jutted her chin out like a child who wouldn't go to bed.

Dr. Conner's face relaxed slightly. "She's right, Hannah. If she wants to see this pregnancy through to term, she has that right. There are a lot of agencies that can help her, if she chooses to give the child up then."

The room again reverberated with the kind of silence that follows a massive thunderclap.

"It's not a sack of used clothes you just give away," Zoe sputtered. "This is my child we're talking about, your *grand*child. Mom, don't you have any feelings for it at all?"

I've died and gone to hell and landed in daytime television Hannah thought grimly.

"Are you prepared to drop out of school, give up your social life and your friends, have permanent stretch marks across your belly, be poor, spend the next two years caring for an infant and the next ten years after that trying to make up for all the time you've lost?" Hannah answered her soberly, ticking off the costs of pregnancy and a new baby on her fingers as she spoke. "Please don't think that this is an easy decision, Zoe. You're still just a kid yourself."

"It so pisses me off how nobody believes in me," Zoe said, rising abruptly. She grabbed her purse before it slid to the floor, a pink, vinyl sack with holsters for cell phones and water bottles, and slammed out of the room.

Couldn't fit a bunch of diapers and wipes in that, Hannah thought, watching her leave. Dr. Conner shook her head. Hannah took off her glasses and set them on the doctor's desk, rubbing her temples tenderly. Her head was pounding. "Do you have *any* suggestions?" she pleaded.

"There are still a few institutions that take in pregnant girls, educate them, and either help them learn how to care for their babies or help them place the child in an adoptive home. Catholic Charities is one…"

"We're Jewish," Hannah interjected. *Not practicing, okay, but still!* She felt indignant at the thought of a Catholic agency sitting in judgment on her daughter and, by extension, on her.

"Jewish Family Services is a fine organization, too. What are you thinking?" Dr. Conner countered impassively.

"I can't think," Hannah confessed. "It's like there's a coal burning in the back of my throat. When I'm not busy doing the stuff of my life, when the future hammers its way into my thoughts, I just want to cry. But what good would that do?"

"Holding back your tears might not be a good idea either," she replied softly. "You have a lot to deal with. I hate to see a kid as young as Zoe have a baby but they do it. Even some younger ones do it, and they do recover. A few even do okay with their babies."

Hannah had seen the truth of this in her work at the middle school but it had never seemed as real, or as impossible, as it did now. She sat thinking for a few minutes until her practical, problem-solving self awoke. Dr. Connor sat in companionable silence, entering patient information on her little silver laptop.

"Well, we're obviously not going to throw her out, though I would dearly love to wring her neck," a resigned Hannah said finally. "So we'll just have to deal with it."

"I'll write up an order for a sonogram," Dr. Conner said briskly. "Oh, and she should start taking prenatal vitamins."

When Hannah reached her car in the clinic's small lot, Zoe was nowhere to be seen. Hannah doubled back in to the receptionist, Sandy, a kind and efficient woman whom she had known for years and asked if she had seen Zoe leave.

"Actually, yes, one couldn't miss her. She stormed out of here as if the devil was on her heels and hopped on a Delaware Avenue bus."

"Of course she did," Hannah muttered.

Sandy smiled, "They grow up and you can't believe how much you miss them."

Hard to picture at the moment, Hannah thought to herself but gamely she smiled back, and murmured, "I'm sure you're right."

A half hour later, she was in the Northside Apothecary, standing before shelves of brightly colored bottles of vitamins, rocking from foot to foot like a woman who had just left a baby at home. *Grandchild* hammered against the inside of her skull, above her eyes. She couldn't read the labels through the tears streaming down her face.

The pharmacist approached her gently. "Ma'am?" he asked. "Ma'am? May I offer you some help? Would you like to sit? Some water?"

"Prenatal vitamins," Hannah choked out softly.

"Oh!" he said, surprised. He stepped back as his eyes slid to her waistline. Hannah was wearing her favorite navy cable knit sweater that easily added ten pounds to her full silhouette.

"Good grief, they're not for me!" Her tears stopped abruptly as she comprehended the solicitous alarm on his face. And then her laugh erupted, a hearty rumble starting deep in her diaphragm. She tried to stop and explain but instead began gasping for air, laughing harder as her cheeks flushed. The pharmacist was clearly alarmed: here was a crazy person losing it in his vitamin aisle.

"I could hug you!" she exclaimed. "But don't worry, I won't. Just know that these vitamins are not for me and that's something to celebrate."

29: Classix at the Knox

Buffalo's glittering neoclassical palace, the Albright Knox Art Gallery, ironically a trove of modern and contemporary art, hosted a hugely successful classic film series cloyingly dubbed "Classix at the Knox." Hoping to attract new arts patrons, it enticed filmgoers to linger after the movie with $5 wine and a discussion group facilitated by luminaries from the local theatre scene. Buy a subscription to the whole series and the first glass of wine at every show is free.

Ellen and Hannah hadn't missed a single movie, nor a single glass of wine, in two years. Even though Ellen had seen the current flick, *The Philadelphia Story,* at least four times on cable, she relished the whole of the theatre experience: the hushed room, the larger-than-life screen, the immersion, anonymity, and intimacy with the actors one never feels in one's own living room, no matter how large your flat screen.

After Hannah had turned her away at her door, Ellen was leery of calling her friend. Confirming their implicit date to the movie, however, seemed an innocuous way to restart their friendship, were Hannah amenable. As she called the Feldmans' number, Ellen mentally prepared to leave a bright, cheerful message on the answering machine and was disconcerted when Beth answered the phone on the first ring.

"Oh," Ellen said, flustered. "Hello, Beth."

"Hey, Ellen," Beth's voice dripped boredom. The Feldmans had caller ID so Ellen was surprised that Beth had even bothered to pick up her call.

"Ummm, Beth, is your mom there, please?"

Beth sighed heavily, the weight of the world almost too much for her to bear. Ellen could picture her rolling her pretty eyes. "Mom's napping."

Right, Ellen thought. *Like Hannah ever has time to nap.* "Could you leave her a little note asking her to call me when she wakes up? I wondered if she remembers the Knox movies tomorrow night."

"Oh! *All* of that?"

"If you could, please," Ellen said softly, hoping to disguise the edge creeping into her voice.

"Got it…" Beth seemed to be writing a note. "Okay, bye, Ellen." She clicked off.

The following day passed without a call from Hannah. Ellen, with another evening looming empty and lonely, decided *hell with it.* Her family was dispersed at various male-centered venues all over town (Rotary Club for William, girlfriend for Cole, wrestling practice for Jon). Standing before her bedroom mirror, Ellen brushed her shiny, straight hair. Horizontal lines grooved her forehead, the legacy of a lifetime of fretting. Plucking a few errant hairs from her eyebrows, she wondered if the time had come to start dying her hair. *To hell with that, too.* She brushed some bronzing makeup over her pale face, added some dark brown eye shadow and plummy lipstick, and gave herself a smile. *Not bad,* she thought.

Shortly, she was at the Knox where she made her way to an empty row in the middle of the theatre. Settling comfortably into the well-padded seat, she cast a furtive glance around for Hannah. Her best friend was nowhere in sight, but Ty was there, looking bemusedly back at her from his seat three rows up and a few seats to the left. Ellen waved weakly, which he immediately accepted as an invitation to join her.

"How about that?" he drawled, folding himself companionably into the next seat. "Haven't seen you in decades and now three times in a week! You by your lonesome again?"

"I am," Ellen admitted slowly. "Everyone's busy."

"Well, you're busy, too," Ty pointed out softly as the lights faded and the previews came up. "You're at the movies."

With you, Ellen thought as her face flushed. Five minutes into the movie, she realized that if she were to choose a movie to see with Ty, it wouldn't be one of these old puffballs where women – strong smart women like Katharine Hepburn – struggled confusedly about love. Why did she enjoy this flick so much in the privacy of her own living room only to find the whole premise appalling with Ty seated on her left, their knees occasionally touching as one or the other shifted in their seats? *Stop* she scolded herself silently, willing her eyes to fix on the screen and her mind to focus on the narrative. And soon, riveted as always by the luminous performances of the old cinematic greats, she was swept up in the movie.

"There's still nobody who can hold a candle to Cary Grant or Jimmy Stewart!" Ty asserted as the lights came back up during the final credits. Ellen shook herself back to reality. "Nobody fills the screen like Katharine Hepburn either." She gave him a sidelong glance.

"For sure," he agreed. "Wine?"

"For sure," Ellen echoed as they headed toward the restaurant where the wine tastings and movie post-mortems were held.

"Actually, that's a piss-poor selection," Ty said upon surveying their choices.

"But it's free." Ellen picked up a glass hopefully.

Ty lifted it gently out of her hand. "No, no. They should've left that swill in Australia! Let's get out of here," he said. "Anyway, I wanted to show you something and this is a perfect opportunity." He placed her unused glass on a table and steered her toward the exit and into the cab of his pickup truck where they took a short drive up Elmwood and into the tidy, well-tended neighborhoods of Kenmore.

Stepping into Ty's foyer was jarring. Ellen felt like she had tumbled through time and landed thirty years ago, when she had been a frequent visitor to this house. The familiar leafy rose pattern on the foyer wallpaper was just slightly more faded than she remembered, and the marble-topped occasional table to the left of the oak door was positioned, as it had always been, in the perfect location for keys and purses and stacks of mail. Glancing toward the kitchen, she spotted a huge bag of basmati rice leaning up against a cupboard, probably too fat to fit on one of the old, narrow shelves. To the left was the dining room, set off by a wide arch of gleaming oak molding that had never been painted white, unlike thousands of its contemporaries throughout the city. The dining room table was strewn with black and white photographs. Additional picture groupings were tacked on two walls – faces and places Ellen remembered with sudden, sharp pangs. Where had everyone gone? When she had said "I do" to William, had she really meant "I don't" to everything else in her life?

Ty disappeared into the kitchen and returned with two steins of foamy beer, a pale pilsner, her favorite when she was a co-ed, for her and a dark brown porter for himself. Handing her the foamy brew, he said, "Take a look at these prints. Takes you back, doesn't it?" He circled proudly around the room, pointing. "There's a method to my madness. I put the shots of the music freaks on this wall and the foodies are over there. I wondered if we would all still cluster in the same groupings as we did back then, and we do!" He gestured excitedly. "Dean, from the record co-op, has an amateur recording studio in his basement. He must have at least twenty guitars, plus his own synthesizer."

"Uh-huh," Ellen sipped her beer, savoring how much she liked the light, crisp taste of a quality pilsner. Her fridge was stocked with the heavier brews Will preferred.

"It's amazing," Ty continued, "or then again, maybe it's not. Maybe it is exactly what was always in the cards. Just look at him at nineteen, happy as a clam, in the midst of all those records and tapes."

Ellen stood in awe, as names and faces from two decades ago were called into a celluloid present.

Ty pointed to an adjacent photo of a studious, bearded young man with a flute. "And that's Luke, remember him? Good with cars and inspired with a flute in his hands; he did Jethro Tull tunes better than Ian Anderson!"

"Well, that's a little over the top. Ian Anderson performed at Chautauqua, it was incredible, nobody can touch him! But I do remember Luke, I do! You've talked to him?"

"Yep, I found him on Facebook. He's some kind of computer nerd by day but he also plays in a garage band. I drove out to Rochester to hear him and they're *really* good. They do all sorts of gigs, from bar mitzvahs to biker bars and he's still loving it! Almost bald, too, but he has a great, long, curly beard."

Despite being coupled to William since their high school days, Ellen had a huge crush on Luke in her first year at college. With his brightly polished silver flute swooping and trilling, he improvised melodies that took her breath away. He was also gay and gently let her know that her sexual attraction could not be returned. If she ever had to give an honest accounting of her life's big moments, that conversation would be near the top.

Nodding toward the other wall, Ty continued. "There's where I put you co-opers and food pantry types. Lauren, remember? Today, she's running an inner city program in Baltimore, a soup kitchen, day care, emergency referrals, on a shoestring budget. It's a righteous place, a regular United Way wet dream. So, it is *unfair* to call us all 'slackers.' And that's my angle for my photo spread!" Ty's grin was wide. "Come on, El. Be a part of it. You've kind of followed your path, no? Rescuing souls? Social work as your calling?"

Studying the faces in those photos, Ellen smiled wistfully. They looked impossibly young and fresh. "I don't belong in your happy photo spread, Ty. Rescuing seems to have used me up. My life feels small compared to this."

"What do you mean?"

"Oh, hell, I don't even jay walk! I take my vitamins and fish oil supplements and extra calcium. In bed by 10. Same job forever, I could do it in my sleep. Sometimes, I even *do* do it in my sleep. Can't say I have much passion left for helping people. I rescue for pay."

Shaking his head, Ty pulled from the stack a picture he had taken a quarter century before. It was of Ellen, with hair cascading down her back, in a denim apron and jeans so tight a paperclip wouldn't slip under the waistband, standing in front of a display of discarded-but-usable canned goods that she had talked local grocers into donating. She was smiling and proud. He angled the photo for better effect.

"Look at this," he said. "Damn nice! And this is you."

"Yeah. That's me," she said ruefully, "completely into it."

Ty frowned. "Come on, what's the matter, El?"

Shrugging dismissively, Ellen waved his question away. "Nothing's really the matter. I'm just feeling a little past my prime. Sell-by date's long past, you know what I mean?"

"No, I don't, and you didn't used to care about sell-by dates. If you're lucky enough not to be dead already, I think you should be alive. And I mean *really* alive, not camped on the permafrost, watching the hourglass run down."

She drained her beer and sighed. "Well, aren't you the philosopher! Most of my life is fine, really it is. My kids are great, I love being a mom. It's just that," she sighed, then stopped.

"Okay," he said softly. "It's just what?"

The words tumbled out. "Well, my marriage is... it's wobbling pretty badly and I keep pretending that it's going to right itself, like a spinning top that's still got momentum. But it doesn't and, being honest, it isn't!" Fighting watery eyes, she continued, "I had real, solid plans to leave William nineteen years ago, but I got pregnant, after trying and trying and finally giving up! Then I had the pregnancy from hell. Cole came five weeks early and we were scared to death that he'd die and I promised that I would never cause this tiny baby any grief if he could just live."

"Who did you promise?" Ty asked gently.

Ellen shrugged. "Like, the universe. I don't know, God maybe?"

"You promised God?" he repeated her words. They hung in the air like helium balloons. He asked gently, "So, God makes deals with you?"

"Well," Ellen stumbled, "not literally, of course, but, Cole lived!"

"Come on, El!" He was softly incredulous. "You don't honestly think your baby survived because you promised God or the universe something that involves you staying in a lousy marriage?"

She shrugged, wishing she had worn more layers so she could take one off. The room felt hot. "Of course I don't *think* it. But I made a promise. I kept it." Ellen shook her hair and continued, "So rational or not, here I am."

Ty grimaced. "El, *really*! Life is too short to live it knowing you're miserable. That's all I got to say. It's too fucking short."

"I need another beer." She jiggled her empty glass.

"Uh-huh, you need more than that," he murmured over his shoulder, heading off for her refill.

Yup, Ellen thought, *I surely do.* She began sifting through the photos, smiling at faces she remembered fondly, squinting hard at others as if to pry their names out of some iced up corner in her memory's freezer. She lingered over Dorr, the peach-fuzz-faced kid with the most exhaustive record collection of anyone she'd ever known; Denyse, brilliant and neurotic, obsessed with her cup size; and JB, the radiohead who turned beet red and made painfully inappropriate remarks about his sexual tension. He was a person who should never have been introduced to drugs or alcohol!

Fresh beers in hand, Ty sauntered back. "So, will you do it?" he asked angling his head toward the photos as he placed the glasses on the table. Turning and smiling, Ellen was on the cusp of yes. Their eyes met, and Ty could see that there had been a shift. Her posture was less rigid, facial muscles more relaxed, eyes wide open. He reached for her hand. Ellen stepped willingly into the path of his body as he pulled her gently toward him. Their lips met, urgent and hungry. They shared a long, longing kiss but when Ty's hand found its way under her blouse, Ellen shuddered involuntarily and pulled back.

"God, that was amazing," she whispered, feeling alive in a way she thought only the young could feel. "I could kiss you forever. I just can't. I just can't."

Putting a finger gently to her lips, Ty stopped her. "It's okay. I didn't think you could. So," he cleared his throat, "I'll take you back to your car."

"Yes, please," Ellen studied the polished hardwood floorboards. "But I will do your photo shoot, if you still want me. I mean, if you still want me to do it. The photo shoot."

Ty laughed. "Of course."

30: Shopping

Subject	Outlet outing
From	Maggie (OntheBrink99@aol)
Sent	Wednesday 10/22 11:08 PM
To	HannahFeldman (HanaF@whosez.); Ellen Palmer (EPalmer@hotmail); Julie Johnson (Musicat@gmail)

Okay, ladies, after about 50 phone calls, emails, and texts, here's the outlet shopping compromise to fit all: we're going to Niagara Falls Outlet Mall this Saturday, 1 to 5, followed by dinner at Beijing Café, all home by 7:30 so Julie can be sitting on her front porch when Stephan gets back from visiting bad ol' dad, and Hannah can put Matt to bed. Me, when I get home, I'm just gonna hide the receipts. Parking is a bitch, with the Canadians crawling all over (eh, eh?) shopping for American bargains, so we'll carpool, Ellen's nicely offered to drive and be our DD. Be at her place @ 12:30. The other idea we had – a big trip to Seneca Falls – is on hold til next summer. Do shopping and feminism mix, anyway? (sigh) Love ya all, Maggie

Subject	Re: Outlet outing
From	Julie Johnson (Musicat@gmail)
Sent	Thur 10/23 3:00 AM
To	Maggie Brinkman (OntheBrink99@aol.); Hannah (HanaF@whosez.); Ellen Palmer (EPalmer@hotmail)

What...you don't tweet? I love it. I'll give you an in-service sometime but be warned. Your youngsters will be irked. Stephan thinks I should respect his generation by staying the hell away from social networking thingies. I remember the smug feeling I got watching my poor mother try to program her first answering machine. The "comes around, goes around" theory. Anyhow, happy we're on for Saturday. Maggie, thanks for coordinating it all. El, I assume we'll get our run in early? Oh, and I'm sure the first wave feminists would've approved of some shopping. Probably not lacy bras or eyeliner but they would've loved good shoes and elastic waistbands! Going to bed now, nighty night, Julie

Subject	Re: Re: Outlet outing
From	Ellen Palmer (EPalmer@hotmail)
Sent	Thur 10/23 5:22 AM
To	Maggie Brinkman (OntheBrink@oal); HannahFeldman (HanaF@whosez.); Julie Johnson (Musicat@gmail)

Yup, Jules, Run's on for 8. I think the early feminists would have been beyond thrilled with a great pair of running shoes. TTYL, El

Subject	Re: Re: Re: Outlet outing
From	Hannah (HanaF@whosez.)
Sent	Thur 10/23 6:00 AM
To	Maggie Brinkman (OntheBrink99@oal.); Ellen Palmer (EPalmer@hotmail); Julie Johnson (Musicat@gmail)

I can't wait to eat out! I think the last time Simon asked me out to eat, he wanted a Ted's hotdog. Anyway, I need a new bra (lacy would be fine, as long as it feels good, too) and boots. Does the outlet have any good lingerie stores or departments? I haven't been there in ages! See you all Sat. H

Subject	Re: Re: Re: Re: Outlet outing
From	Ellen Palmer (EPalmer@hotmail)
Sent	Thur 10/23 8:10 AM
To	Julie (Musicat@gmail) Maggie Brinkman (OntheBrink99@oal.); HannahFeldman (HanaF@whosez.)

This'll be fun! There're a few good outlets for lingerie, Hannah, and some great shoe stores. And don't you just wish we could hear the first wave feminists talk about our footwear options! Til Saturday, EL

Subject	Re: Re: Re: Re: Re: Outlet outing
From	Maggie Brinkman (OntheBrink99@oal.)
Sent	Thur 10/23 4:00 PM
To	Ellen Palmer (EPalmer@hotmail);Julie (Musicat@gmail); HannahFeldman (HanaF@whosez.)

Would love to hear the first-wave feminists talk about *anything*!

Saturday sailed into the region on a chill, harsh, wet wind. In the anthill-busy parking lot of the Outlet Mall, people poured from their vehicles and scurried toward the gaudy entrances, into the thrum of families rushing among a hundred stores luring them with pre-holiday deals. After scrutinizing their shopping lists at a sticky table in the food court, the women separated. Ellen and Julie set out together in search of new computer accessories and sports gear for their sons while Hannah and Maggie headed for a store catering to teen girls, where tight sweaters, bright scarves, and overpriced bangles were on their daughters' wish lists. Nothing the first-wave feminists could have even imagined.

Several sweaters, a pair of sleek black leather boots with double buckles for Maggie, a perfect-fit crimson bra for Hannah, a silky black nightgown for Ellen (not on her list), an MP3 player, and a random assortment of candles, kitchen gadgets and other stocking-stuffers later, they reconvened in the food court. With the exception of Julie, who was more buoyant than ever, the day had worn them thin, and they struggled to fully admire one another's successes. Maggie was troubled by the strange tension in Ellen and a distracted aspect to Hannah that she had never noticed before. She tried to bridge the gap with a comment about how tiring it really is, that shopping always seems more enticing and fun in theory than in practice. Ellen and Hannah quickly embraced that explanation. "Really?" Julie asked, "I thought it went great. It's going to be so much fun to see the look on Stephan's face when he opens his new Bluetooth wireless speaker!"

31: Ice and Fire

Heavy clouds scudded across the horizon and piled up against one another as if slamming into the inner harbor's retaining wall. Eying them apprehensively, Ellen wedged her shopping bags into the trunk on top of her friends' collective haul. Her new black nightgown was tucked discreetly into the bag with a cashmere argyle sweater for William. It had been a successful shopping trip, if not a joyful one. Despite the worrisome sky, they stuck with their original plan to indulge in a restaurant meal, weather be damned.

At the Beijing Café, Hannah and Ellen took pains to be seated opposite one another, eliminating the possibility of any sidebar conversations. Searching to make conversation, the friends exclaimed over the restaurant's gorgeous photos of the Great Wall, sampans on the Yangtze **River**, and scenes of tiled mosques tucked among snow-capped, soaring southern mountains. Then they lapsed into silence, contemplating their menus and listening to their own thoughts. For a week, Hannah had known that Ellen *knew,* and she yearned for the time when she could talk freely about everything with Ellen; the halcyon time before her Zoe had turned up pregnant.

The possibility that her marriage was imploding was emerging into sharp focus for Maggie, and no amount of dope was taking the edge off that. She disguised her feelings, but she felt literally sick about it and wished her friends were more "there" for her. She didn't want to share if they didn't want to hear. Having Hannah and Ellen each be so preoccupied completely disturbed the group's symmetry and uncomfortably reminded her of earlier times of feeling sick and abandoned.

Julie yearned to parse the particulars of her dates with Nathan and hear her best friends gauge "how it was going," but they all seemed slightly weird and a bit dissembling. She held her tongue.

And Ellen, by long-ingrained habit, murmured affirming clichés to whatever her friends said, while feeling herself detached and self-absorbed. Minutes and food ticked by and they survived the meal, possibly the most uncomfortable and disingenuous time the four had *ever* spent together.

By the time they finished their cashew chicken, spicy bean curd, and Shenzhen vegetables and rice, divvied up the check, and buckled themselves back into Ellen's car, the sky was awash in inky banks of clouds directly overhead. Explosive thunder shook the ground beneath them.

"It shouldn't be doing this in October!" Julie said in alarm, as lightning ripped the sky into shards of black and white. Driving rain pelted the road while Ellen cautiously threaded her way onto the Robert Moses Expressway. The Niagara River, just a few yards from the expressway, was splattered with frothy whitecaps as it hurtled itself toward the thundering falls. The four women sat in tense silence listening to the wind buffeting the car. Ellen gripped the steering wheel with all her strength, by sheer will holding the car in its lane. "Don't worry," she said with thick anxiety. "I grew up driving in this shit. We'll be fine."

They reached the merge onto Interstate 190 and began the ascent up the high, narrow bridge that spans the Niagara River and leads onto Grand Island. The river churned beneath them now, violent white caps sparkling in the muddy water. "Bridge freezes before roadway," Ellen read the sign silently, glad for the human ballast in her car as they crested the arch of the bridge. In the distance, a black wall seemed to drop over the Thruway and curtain off their view. Julie and Hannah, buckled into the back seats, shivered and exchanged worried glances.

Grand Island lay flat and defenseless against an early winter storm barreling its way through the desiccated orchards and barren fields around the Great Lakes, gathering force and moisture from the still warmish waters of Lake Erie. Usually the fine old city of Buffalo hosted these freakish, demonic storms but this time, nature turned the wheel slightly and the Island would feel the brunt of its fury. A mile down the road, the rain metamorphosed into mesmerizing snowflakes that danced seductively in the car's headlights. "Follow me," they beckoned as landmarks disappeared. The white lines demarcating the edge of the highway were hidden under a one-inch and then, quickly, a two-inch coating of snow and slush.

Gluing her eyes to the rear lights of a monster SUV in front of her, Ellen prayed that its driver could see the road better than she. She wished he would slow down. The burly vehicle charged ahead, creating a frothy wake that imperiled the drive even more. Ellen reduced her speed from forty to thirty-five to twenty-five miles per hour and would have slowed even further but she dared not completely lose those taillights.

Until she did. First, the snow changed from fat, slushy flakes to grainy, driven pellets hurtling furiously at the windshield, as if they earned points for velocity. The taillights in front of her suddenly disappeared then reappeared to sketch a crazed pattern as the brake lights blinkered off and on. Then, almost in slow motion, the big vehicle swerved and skittered to the right, bounced against the guardrail, flipped on its side and slid back toward Ellen's lane. Ellen veered left and managed to pass alongside it as Julie let out a strangled yip.

"Call 911!" Hannah yelled, as she hopelessly tried to retrieve her cell from her overstuffed purse.

"Shouldn't we see if there's some way we could help?" asked Maggie, peering back into the darkness where the other vehicle had disappeared.

"How in hell can we do that?" Ellen asked miserably. "I swear to God, if we get out of this alive, I'll never drive again. There's no way to go back on this highway. But somebody call it in! Tell them there was a wreck about two miles south of the North Grand Island Bridge."

"I'm ringing them now," Julie trembled.

Ellen's car, leaving the SUV to its fate, fishtailed back and forth, back and forth, while she fought the impulse to overcorrect her steering. She popped the vehicle into neutral and hung on to the steering wheel, the muscles in her jaw, neck, and arms as tense as bridge pylons. Inexplicable licks of flame appeared and disappeared in the gloom ahead. Behind them, the SUV was swallowed up by the blackness of the night. The Accord slowed and straightened out and Ellen eased it back into second gear. Emergency lights pulsed in red flashes ahead in the whirling snow. Creeping along at less than five miles per hour, Ellen could hear and feel the rumble strips embedded on the shoulder of the highway so she corrected mildly to the left, into what she hoped was a lane. The road was a wretched slop of ice and slush.

The back-and-forth flicker of hand-held emergency lights appeared, along with a dim human shape, waving them toward an exit. Gratefully, Ellen obliged. Stopping at the end of the exit, they waited while a young volunteer fireman approached the car, and they quickly told him about the accident they had witnessed. He replied, "Bad night to be out! There's been a big accident on this side of the bridge to Buffalo. A fuel tanker is on fire blocking both lanes. Nobody's crossing that bridge tonight. You can either turn around and go back to Niagara Falls and try to get to Buffalo through Tonawanda or you can take a left at the light ahead and take that road down to the end. There's a hotel down there, maybe they'll have rooms."

"We'll find that hotel," Ellen decided. "I *have* to get out of this car."

Her three passengers, like a chorus, breathed a collective "Yes!" Texting home, the three left their husbands or children some version of: "I'm okay but can't get home. Spending night at hotel. TTY tomorrow. Please text back and let me know everybody's safe. Love you." After Hannah sent her own message, she commandeered Ellen's phone and texted Will, Cole, and Jon that Ellen and *In Accord* were riding out the storm at a hotel on Grand Island. The three-mile drive across the island took half an hour. Finally, the hotel's familiar cream and green façade materialized in the madly swirling whiteness.

"Vacancy!" Julie read, rapturously.

Mobbing the reception counter, they were relieved to hear that there was one vacancy, a room with a double bed and a fold-out couch. "We'll take it," Hannah shoved her credit card at the clerk. "I don't care where I sleep as long as it's out of this storm!"

"Let me buy you a drink," Julie slung a strong arm around Ellen's shoulder and gave her a warm squeeze. "You are a warrior woman, getting us here with nary a scratch. That was horrible."

"I'm so shaky, my legs feel like they're going to give out," Ellen nearly sobbed.

"Great job, really," Hannah added warmly. "I was scared shitless!"

Making her way toward a table, the tension started to recede from Ellen's shoulders and neck, a slow tide washing back out to sea. A drink sounded heavenly.

32: Night at an Inn

Plastic palm fronds interwoven with strands of multicolored lights dangled from the bar's ceiling. The cavernous room was jammed with refugees from the storm and revelers in party dress, spillovers from an earlier wedding reception in one of the hotel's banquet rooms. All were fixated on the bar's huge, flat-screen televisions with their news outlet's moment-to-moment coverage of the horrific progress of the storm. Ellen collapsed into a chair at the last empty table, a small oval with seahorses and sand dollars embedded in its Plexiglas top, and rubbed her temples. "I hope those people in the SUV are okay." The image of the vehicle she had been tailing like a puppy, caroming off the guardrails and sledding toward her on its side, replayed itself in her mind.

"At least they weren't going fast," Julie offered weakly.

"Yeah," Maggie shuddered. "That was a nightmare. I've always been scared to death of *being* in an accident but I've never watched one. It seemed so weird, like everything was going slow and fast at the same time."

Their drinks arrived – a Southern Comfort Manhattan on the rocks for Ellen, red wines for Maggie and Hannah, lite beer for Julie. Ellen drained hers in one long gulp.

"Slow down, baby," Maggie advised in a universal mother voice.

"Okay, one more and I switch to water," Ellen smiled.

Drink refills kept arriving, courtesy of revelers who ordered rounds each time the perky news anchor offered a new bulletin about the blizzard. "Snow falling at two inches per hour." Drinks! "A snow emergency has been declared on Grand Island. All unnecessary travel banned." Drinks! "The I-90 is closed from Silver Creek to Batavia, and the Red Cross is opening emergency shelters for stranded motorists." More drinks!! The friends were well-lubed when a pregnant woman crowded by their table, her enormous belly protruding like basketball under her tight black cashmere sweater.

"Oh, cool, you're having a baby girl, hi little baby girl!" Maggie jiggled her finger at the belly with drunken authority as the alarmed woman waddled quickly away.

"How do you know its a girl?" Julie tried to downplay her lisp.

"Look at how she's carrying it: *all* the weight in front. With boys, it gets spread around from your butt to your belly button."

"Silly!" Ellen tisked-tisked. "If that were true, we wouldn't need sonograms, would we?"

"It's as good as a sonogram!" Maggie slurred slightly, "I'll prove it! Who do we know who's pregnant? I'll bet you a hundred dollars." Her eyes were twinkling, ready to make a large drunken wager. "Ready to put some money where your mouth is, Ms. Palmer?"

Involuntarily, Ellen's gaze slid searchingly to Hannah.

"Hannah?" Maggie followed Ellen's eyes, delighted. "Oh my God, Hannah, are you preggers again? Dear, you shouldn't be drinking that," she reached for Hannah's wine.

"Oh, for heaven's sake!" Hannah grabbed her glass back snappishly. "I am NOT pregnant."

"Then what's that guilty look on your face?" Maggie was a coonhound on a scent.

"Goddamit!" Hannah glared at Ellen.

"I didn't say anything," Ellen defended herself softly.

"Okay, that's it, out with it. Something's going on. I knew it! I knew you two weren't right. You've been *off* all afternoon. So, who's pregnant?" Maggie barely paused for breath then answered herself, "Beth? Oh my God, is it Beth?"

Julie looked perplexed. "I thought Beth got caught *drinking.* Didn't she? In Quebec?"

Hannah's shoulders slumped as the air escaped her lungs. "Beth's not pregnant. It's... it's Zoe."

Despite the wild revelry in the background, the air went silent around the four women. Hannah slumped in her seat, eyes downcast.

Shaking herself back into the moment, Maggie argued in disbelief, "Zoe! You got to be fucking kidding. Zoe's...what, fifteen?"

Hannah and Ellen answered nearly together: "Fourteen."

Julie paled. All eyes were on Hannah as she stared at the table and stroked the stem of her wine goblet.

Maggie took a slow sip of her wine and pursed her lips. "So, shit, Hannah, what's going on? Zoe's really pregnant? Why haven't you said anything?"

Hannah snagged her left lower lip in her teeth as tears leaked down her wide cheeks. She fought to control her feelings.

Softly, tentatively, Ellen reached out and touched Hannah's arm. "How awful. So what are you going to do? She's still practically a baby."

Her face etched with misery, Hannah replied, "It's actually not my call. She's the one who's pregnant."

"I'm so sorry. But..." Julie stammered. "You're her *mother*. What do you want her to do?"

Sagging even more, Hannah repeated, "It's really not my call."

Maggie's voice was challenging. "So is she, like trying to decide all on her own? Thinking *abortion*? *Adoption*? She couldn't possibly..."

A low rasp escaped her throat as Hannah raised her head and scanned her friends' concerned faces. "I can hardly say this out loud, and I'm pissed that you're making me! Zoe says it's *her baby* and she plans to keep it. She says we can throw them both out onto the street if we want to but she will not give up," Hannah made quotation marks in the air with her fingers, "her baby."

"If Leah came home pregnant, I would completely freak out," Maggie pronounced.

Silently, Julie pictured her own abortion at fifteen, a decision forced on her by her mother, along with a compact that they must never tell her father, or anyone. A promise kept.

Ellen mumbled, "Wow." She turned her full gaze upon Hannah and spoke gently. "Hannah, how are *you*? I guess I can see that it's not your call, *choice* and everything, but really, how are *you*?"

"I'm exhausted. I haven't slept a solid night since she told us. First thought in the morning my brain goes to: my daughter's having a baby and it makes *me* nauseous. I'm scared for her when I'm not thinking how much I want to wring her neck. She's ruined her life and tossed away our dreams for her like they were garbage." The words had come in a torrent, and now she stopped. "And none of that matters." Hannah straightened and said with a defiant glare, "So don't judge me. I'm doing the best I can. "

Maggie scowled. "Who's judging?"

"What? I'm not judging you!" Ellen protested simultaneously.

"Oh, don't give me that crap," Hannah shot back at Ellen. "You are, you know you are, you with your perfect life and your answer for everything. You are thinking that I have let my girls walk all over me and this is the logical result. *As ye sow, so shall ye reap.*" She mimed Ellen's lilting voice. "It's one of your favorite sayings. I hate your pity."

Julie sat up angrily. "I don't know what you're talking about, and neither do you. You're the one with the perfect life. Nobody pities you!"

"Man, Hannah, that is just off the effing wall! Where do you get that we pity you?" Maggie challenged.

"It's me," Ellen confessed. "I brought her coffee. She thinks that's pity." Ellen's eyes were glittery. "Well, for your information, I don't pity you. I was trying to support you. But forget it. It's your drama. Go ahead and star in it!" She pulled out her room key and pushed herself unsteadily to her feet. "I'm done."

"Me, too," Maggie said, rising unsteadily to offer her arm. "Let's go."

"Come on," Julie pleaded looking back and forth between these friends whom she hardly recognized tonight. "We're frazzled, we are lucky we didn't get into a horrible accident. Let's get some sleep."

Hannah gripped the edge of the table and continued to sit.

"What are you going to do? Put your head down and sleep on the table? Come on!" Maggie nudged Hannah.

Unsteadily, the four women made their way to their room in the harsh light of the narrow corridor. Ellen fumbled and swiped the key three times before they gained entry. The room was furnished in the spare simplicity of a two-star hotel: beige stucco walls, a faux oil painting of an old red barn surrounded by a dozen placid Holsteins, a multihued carpet, and a bed covered in a stiff, patterned comforter likely hiding stains better left unnamed. A couch backed up against the long wall and two small chairs were crammed under a tiny round table with more plastic seahorses embedded in its top, tucked against the far corner of the room.

"Sweet," Maggie whistled as she dropped her purse on the bed.

Standing in the small, hot, full room, Ellen turned to Hannah and pumped both hands in the air, "You *do* let your girls walk all over you. And I have always supported you, no matter what. The *as you reap, so shall you sow* thing is something you've said a hundred times, too, by the way, whenever you talk about the troubled students at your school. It should be on the wall of your office! So this really sucks. It sucks for you *and* for me." She took a deep, tremulous breath and continued, "And by the way, my life is *not* perfect. My husband isn't speaking to me and last week, I went out to a bar alone and I ran into Ty, you remember, that guy from my college days…"

Maggie jumped in, "What? Will isn't speaking to you? Weird how our lives sometimes sync. Brian isn't speaking to me either. That is one goddam sucky way to live!"

Julie frowned, looking back and forth between Maggie and Ellen. "Why aren't your husbands speaking to you? Are you having an affair, Ellen? That doesn't seem like you! I'm so sorry about Zoe, Hannah. I really did think you all had perfect lives."

"Brian found my stash." Maggie confessed quickly.

Ellen's eyes widened. "Shit! No way!"

"What?" Hannah demanded.

Dramatically, Maggie collapsed on the bed. "I hid it in the kitchen, in an old casserole I never ever use, but Brian was looking for coffee and stumbled on it. He blew up, he really pitched a fit. I've never seen him so pissed off. He hasn't said one word to me in three days."

As Julie sympathized with a soft, "That's awful," Hannah spoke over her, insistently. "Excuse me, but he found your *what?*"

"You heard me," Maggie's voice was whispery. "He found my stash. My pot. My grass. My weed." Her tone strengthened as she ticked off some common names for cannabis. "Don't go all shocked, Hannah. I smoke a little dope now and then, gets me through the long nights. Used to help with the nausea from the chemo."

Hannah was indignant. "Christ! Maggie, where do you get marijuana?"

Maggie drew herself up regally and gestured toward Ellen. "Our own Ms. Palmer is my dealer, actually. Well, not my dealer. She's my supplier."

Eyes blazing, Hannah looked from one friend to the other with that interrogator's gaze so well practiced by middle school principals. "Dealer! Supplier! What the hell's the difference? I don't believe this, I don't freaking believe this. I mean it! Are you two out of your minds?"

Ellen quizzed, "Why are you so hysterical?"

"I am not hysterical! But we *all* have teenagers. Impressionable teenagers. That should be enough said."

Ellen shrugged. "I hide it. I don't smoke around my boys or even in my house. And it's not like anyone here is a drug virgin."

Shocked, Hannah sputtered, "How stupid are you? Don't you think your boys smell it a mile away, on your clothes, in your hair?"

A slight smile played on Ellen's lips. "Apparently *you* never have…"

Already flushed with wine and anger, Hannah reddened another shade.

"And look who's talking about impressionable teenagers! I don't see how *you* can play that card at the moment," Ellen finished and instantly regretted her sarcasm, as Hannah's gaze narrowed.

Anxious as a caged stray, Julie paced in the four-foot space between the couch and the television. "So let me get this straight." She faced her friends, hands on hips. Hannah was glowering at Ellen. Maggie was collapsed over herself on the bed, holding her head. Julie ticked items off on her fingers as she spoke. "Ellen and Maggie are potheads and your husbands aren't speaking to you. And Ellen, you're – what? – dealing drugs and sneaking out to see an old boyfriend? I thought I saw you buying something sexy at the mall. Did I? And Zoe's pregnant so you, Hannah, are not speaking to *anyone*. And Ellen's stalking you with coffee, which is pissing you off!" She sucked in a deep breath and then, with a fluid catlike motion, grabbed a pillow from the couch and flung it at Ellen. "This is crazy! You are all crazy!"

"Shit!" Ellen grabbed the pillow out of the air before it struck her. "What the hell are you doing?" She flung it back, hard, as Julie heaved a sturdy little bolster toward Hannah, who ducked, lost her balance, and crumpled awkwardly across Maggie on the bed.

"Damn!" Surprised, Maggie pushed reflexively, landing Hannah with an "Ooowww!!" in a pile on the floor.

"Hey!" Ellen protested, yanking a pillow out of Julie's hand before she could launch another one. "That's enough! We're not five years old!"

Backed up against the window, Julie held her own face with both hands. "I'm sorry!" she cried, "but I can't stand this. I hate all this bickering and fighting. You're making me sick!"

"People fight!" Hannah replied as she gingerly gathered herself up off the floor and sat on the bed beside Maggie. "Sometimes, they have to. I'm sorry but you live in a bubble if you think they don't."

"Not where I come from, people don't fight," Julie defended herself. "My parents never even raised their voices, and neither do I."

"So you think they never got mad? Are you saying *you* never get mad?" Astonishment frosted Hannah's question.

Julie opened her mouth to speak, then remembered all the pained silences that marked her sad adolescence.

"Then why won't *you* fight with me, or, or, at least talk with me?" Ellen pointed her question at Hannah, oblivious to the red tide creeping up Julie's neck.

"Oh, for Christ's sake, Ellen," Hannah said, "I am not your *mother,* I have a lot on my hands right now. My fight is not with you."

Ellen plopped down on the couch with pillows still clutched to her chest. "Jeez! That's not fair. That's you copping out."

The room was calm and quiet except for the labored breathing of all four women.

As her fingers traced the chevron pattern on the quilt, Hannah spoke soberly. "I know you're unhappy, El. But sometimes you need things I can't give you. No one can do your breathing for you."

"Oh, wow, come on, both of you!" Maggie said quietly.

"Let's talk about friendship! What is actually going on here?" Ellen glared at Maggie. "It was okay for you to feel bitter about everyone abandoning you back when you got sick the second time. Now you're on my case?" She turned to Hannah. "This is a real problem for me. Are we just pretending to be friends? Or do we put ourselves out there for each other when it's *not* easy?" As she shook her head, her hair fell in loose strands. "See, you guys are as important to me as family. Everyone else moves away, children, sisters. Husbands, they're in their own universe. But we have chosen each other. The support, the love…I mean, I talk to you guys in my head all the time! That's the thing that keeps me going."

Distancing herself as much as possible in the cramped room, Hannah stood between the oversized mirror and the fake mahogany armoire, arms crossed tightly over her chest, eyes narrowed to slits. "I can't live on your terms," she enunciated slowly. "I love you, Ellen, but honestly, blood does trump everything. Simon and Matt and the girls gobble up the first and biggest part of me. They just do, I won't defend it. I'm sorry if it hurts you." There was no apology in her voice.

Looking back and forth between Ellen and Hannah, Maggie searched for a way to span their gulf. "Really?" she asked quietly. "I don't get the 'either/or' thing, Hannah. Of course our families have first dibs on our *time*, that's simple physics, but being friends does mean something, too. Ellen can be annoying," she shot an apologetic glance at Ellen, "but we are all annoying sometimes! At least she's always there for you. She was there for me. It's hard to watch you shut her out."

Fists balled tight, face flushed, Hannah argued, "Even friends have to get that there are limits, boundaries. I will *not* be ordered around by anybody!"

Ellen coughed to suppress a laugh, thinking of all the times Hannah took orders from her girls.

Annoyed by that small laugh, Hannah continued, "And besides, Ellen, sometimes it seems like you use me to take the pressure off and you say things to me you really should say to your husband. It's okay to practice on me but honestly, if you're seeing what's-his-name from college because Will's gone off on one of his pity parties again, well, that's not something I can do anything about for you. You got to live it yourself."

As if struck, Ellen sucked in her breath. This was an icy blast, startlingly at odds with her view of herself as reasonable, self-responsible, a giver rather than a taker. Her mind raced. "*Seeing* what's-his-name" was almost on the table but Ellen decided to duck that question. This is not about that, she thought. This is about the deepest of friendships, about an encircling web of unconditional support that she imagined was the defining characteristic of this band of women. But was she – were any of them – assured of that level of connection and support? She couldn't think of Hannah as the master of her own life, but it was also true that Ellen used Hannah as a pressure release valve, indulging in the pleasure of saying out loud those things that she never summoned the courage to verbalize to Will. And why not, she asked herself. What was she afraid of?

A raucous group singing Janis Joplin stomped past the door belting out "*Freedom's just another word for nothin' left to lose.*" At first she was annoyed, but then Ellen yearned to be one of them: free, wandering the halls of a big hotel with friends, safe from a storm, no worries. Even when she'd been a teenager, she yearned to be free. She turned an uncomfortable thought over in her mind, like a new taste. *Freedom is when you stop trying to bend others to your mold.* And she could be free right now, right this second, if she would just release her demands. In some ways, Will was correct. She *did* have everything she needed, without having to run to a girlfriend for justification or validation. Ellen wrestled with this insight, this hot sun burning off a fog. "Okay," she exclaimed. "You're fired!"

"What?" Irritation graveled Hannah's tone.

Ellen threw her hands up in the air. "I get it, I finally get it. There was something I wanted from you, something I thought I deserved but that's not going to happen and guess what I just realized? The sky isn't falling. The fucking sky is not falling. And I'm okay." She scanned face-to-face, feeling a simple gratitude to be alive at this moment in this room with these three. It's amazing, she thought, how everything can change in an instant, a moment of awareness washing away a mountain of self-inflicted anguish. She smiled warmly. "It's been one fuck of a terrible night. Let's get some sleep."

Julie shook her hair. "That's *it*? Are you serious? *Let's get some sleep?*"

"Yes!" Maggie enthused, offering a hand up to Ellen so they could convert the couch to a bed. "Yeah, that's it. It's been a long crazy night. Although I do want to hear all about the old boyfriend, El. Just not tonight." Tossing the seat cushions aside, she yanked on the crossbar to open the metal frame and release the sofa sleeper's thin, deeply creased mattress. "Whoa, that is going to be a challenge," she observed, "but I'm so wiped I could sleep anywhere. Who's bunking with me?"

They were soon lined up, four logs under blankets, trying not to toss and turn or touch each other. The hotel was still thrumming with the sounds of late night partiers, excited kids careening down the halls, and guests from the wedding bidding each other goodnight in loud, tipsy voices. Winter howled outside their window, vibrating the vinyl blinds so that they swished and clinked against the glass. The furnace clattered on, its fan squealing a plea for lubrication before it reached the steady whir that almost melted into the background ambience. One by one, sleep carted each away to her own dreams. Maggie was the last to fall, thinking just as she dropped off how lovely it would be if only she had some weed and could get a tad stoned.

33: The Day After

The storm howled through the dark hours, dropping sixteen inches of snow before exhausting itself over Lake Ontario. Streaming winds then sculpted the snow into a frozen Saharan landscape with swirled hillocks and deep troughs disguising fields, lawns, and parking lots. The deciduous trees had already dropped their leaves but tall, thin hemlocks and other evergreens bent under the weight of the snow like ancient osteoporotic women. Help arrived from the east, from Rochester and Syracuse, and from the south and west, Pittsburgh and Cleveland, as nearby cities that had been spared the fury of this storm dispatched their plows, front-end loaders, and monster snow blowers to dig out the beleaguered area. Caravans of power company crews and equipment arrived from a 200-mile radius to prune away the downed limbs, deal with the live power lines that lay snapped and dangerous in the streets, and string new cable to restore the lights and heat and life to tens of thousands of cold, dark homes and businesses.

Awakening first, Hannah inventoried her throbbing head, dry lips, and cottony mouth. *Coffee* was her first urgent thought, as she slid gingerly out of bed. It groaned and creaked in protest and

Julie stirred beside her, then settled back into slumber. Across the room on the sleeper sofa, Ellen heard the creak and opened her eyes. Hannah gestured toward the door and mimed having a cup of coffee.

Shortly, the two women were seated in a booth in the hotel's busy coffee shop. Each felt a little nervous and tentative, grateful to have storm news as a safe distraction. Loud televisions dominated the restaurant area, reassuring viewers that clean-up was well underway, most major roads would soon be open, and life was on a fast track back to normal as temperatures rose into the high 30s.

"The kids are gonna be pissed if they don't get a few snow days out of this, and the teachers, too," Hannah observed flatly, gazing at the screen.

"Surely everything will be closed for a day or two while they find a place to dump all this snow." Fumbling in her purse, Ellen pulled out a small vial. "Ibuprofen?" she offered.

"Perfect, wonderful," Hannah gratefully accepted.

A ponytailed waitress with streaks of electric blue zinging through her blond hair brought steaming mugs of coffee and sticky, laminated menus. After placing their order, Ellen took a long gulp of coffee, sighed, and stared searchingly at Hannah. "I meant it," she said, "I meant it last night when I said that I get it. I've been putting too much pressure on you, and it's okay. I'll back off. What I didn't say then and I want to say now is that I'm sorry for being such a pain in the ass. I just miss you, is all."

"Well thanks, and I'm sorry, too," Hannah replied with genuine warmth. "I should've made some time or at least called you back. I miss you, too. It's just so *hard* to even talk about what's happening at my house. See? I can't even name names, can't even say it aloud yet. But you were right that our friendship counts for something." Hannah sighed, her attention drawn back to her own family drama even as she was trying to focus on Ellen. She felt anxious to be physically near Zoe, as if by proximity, she could bulldoze some new path through this jungle.

Ellen noticed Hannah's attention wandering. Slowly rotating her coffee mug, she told herself that it was time to practice her new posture of detached acceptance. The waitress arrived with large plates of food. They paused for butter and syrup. Forking a bite of waffle brought Hannah back into the present and she cleared her throat. "So what exactly *is* going on in your life? Something got lost in the shuffle last night. I think I heard a bunch of innuendo about you and what was his name, Ty Somebody?"

A soft smile played across her face as Ellen said, "Ty. Yes, that's his name. Tyler Moynihan."

"So?"

"So, something might be happening. I've met him a couple of times, and," Ellen's voice trailed off and a slight reddening started up her neckline.

Hannah shook her head, startled. "Holy shit! You're *having an affair*? Really?"

"Heavens, no!" Stumbling over her words, Ellen finally said, "No, we had one kiss. I'm not sleeping with him. We were both kind of taken aback."

Ellen was smiling and Hannah noticed that she was sitting up taller than usual. "Wow, look at you," she smiled back.

"Yeah, I know, look at me." Ellen then looked at herself, in yesterday's clothes and yesterday's hair, and giggled. "Maybe it would be better not to look at me!"

Undeterred, Hannah pressed on. "What does 'one kiss' mean?"

"Good question!"

"You haven't thought it through?"

"I've thought about it like crazy but I can't say I've thought it *through*." Ellen cut a bite of omelet and stared at it as if answers were lurking in its yellow crevices.

"So what's this Ty fellow want?"

"Oh, to talk, and sex, I guess."

Hannah snorted rudely. "You're funny. Of course he wants sex. What does he talk about?"

"God! Everything! It's so very different to talk with a man about his thoughts and feelings." She took a deep breath. "It makes me feel like a college girl again, sort of dizzy with the excitement of having someone look at you, really look at you, tell you what's actually on his mind, and wait to hear what you're going to say, like it's important, like you have interesting opinions." She hesitated briefly. "And he wants to take photos for a picture spread..."

"Oh, dear, what sort of photos? Are you sure he's not some kind of perv, softening you up with big doe eyes, so he can get you to let him take porn pictures?"

Breaking into hysterical laughter, Ellen tried to gesture that *that* was simply impossible. Catching her meaning, Hannah also broke into great waves of laughter and it took them both a few minutes to calm down. Wiping her tears, Ellen finally choked out, "Look at me! I'm about as far from porn material as I am from, I don't know, being an astronaut and landing on Mars."

Hannah smiled and gestured for Ellen to go on, ceding the point.

"And you've been reading too many *Educator Alerts* to have thoughts like that even sneak into your brain! Ty's doing a photo shoot for some magazine. It's off the radar, I don't remember its name, might be a local or regional thing, but it's a then-and-now story about our college crowd, how we loved Buffalo then *and* we didn't turn out to be such terrible slackers now. Strictly G-rated."

They sat back and sipped their coffee amiably for a few moments, and then Hannah leaned forward intently. "So, wow, where do you want this to go? Do you actually want to end your marriage and take up with this man?"

"I don't know! It's murky, messy, guilty. I didn't mean to get involved."

"If Will finds out, he'll be furious," Hannah pointed out. "You can't be thinking that you'll get away with having it both ways?"

"May I remind you that when this exact thing came up at our last book club, you said you wouldn't want to know if Simon was being unfaithful? You just wanted it to stay a secret that withered away on its own, not rock any boats. I think about that a lot. How do I know what's worth throwing everything away for?"

"Well, in my case, that was theoretical, and I was just being oppositional. I thought about it later and realized there's no way I could just play dead to it if Simon were to take up with somebody else. And this is real, this is now," Hannah said softly. "I can't believe it, actually. You've always been so loyal."

"That's me, a big golden retriever." Ellen said glumly.

Hannah giggled. "Okay, arf! But I don't see how you could stay in a relationship with Will if you're really as into this Ty guy as you seem to be."

They were interrupted by cheering from a group of youths in one corner of the restaurant as it was announced that Buffalo, Grand Island, Kenmore, and Tonawanda schools would be closed the following day.

"You know, the sad thing is that I'm *not* in a relationship with Will, not really. He's in his own world and isn't the least bit concerned about us. Or about doing anything that would keep our marriage alive. He says that his love is *demonstrated* by his coming home after work. He actually said that, in this fake, patient tone like he was talking to some stupid-ass customer and he had to explain the limits of their policy *again*."

The waitress came by with refills. Absentmindedly, Ellen twirled her wide gold wedding band on her finger.

"Wow. I can't even imagine," Hannah said softly.

Feeling her eyes mist, Ellen squared up her posture like a soldier's. "It's funny. I don't have to work at hiding anything because he isn't looking. As long as I'm physically there, I'm just furniture."

"But I can see that you *are* working hard, if only at seeming to be okay."

Ellen exhaled slowly and continued to twist her ring. As if on cue, Julie and Maggie appeared at the restaurant entrance waving gaily and began maneuvering their way over to the booth.

"Let's talk more later, okay?" Ellen asked under her breath.

Hannah nodded.

"Hey!" Julie sang out as they arrived at the table. "No fair sneaking out on us. Are you guys talking this morning? Work things out?"

Ellen and Hannah nodded. Reading their relaxed body language, Julie was reassured. "Did you hear? Power has mostly been restored and the roads are open, all of the majors anyway. At least we can get home."

"Which makes me *very* fucking happy," Maggie added. "That mattress felt like it was stuffed with pebbles. I'd have been more comfortable on the floor!"

"Sorry! Have some breakfast before we head out." Hannah invited, smiling.

"Avoid the omelet though, it's leathery." Ellen cautioned, sliding further into the booth so Maggie could slip in beside her. They had a quick meal punctuated by urgent texts and phone calls from their families.

"I guess we know we're missed," Maggie observed ruefully. "That's the first time Brian's actually spoken to me in days. He wanted to be sure I was okay. And," she paused dramatically, "and, he's agreed to marriage counseling."

"Wow," Hannah looked surprised.

"I know, I know!" Maggie was effusive. "It dawned on me that we might actually be done, at the end of our rope. *In sickness and in health*, sure, fine, but not in *me* wanting something *he* opposes. I've tried to get him to agree to counseling before and he's always said there's nothing wrong with *him,* any problems we have is because of my fucking shitty attitude." She took a sip of her water and deftly re-wrapped her scarf. "This could be a game-changer, if he really participates."

"That's so great that he's agreed," Ellen said, "but in my experience, it's a big, important *if.*" So often when a couple needed to talk to a social worker at the hospital, only one of them was really engaged in the problem-solving. It always frustrated

261

her, and she couldn't bear to see Maggie deal with another disappointment, especially as she felt mildly guilty for introducing the weed that was the flashpoint for this crisis.

"You had cancer! How can he give you grief about your attitude?" Julie protested. *Men!* She thought, angrily, reflecting on how nimbly Eric had shifted responsibility for his infidelities onto her shoulders.

The drive home was breathtakingly gorgeous. Fresh snow piled on every surface like lustrous whipped cream. It sparkled and glinted brilliantly in the bright sun. The book club friends were all back in their own homes by noon and gratefully taking hot showers by 12:15 – everyone except Hannah who stopped to admire Matt's lopsided new snowman, wearing a scarf knitted for her by a treasured aunt in her favorite colors, waving gaily from their front yard. Hannah gamely bit her tongue and *loved* Mr. Frosty, scarf and all.

34: Maggie and Brian

Discreetly, Brian queried his three most trusted colleagues for references for marriage counselors. He was flabbergasted when all three personally recommended Dr. Anna McLaurin. Marital discord was far more common in the DA's office than he had imagined. It comforted him to discover that his was not the first office marriage to crash and burn. Still, he went to sleep angry and woke up angry (in the lumpy old single bed in the spare room), and he had not spoken to his wife in the week since finding her stash. Feeling betrayed and bitter, he recounted to himself all the times that she had done her own thing, heedless of its impact on his life or career. Office parties – Maggie's worst nightmare. Political fundraisers – Maggie's worst nightmare. Law school alumni affairs – Maggie's worst nightmare. Conservative speech, conservative dress – Maggie's worst nightmare. But the night of the terrible storm had brought him a powerful awareness. While he could not imagine *how* he could reconcile with her, imagining life without her was a bleak, lonely, straight-laced, and boring landscape. He needed her irreverence, her ability to see through pretension. Finally, he could wrap his brain around the painfully exposed idea that they needed professional help.

The psychologist's office was modern and airy, on the second floor of a blocky suburban office building where one could as easily book a Caribbean vacation or buy car insurance as decide the fate of one's marriage. The Brinkmans were ushered into the inner office at once and faced the immediate decision of where to sit. Together on the couch, or in opposing chairs, or in some other combination of near but not too near? Maggie immediately settled on the couch, leaving Brian to declare himself. He hesitated until Dr. McLaurin pointed to the chair nearest Maggie.

"Please, have a seat," she said, "and call me Anna. I'm glad to meet you." After making neutral eye contact with each of them, she asked in a cool professional voice, "Now, how can I help you?"

Maggie hesitated a moment, then waded into the tense, awkward silence. "I thought Brian *told* you why we need to see you when he made this appointment."

"I'd like to have us all start on the same page," Anna replied in a placid, neutral tone.

"I'll go over it again," Brian spoke slowly, as if to a developmentally disabled client. "After 20 years of marriage, raising two great kids, and beating a terrible illness not once but twice, one thinks one knows one's wife. But, I don't! I'm an assistant district attorney and she's a secret pothead." He emphasized *pothead.*

Anna looked at Maggie, silently inviting her to share her version of what they were seeking from her. The room grew still, magnifying the outside sounds of engines and horns and the brakes on the tractor-trailers moving consumables up and down Delaware Avenue. Her heart was racing but Maggie was at a loss for words and emotionally flustered. Finally, in a small voice, she spoke. "I smoke a little weed sometimes to help me sleep. I got started on it when the chemo made me nauseous. Brian is making this into something huge."

Her husband leaned back and gripped the arms of his chair. He could sure use a haircut, Maggie thought, noting the wispy locks beginning to curl over his ears. In normal times, she would already have made the appointment for him.

"So you've been married twenty years," Anna confirmed. "Have there been other times when one of you thought a particular issue or problem was far more important than the other? I'm wondering if you've had to handle anything like this before."

"No," Brian said instantly, relegating his list of Maggie's worst nightmares, and how they've, maybe, deflated his career prospects, to a back burner. They were here to talk about the weed, and only the weed, as far as he was concerned.

"Yes," Maggie said simultaneously.

"Oh!" Anna said, nonplussed. She continued to gather background data, probing for common ground where they might be able to join one another. Issues related to Maggie's cancer were like a toxic dust they were both inhaling. Brian was vehement that the disease – he didn't like to call it by name – had been vanquished. Maggie was equally vigorous in her opinion that the cancer lurked in her body, just waiting for her to relax her vigilance and then it would roar back. As bleak as her vision, his was rose-tinted. The fifty-minute hour flew by and Dr. McLaurin scheduled them for her first opening the following week.

35: Hannah and Simon

Groping in the dark for her bedside clock, Hannah opened one eye a narrow slit and saw, with sweet relief, that it was only 2:19 in the morning. She was entitled to more precious sleep. Nestling back into her one comfortable sleeping pose on her left side, legs slightly tucked, she ordered her mind to quiet. Instead, her awareness gradually sharpened. The bedroom was unnaturally still and silent. Where was Simon? She slid an exploratory hand gently all the way across the bed through cold, smooth, unoccupied sheets. Simon *never* has trouble sleeping, she thought, worried. Pulling her old fleece robe around her shoulders, she tiptoed across the hall and saw that his office was dark and empty. Then she padded downstairs and slipped from room to room. He was not in their family room, living room, or kitchen.

In the dining room, graph paper was strewn across the table along with an assortment of pencils, rulers, and a calculator. At first, it looked like a high school trigonometry assignment from the era before computers. A look of consternation crossed her face as the designs began to shape-shift into the familiar layout of her attic. There was the gabled front window, the open staircase, the deep shelves in the rear that held the girls' favorite childhood books and toys and soccer trophies, holiday ornaments, abandoned knitting projects, and boxes upon boxes of stuff that someone had decided might have use someday. Currently, the unfinished front space held two old rockers that needed to be caned, an assortment of seldom used luggage, sleeping bags, a tent falling out of its disintegrating box, a foot locker crammed with camping gear, Matt's crib and changing table and infant swing, three bulky monitors and CPUs, and a saxophone that Simon had played in high school and still couldn't bear to part with.

Reaching onto the table, Hannah picked up the most developed of the sketches and angled it toward the light. Simon's intentions were unmistakable. He had sectioned the front space into one large and one smaller room while across from the stairs, he had penciled in a small bathroom. She held the paper tightly in her hand and again circled her first floor rooms, perplexed. Finally, she spied the dim outline of Simon's head though the back window, sitting still as a statue outside on the steps to their back yard.

"Simon?" she stuck her head out the door and called as loudly as she dared, "Simon! What the hell are you doing?" Then she smelt sweet, acrid smoke and saw the glow of a lit joint between his fingers. "Oh my God, you're smoking *weed*! Did Ellen give that to you?"

"Ha! No, no! What are you talking about?" His face was hidden in the shadows of the night. "Fella at work said I was too stressed. He gave me this one joint, just wanted to see if I'd like it. Have to say, my lungs don't do this like they used to."

"It's cold out here, Simon, put that stupid thing out and come in." Hannah demanded.

"No, uh-uh. Put on a jacket and come out. It's not that cold. Or go back to bed. Do what you want."

Hannah hesitated then grabbed one of Simon's heavy jackets, slipped on her garden boots, and went out into the bracing night air. Autumn stars were in full display on the black sky's canvas, winking and twinkling like distant fireworks. The sight of them made her feel infinitesimal and humble. She plopped down beside her husband and rattled the drawing clutched in her hand.

Glancing at her discovery, Simon smiled and extended the joint toward her. Two weeks ago, she would've been full of righteous sputtering at the proffered pot but tonight...tonight, it seemed like something worth trying. Maybe New York would legalize it. Maybe she and Simon would drink less alcohol and stress their livers less if they could substitute a little weed when they needed to self-medicate. She accepted the joint and held it in front of her tentatively, sighed, and took a slow, cautious drag. Holding the smoke in her lungs while her eyes watered and her throat rebelled, she calculated the last time she had been stoned. Decades ago.

"So..." Simon drawled, tilting his head toward the rough sketch his wife held. "What'd'ya think of my idea?"

"Is this what it looks like?" she asked as the smoke escaped her lungs and snaked up into the cold night air like a charmed cobra. "Are you thinking of building a nursery in our attic?"

"Bingo! Exactly. Why not?"

"Simon." Hannah was full of exasperation. "Damn it! I can't believe what I'm hearing. Having a pregnant fourteen-year-old daughter is spinning me in circles and you're turning it into a fucking *this old house* project!"

"Hannie," he said patiently, "I have *got* to *do* something."

"How about rebuilding the deck?"

"That'll have to wait until next spring."

She faced him. "We have to talk to the boy and his parents, you know. That can't wait. You could do that."

Simon put his arm around her and pulled her close. "That'll come. That's a whole other ball of wax and I don't feel like I have any control over how that goes. This project gives me something to do with my hands. I need it!"

They sat in silence while Simon puffed on the joint. Hannah declined another drag. Finally, she sighed and admitted, "I can't *do* anything. My brain is paralyzed."

He gave her shoulders another squeeze. "It's okay. You don't have to do anything. But would you listen to what I'm thinking?"

Hannah looked at the wide sky again. Was that the Milky Way, a creamy swath in the bejeweled heavens? How many stars in the sky? Was anything on her path *that* important? Surely she could listen to her husband. She nodded.

Encouraged, Simon explained, "Putting a nursery up there says to Zoe, okay, here's how this works. You get an upstairs space, you and *your* baby. When *your* baby cries, you'll be the first to know. When it doesn't want to sleep, you'll be the first responder. Because," Simon sighed deeply and took another drag on the diminishing joint, "I feel too old to raise another kid and I don't want to lose you to another baby either. Even my own grandchild, damn it! Zoe *has* to become responsible and that's going to take a herculean effort for you to *let* her, to guide her, and to force her."

"Herculean?"

He rolled his eyes. "Okay, Amazonian!"

Smiling, Hannah reached for the joint. She took a hit and sat quietly, thinking and beginning to relax. She released the smoke.

"We're end-played, okay?" Simon continued. "No way we would actually throw Zoe and this baby out, and it's well past the point where anyone can discuss abortion. Even adoption is hard to imagine. So how do we make it work? I keep asking myself, *how do we make this work*? And then it hit me. We have to help her grow up. We need to be there for the practical shit and back her up so she doesn't screw up the child. But, we also need to make her put in the time, be the mom. Because when she's twenty-four, she's going to have a nine-year-old. And at that point, she isn't going to want us raising her child. She fights us – you," he corrected, "on everything already. So we just have to help her and have some faith that she'll grow up okay. She's a strong kid."

"Shit," Hannah said, taking another puff. "You're right. I'm still spinning on the denial/shock wheel, and you've moved on to acceptance. My practical, wonderful husband!" She leaned against his shoulder and relished knowing that he was her rock – strong, steady, easy. How nice it was that he didn't want to lose her to another child. They would roll with this. Yes, they would. She giggled, slightly stoned and feeling relaxed for the first time since before her arduous trek to Quebec. "We'll never be able to retire and take that trip to New Zealand," she said lightly. "I so wanted to see the sites where they filmed the *Lord of the Rings*. And Hawaii. And what about the Great Wall?"

"New Zealand? You want to go to *New Zealand*?" Simon, aromatic of scotch and weed, pulled her close. "We'll go to New Zealand, I promise! For our next big anniversary, that's what we'll do!"

36: Buttons

"Hi, Ellen, let's do the photo shoot at your office after work Thursday," the message on Ellen's office phone suggested. "I'll bring a couple of cameras and some extra lights. Don't worry about a thing. Just be yourself. This'll be fun!"

But worry she did. She replayed the message from Ty four times, trying to extract meaning from his light, noncommittal tone. Anyone could've listened to his words and thought nothing of it, no hint that this might be something of a date. Still, she liked listening to the warm resonance of his voice. Skipping lunch, she rushed to the mall and had her upper lip and brows waxed and then fretted that her patients would wonder about the puffy, inflamed skin above her lip, almost the shadow of a moustache. No one noticed, reminding her that they were pretty obsessed with themselves and the challenges in their own lives. After work, she had her hair trimmed slightly, resisting the urge to go all out with highlights and lowlights because she feared that Ty *would* notice and would find her silly. Really, all she wanted was to look good in a natural, casual way.

Later that night, as she was sitting on the couch trying again to write her ending to *Mariner's Cove*, Jon halted on his way upstairs and stared at her quizzically. "What are you doing?"

"Trying to write a new ending to a book."

"Why would you do that?"

"My book club didn't like the original ending."

"Why?"

"Oh, it was about a married couple that was unhappy and were deceitful and it just kind of went on and ended like that."

Jon scoffed. "That's stupid! People shouldn't stay married if they're not happy."

"Oh?" Her voice was bland but her heart was beating loudly in her ears. What did he know or suspect?

"Really." His answer belied no ulterior anythings. "Why stay miserable?"

"I'm surprised that you've thought about that." She gazed up at her lanky son anxiously.

He shrugged. "I got a big wrestling meet Friday after school. Can you come?"

"Wouldn't miss it." Ellen smiled brightly at him. Privately, she yearned for a healthy end to his wrestling phase. So much testosterone concentrated in one place at one time! Boys starving themselves to "make weight," which, oddly, meant being able to fight at a lighter weight, *losing* it rather than making it. She could never really breathe until Jon's matches were over.

"You look different." He peered at her intently. "It's your hair, maybe. Are you doing something different?"

"Wow, you're observant!" Lord, she didn't want to converse about her little makeover with her son. She needn't have worried. His cell phone chimed and he sprinted up the rest of the stairs, diving into the private sanctuary of his room.

On Thursday, the day of the planned photo shoot, both Ellen's co-worker and her administrative assistant called in sick. Ellen spent the whole day scurrying madly to compensate for being short-staffed while patients' needs and demands stacked up like last week's newspapers. She wrangled with insurance companies, nursing homes, and charge nurses, and tried in vain to talk sense to one particularly sweet ninety-pound, ninety-year-old lady who was determined to bring her husband home despite his advanced Parkinson's.

When she looked up at 5:30 to find Ty filling her doorway, a ragged duffle bag filled with photographic equipment dangling over his shoulder, she was aghast. "Oh my God, already?" she cried.

"Um, hello?" He smiled crookedly and sighed. "It's 5:30. Not good?"

"I'm sooo sorry, it's been crazy-busy and I lost track of the day!" She took a deep breath, forced a welcoming grin, and started over. "Hello! I'm sure I look like hell, but we did say *now*. I would never ask you to schlep all that stuff again. What's in there, anyway? I thought you said you were bringing a few cameras. That looks like enough gear to go camping for a week."

"Why? Would you like that?"

Laughing, Ellen relaxed. "Yes, I would. I absolutely would!"

"Well, that's what I'll put in it next time," he said lightly. "I just have some lights, a tripod, and a reflector to soften the shadows. Nothing too elaborate but office light can be pretty brutal." He cast a critical eye at her fluorescent lights, buzzing annoyingly in the white fiberglass ceiling panels overhead. "Like those. We need to soften this place up, make it look warm and inviting."

"Good luck with that! This is a *hospital* social work department."

Ty was scowling at her shelves, overflowing with books and official-sounding manuals such as *Health Care Financing Administration (HCFA) Policies and Procedures*. A small column of magazines (*Hospital Social Work Today*) grew up from the floor, nearly three feet high. She shut her eyes to avoid watching him observe her clutter.

"Tell you what," he suggested, lifting a stack of books off the end table by the small couch. "Let's create one small area where the space looks inviting and comfortable, like *you* own it. And, um, your blouse…"

"What? What about it?" Ellen quickly looked to see what she had spilled on herself during her daylong flurry.

"Well, do you happen to have anything in a less vibrant color? Or a jacket? It looks great on you, but I'm afraid that color is going to compete with the olive tones of the walls in here."

Ever since Ty's call, Ellen had planned on wearing this particular silk blouse. A deep jade, it accentuated her hazel eyes and its silk felt like warmed lotion on her skin. But she did have a fitted off-white linen blouse in her coat closet, on hand for lunchtime emergencies involving sauce or salad dressing.

"How's this?" She pulled out the white shirt and held it up to him.

"Perfect." He closed the door to her office and shut the interior window blind. The hustle and business-professional air of the hospital instantly disappeared behind the closed blind.

Brain-freeze set in. Ellen wondered if she should change her blouse on the spot as if this were an insignificant wardrobe swap, or if she should trek all the way to the ladies' restroom at the far end of the corridor. That seemed silly, with Ty so focused on trying to create peace within her chaos. A series of four miniscule buttons on the cuffs held each sleeve tightly in place. Ellen undid the left sleeve easily but she fumbled with the buttons on the right, her non-dominant hand sweaty and clumsy. Ty had his back to her, busily straightening out her office, moving the stacks of manuals and magazines off camera, plumping her one decorative pillow, and positioning his reflector. Eventually, however, he had to notice that she was struggling without success to get the buttons on her sleeve undone. As he grinned, she forgot to be embarrassed and simply noticed his beguiling smile.

"Here, let me help you." He faced her, gently took her wrist in his left hand and efficiently worked the buttons free. His touch on her wrist ignited an ardent, spicy shiver down her spine. He lingered to stroke her wrist for a long, wordless moment and then tentatively unbuttoned the tiny button nearest her throat. Now his eyes found permission in hers and he unbuttoned the next, then the next. When the blouse was hanging fully open he slid it off her shoulders, and spent a long moment just gazing at her shoulders, collar bones, and breasts swelling out of her bra. Then he sighed. "I am a happy man," he whispered, leaning in and outlining the swell of her breasts first with his finger and then with his tongue.

Closing her eyes, Ellen wished this moment could be her eternity. Ty leaned closer and kissed her gently on her lips. His first kiss was soft, dry, and tentative. Thirstily Ellen returned that kiss, her arms reaching around him and pulling him tight to her body. Her hands found his belt buckle, easily released, and the zipper to his jeans. She slid her hand inside his boxers. They swayed wordlessly while she stroked him and he kissed her deeply, both astounded by their urgency.

Her couch was a hospital-issue, small, uncomfortable thing, but she had a lovely afghan draped over the back cushions. They spread that out on the floor and made love on it. Afterward, they lay hand-in-hand in sweet quiet for several minutes.

Finally, Ty asked in a sly voice, "So, we going do this?"

Ellen giggled, "Pardon?"

"I want to record this moment. You look…"

"Like I just had fantastic illicit sex?" she finished the sentence for him.

"Well, yes."

"Is your camera going to tell on me?"

"It just tells the truth. I could take some awesome pictures of you now. If you're okay with that?"

Ellen gasped. "What? No pictures of me naked!"

Eyes sparkling, he reached out and traced the line of her chin, ending with his index finger softly resting against her lips. His words were soothing. "Shhh, Ellen, no worries. Of course, put your clothes on. I just want pictures of your face, of you. You look incredibly beautiful."

37: Rafael

The boy stood in the doorway of his father's study, nervously shifting from foot to foot. His father, Erie County Court Surrogate Judge Jorge Cordero, was pouring intensely over a brief that a law clerk had given him that afternoon. Books of legal code, practice, and scholarly journals neatly lined the floor-to-ceiling cherry shelves built into one wall of his immaculate study. An original Picasso lithograph graced the opposite wall above a burgundy leather couch while the judge's elegant desk was centered on the back wall overlooking the family's garden. The desk was clear, except for papers associated with the case before him. His Honor did not like clutter.

"Dad?" Rafael spoke quietly.

The judge looked up from his brief and smiled. "Come in, come in." He noticed that his son's glasses were slipping down his nose and that the boy's face seemed shiny, almost sweaty. "What's on your mind?"

"If you're busy, I can come back," Rafael offered, shoving his glasses back into place and nodding toward the paperwork that had been consuming his father's attention.

"What did you want to say, son?" the judge asked, a

sternness in his voice.

Rafael cringed. "I, I need to tell you something." He swallowed and stared resolutely at the floor. "I don't want to but I have to." His voice was shaking as he remained standing just beyond the door.

Concerned, the judge motioned his son to the couch. Then he closed the door and settled into a nearby chair, leaning forward to indicate that his full attention belonged to his boy, his only child, the shining centerpiece of his marriage.

Rafael felt as though his mouth was full of dry granola. He struggled to swallow, and croaked in a whisper, "A girl is pregnant."

Highly attuned to the nuances of what people (mainly, witnesses in criminal trials) did or did not say, the judge nonetheless did not comprehend his son's drift. He waited for Rafael to finish explaining the problem. Eventually, exasperated by waiting – he was a famously impatient man – he finally prompted, "A girl is pregnant. What's that got to do with you?"

"She says, she says, she says I'm its father," Rafael confessed hoarsely, in a nearly inaudible rush of words. He was unable to look at his father.

The judge exhaled a loud "ooof," and slumped back in his chair, not quite believing what he had just been told. Rafael was sixteen, a track star, an excellent student, a dutiful son who had never given trouble to his parents. This was inconceivable. Jorge Cordero ran his fingers through his thick, wavy, salt-and-pepper hair and held his head. His years of hard work, his sacrifice, and his triumph all seemed to drain away.

"We raised you right," he said with a steely edge in his voice. "Tell me how it happens that you have *this* to say to me."

"I'm so sorry, so ashamed," Rafael replied softly.

"As well you should be! But that doesn't answer my question. How did this happen?" There was no mercy in the father's voice, no kindness in his eyes.

In as few words as possible, Rafael described the summer party and how his friends kept putting drinks in his hands, finding it hysterical that he'd never been drunk before. Then a girl wanted to dance and he did, too! "Everything after that's sort of a blur," the boy confessed.

"Still not an answer," his father responded, eyes narrowing even further.

"It's hard," Rafael stumbled for the right words. He was sitting opposite his father's grandfather clock, an imposing carved masterpiece in walnut burl. The rhythmic pendulum swept back and forth across the astrological blue moon phase on the background. The family name was engraved on a solid brass heirloom plate affixed to the clock. His father cherished it. Reluctantly, Rafael dragged himself back into the conversation. "So this girl was dancing like she belonged on a TV show or something and it was really sexy, like she was trying to seduce me." He paused and remembered and concluded dramatically, "She seduced me!"

The judge was on his feet then, his finger stabbing his son in the chest. "Don't you ever, *ever* say that someone else is responsible for what you did. That girl could've been butt naked with her legs spread like an open book and you still had a choice. We don't, in this family, we don't ever blame other people for our actions!"

Rafael twisted away from his father's jabbing finger, humiliated. "I know, Dad, I know. I'm sorry," he choked out.

Abruptly, Jorge sat down and began tapping his fingers on the arms of the chair. He looked darkly at his son. Rafael stared at the clock, his face flushed and perspiring. Finally, the judge spoke. "So?" he asked. "You got a girl pregnant. Who is this girl?"

"Her name is Zoe Feldman. She's a freshman."

"Are you sure you are the father?" Jorge's innately suspicious and analytical mind began to assert itself.

"Um, yes?" Rafael's eyes were wide with shock at his father's innuendo.

"She claims you made her pregnant. You better find out if that's true."

Rafael sat quietly, staring fixedly into space and wishing he could disappear. There was no way he was going to ask Zoe if she might be pregnant by someone else. That thought was mortifying.

"I was a family court judge back before you were even walking," Jorge said, recalling all the painful family dramas he had presided over, the divorces and custody battles, so many children caught in the crosshairs. "It is entirely possible that this girl is trying to trap you because she thinks your family has wealth and prestige."

Shaking his head, Rafael almost smiled. "I don't think she was thinking that!"

Jorge noticed the stifled smile. "Wipe that smirk off your face. There's nothing funny about this. Maybe she wasn't thinking like that when she was with you," he said harshly, "but when she found out she was knocked up, she thought, who could I blame? Who could I get to pay for my abortion?"

"Oh, stop! Dad, stop!" Rafael shook his head vigorously. "She's having the baby. She was clear on that. There's not going to be any abortion. "

"What?"

Rafael described the phone conversation he'd had with Zoe. First, she had reminded him of who she was, and then she told him she was just in the second trimester of the pregnancy. Declaring that she planned to have the baby, she had also admitted that calling him wasn't her idea: her parents had insisted upon it.

"What's her name again?" the judge had asked. Then he remembered. "Feldman, you said? She's Jewish?"

"I don't know. I guess," Rafael answered, unsure of his father's implication.

The judge quickly calculated that a healthy infant would be snapped up through a private adoption by some modern, eager, childless couple. He grilled and upbraided Rafael until there was nothing left to say. His finally commanded his despondent son: "You must convince this girl to place the baby for adoption. I will cover whatever pregnancy and delivery costs she incurs, once there is proof of paternity. But you must insist that it is given up for adoption for its sake as well as for your own future. And you must *not* tell your mother. Ever! Are we clear on that?"

"Yes, sir," Rafael answered miserably.

38: Reckoning

November days can be as short as a dream. With no moon to light the sky, an ink-black night had fallen like a blanket over the city by the time Ty finished taking dozens of photographs. He carefully packed his gear back into the duffle bag, kissed Ellen slowly and longingly, and left.

Having sex with Ty had been like being awakened from the dead. Ellen felt nerve pathways pulsing joyfully from the core of her pelvis out through her fingertips and down her thighs all the way to the soles of her feet. Afterwards, she and Ty had laughed easily while setting up the poses for his photo shoot, with Ellen willingly accepting all of his directions. Tilt your head. Raise your chin. Now sit behind your desk looking serious and studying a patient's file. Look a little more concerned. Okay, enough of that. Unbutton those top three buttons. As if bound by an implicit pledge to sustain the magic, each stayed and played completely in the moment. All questions, all thoughts of the future, were shelved for some other time.

When the door latched behind Ty, Ellen moved to the window and opened her blinds. She stood, looking down as lights twinkled up and down the streets near the hospital. High-heeled shoes click-clack-clicked as a woman hurried past Ellen's door. An ambulance careened into the emergency entrance, sirens screaming. Muffled voices rose and fell from the end of the corridor, thick with urgency about some life-or-death matter.

Ellen didn't feel urgent. She felt as though she could spread her beautiful, invisible wings and fly. "A moth to the light," she whispered, recalling Ty's naked body, the curly grey and black hairs on his chest and the confident feel of his muscled arms. It was unreal that this was happening. And yet, God! He, it, this was irresistible. She had been so parched for so long. With her eyes closed, she lightly stroked the faux granite window ledge with her finger, noticing how pleasantly smooth and soft it felt. She had never, in her ten years in this office, appreciated a single tactile sensation here. A smile softened her face and she opened her eyes to the cityscape.

Buffalonians must despise the dark, she thought, observing the mushrooming displays of garish blow-up figurines (turkeys, pilgrims, and some early Santa's) and colorful strands of lights adorning front doors and shrubs as far as her eyes could see. By late November it was a rare house that flaunted no holiday-themed decoration; such a place seemed sullen and reproachful in this festive town. Neatly coiled in plastic bins in her own attic, at least a dozen strands of white or colored lights waited for her to embrace the holiday mood. In years past, she spent hours stapling them artistically around her windows and porch railings, adding little stars and curlicues for effect. A cold pall settled over her as she pictured those lights nesting in her attic, waiting to be strung. Suddenly, she was imagining her home. *Home*: husband, sons, commitments, memories, responsibilities.

As a girl, Ellen spent hundreds of hours playing with an elaborate Victorian doll house, rearranging the furniture, setting a diminutive family at the mahogany dining table, putting them to bed under dainty lace coverlets, getting them up and sending them forth on their daily rounds. Any cash she accumulated was spent on accoutrements for that dollhouse: tiny Lenox vases with tinier porcelain daisies, miniature wool Persian rugs, even copper sauce-pots and frying pans. She had nourished herself by creating and controlling a stable family life in that dollhouse. Even into her teens, she put out the Thanksgiving feast in November and in December she strung pearl-sized ornaments on a small twig of evergreen clipped from her real family's real tree. She had loved the entire holiday season, from Halloween to New Year's Day, and she had fantasized that in her perfect future, her holidays would be as blissful as playing with her dolls. Everyone would cherish everyone.

Awareness of the chasm between her fantasy holidays and her reality suddenly filled her with a cold, punishing dread. Thanksgiving and Christmas were galloping at her like a team of Belgian workhorses pulling a sleigh of traditions and expectations. During the early years of her marriage, the practical custom of alternating Thanksgiving and Christmas celebrations between her family's and Williams' parents' house became set in stone. When

William's mother died a decade ago, it passed naturally to the younger generation to host these family events.

So now, it was her turn to prepare and serve the Thanksgiving feast. Her parents, her sister's family including a newly married nephew, his bride, and his bride's eight-year-old twins, Will's father, sister, and her overbearing husband, plus their three teenagers would all descend on Ellen's home. They expected to gorge on smoked turkey, fruit compote, sweet potato pie, and Ellen's specialty, homemade salt rising bread. The house would feel like it was bursting at the seams and by the end of the evening, Ellen would have had too much to drink and would be utterly frazzled. Traumatized by the horde of intruders, Romeo and Juliet would hide for days afterwards. Romeo might even leave a "protest pee" in somebody's shoe, though never Ellen's.

Following on the heels of Thanksgiving, the first Friday evening of December was always reserved for William's office party. Said party required Ellen to produce artfully wrapped, thoughtful gifts for his key staff, as well as find something to wear that was festive and flattering but not attention-grabbing. Her role was to be charming and all-but invisible. Then, Christmas would be at William's sister's house up in Lewistown. Christmas, Ellen could not bear to think that far into the future. Her head began to throb as the lovely sexy tingling she had felt moments before evaporated.

"What am I to do?" she wondered aloud. Unbidden, the words "home wrecker" danced across her awareness. Examining the words in her mind, she felt as insecure as a tourist who discovers she's lost in a dangerous and vulgar place.

Her thoughts raced ahead. Home. Wrecker. Was that what she was? Could you wreck something that was already in ruins? But the boys? One could wreck one's children; all the clinical articles about childhood depression were unequivocal about that. Could she go home, then, and shut this afternoon out of her mind, carrying on as if nothing had happened? At least until Cole and Jonathan grew up and moved out? Why not? The only difference between her usual charade and that scenario was that she had indulged in a few moments of pleasure. *Pure pleasure.* Well, okay, it probably wasn't kosher to call it "pure." *Genuine?* That was it! Wasn't she entitled to some *genuine* pleasure? No, of course she wasn't. Her Protestant upbringing made no bones about the responsibilities of married women with families. But, oh, it had been so sweet. It had felt so right. Guilt, she knew, must be hovering like a helicopter nearby, but it hadn't attacked the place where she lived. Not yet.

A light snow began to fall, leaving a wispy coating on lawns and cars. It wasn't cold enough yet for the snow to accumulate. Soon, too soon, Ellen thought. She stood transfixed at her window for a full hour after Ty's departure, thinking and watching. Finally, she arrived at that the cold truth that she had nowhere else to go, no one to confide in. And far more importantly, she had sons who deserved, and maybe even still needed, their mother, even the flawed version she now knew herself to be. Slipping on her coat and a jaunty white beret, she stepped out onto the brightly polished corridor and headed home.

39: It's a Girl

Beads of sweat popped out like hives across Simon's brow as he sliced several varieties of gourmet cheese and tried to artfully arrange a platter of crackers and appetizers. He cast a nervous eye toward the clock. The Cordero family: Jorge, his wife, Elena, and their son, Rafael, were due to arrive in fifteen minutes for a face-to-face meeting of the two families.

Moments ago, Hannah called to say that she and Zoe were stuck in traffic on the Scajaquada, a curvy expressway bisecting north and west quadrants of the city. Up ahead, an overturned garbage truck had spilled its contents onto the roadway. All exits toward home were closed. "The police and the fire department are all over the place," Hannah reported, "but I have no idea when anything's going to move again. Maybe Rafael's family's stuck, too?" she added hopefully.

"That would *not* be the kind of break we're getting lately," Simon grumped. Then Hannah's ears were blasted by the sounds of a small boy wailing. Matt tore into the kitchen holding a bloodied finger up to his father. "Daddy, I'm bleeding! I need a band aide!" he gasped with exaggerated anguish.

"Gotta go," Simon barked as he quickly hung up.

The meeting hadn't even begun and already it was a disaster. When Zoe finally informed Rafael that she was pregnant, he'd been stunned and defensive. Wildly inebriated during his brief time with her, it didn't seem possible that she could've become pregnant. Zoe intuited that he might be afraid to tell his parents but her sympathy dried up when he called back to request that she get a paternity test. Later, when he informed her that his dad would cover her medical costs if she placed the baby for adoption, she lit up like Riverside Park on the 4th of July. She barraged him with text messages that ended with "F off! U r a jerk. Baby ok without u." Unfortunately, Rafael's mother intercepted the messages on her son's phone and insisted on knowing to what this young lady was referring. When Elena insisted, Elena prevailed. Painfully, Rafael revealed his secret to his mother. As angry and disappointed as they were with their own son, the Corderos had also formed a horrible first impression of Zoe Feldman.

Her daughter's text-messaged introduction to the Cordero family was not known to Hannah when she called them to arrange a get-together. She thought that Elena sounded as cold as ice. When Elena mentioned that she'd been involved in a foster parent organization, and had seen first-hand the unfortunate results of babies raising babies, Hannah was offended. Realizing how deeply she was already attached to this ill-timed and ill-conceived baby, she mentioned that she was a school principal with two master's degrees and that her family would certainly be able to provide a suitable home for any child.

"My daughter has a *lot* of growing up to do," she conceded, and added: "But I have confidence in her. She's basically a good kid. She'll step up and we're prepared to fully assist her."

Hesitantly, the Corderos agreed a family meeting to talk about their mutual problem.

The dump truck mess was cleared away quickly, allowing Hannah and Zoe to pull into the driveway just moments behind the Corderos. Matt was proudly showing Mrs. Cordero and Rafael the fresh neon green bandage on the finger that he'd pinched in an antique toy box hinge, when Hannah walked in. He sniffled as much as he could manage for effect and then, with Beth supervising, went back to watching an animated movie featuring bilingual Tamarin monkeys that Simon downloaded for the occasion. As he hung up their coats, Simon offered the Corderos drinks. All refreshments were promptly declined. Zoe, clutching a sheaf of papers, hung back and avoided eye contact with anyone, her face an inscrutable mask.

Hannah put on her warmest smile as she welcomed the three strangers standing in her vestibule. Her first impression was that Rafael was gorgeous. His blazing eyes were fixed on Zoe. Hannah could see that he had inherited the fine bone structure of mother's face and the athletic figure of his father. It occurred to her how proud the Corderos must be of this son.

"Please, come in," she said graciously, leading the way into the living room. Zoe trailed behind as if uncertain of her place at this conference. Sitting primly on the edge of an upholstered chair, Elena held her purse tightly in her lap. Her thick, dark hair was swept up in front and captured in a French braid down her back. An elegant woman, she was lightly made up except for dark, glistening berry lipstick. A lovely gold necklace, diamond earrings, and beautifully manicured long red nails conveyed an aura of prosperity. The judge's exquisitely tailored suit, Rolex watch, and thick gold wedding ring similarly spoke of wealth and taste.

Hannah remembered that the judge was re-elected to the appellate court last year after a bruising campaign in which he promised to restore public trust and confidence in the legal system. He had a reputation for being tough enough for the raucous politics of the local scene and smart enough to do a fine job. A local redistricting mess was sure to land in his court sooner or later and Hannah, on any other occasion, would have loved to pick his brain about these upcoming battles. Not a good time for that, she thought. Simon, rather dressed up in a brown herringbone blazer, beige sweater, and pressed khaki pants, set the platter of snacks that he had prepared on the coffee table and offered to make coffee. Hannah shot him a furtive "don't you dare leave me" look but she needn't have bothered as the Corderos again declined to be served.

"Well," Hannah said when they were all seated. "Well, so here we are. Thank you for coming." She was feeling as guarded as a school official at a disciplinary meeting with litigious parents.

The judge cleared his throat and looked at his son. "We have talked with Rafael and with our priest and we have prayed," he said gravely. The room grew still in keeping with the solemn tone of the judge's voice. No one shifted in their seat. He waited, a man accustomed to a respectful audience. Finally he spoke again. "We cannot come to terms with the idea of our son, our *sixteen*-year-old son, having a child with, with…"

All eyes turned toward the pregnant girl, her parents in shock at the judge's unfathomable statement. *Come to terms?* What did that even mean? Rafael's face registered misery in his tightly pursed yet trembling lips. Simon scowled, his shoulders hunched up as if readying for an attack.

However, Zoe straightened in her chair and locked eyes with the judge. "My name is Zoe," she said. "Zoe! And I am having a baby. This baby." She shuffled through the papers still clutched in her hand and dramatically placed three printouts of sonograms on the coffee table in the center of the room.

"Oh, my God!" Simon exclaimed. "You had the ultrasound? I can't believe I forgot that in the crush of everything else. I'm sorry! How did it go?"

"It went great!" she practically sang. "It's a girl! I'm having a baby girl!"

She patted her still-flat tummy and stood protectively over her sonograms, her long hair pulled casually back in a ponytail. Sliding one of the prints towards Rafael, she said, "Look! There's her tiny hands all bunched up in fists. And there, that smudge is her heart." She smiled her most dazzling smile, sat down beside him and turned toward him as if to block out the rest of the people in the room. "Listen to me, please. I'm sorry. I'm so sorry I freaked out on you. It was a shock to me, too, when I found out that I am pregnant. I should've given you some time to get used to the idea."

Rafael was shifting his gaze between Zoe and the grainy images of the fetus spread across the coffee table.

"Go ahead, you can touch them," she encouraged. "They're cool!"

He reached out and took one, peering at the coarse outline of a human fetus. The paper shook in his hand and his eyes were wide. "Mom?" he said, looking toward Elena. "Look."

The judge stood up abruptly. "Put that down!" he barked toward his son, who dropped the paper instantly. "I thought we could talk this through like rational people but I see that I was mistaken. It's time to state things clearly. You cannot seriously be planning on keeping the baby, young lady! There are lives you will destroy if you do that. My son has a future. You might have a future. That infant should have a family who can provide for it, give it a future, too."

Although he was voicing sentiments Hannah had felt just weeks earlier, anger rose in her when he spoke to Zoe as if she were a felon whose fate he could dictate. And as though the Feldman family was trash who couldn't, or wouldn't, provide for this child, this baby girl! She caught Simon's look from across the room.

"It's not up to you," Hannah and Simon spoke nearly in unison, their anger barely disguised.

Zoe jumped up and faced the judge with defiance flashing in her face. "Sir," she said with exaggerated politeness, "I don't actually see where this has anything to do with you. My *parents* thought we *should* have this meeting as a *courtesy* or something. I knew it was a bad, bad, *bad* idea."

Taken aback, the judge furrowed his high, regal forehead for a moment. "Think!" he commanded, his eyes boring into her. "The future for this child, for you, and for Rafael is bleak. You're only a child yourself, you can't possibly give a baby what it needs. You don't even know what that means." His voice dripped icy consternation. "What happens when that baby cries all night long? What happens when you want to party with your friends?"

Holding herself as ramrod straight as the judge, Zoe stepped toward him and held up her palm like a traffic cop's. "Stop!" she ordered. "If you don't think I've heard every word of that lecture a million times already, you are crazy!"

Gasping inwardly at Zoe's impertinence, Hannah also felt a surge of pride at her assertiveness. Sitting with her daughter at the obstetrician's office less than two hours ago, she had seen the image of the tiny fetus hiccupping and swimming around in Zoe's uterus, its miraculous pea-sized heart beating perfectly. The sight inspired awe. Zoe had seemed changed, as well; she seemed to grasp the astonishing and terrifying reality of the material existence of this other being. It wasn't simply something that had made her nauseous and ashamed; it was someone innocent who would have a life's journey of her own.

"No one speaks to me like that! We are leaving," the judge took three steps toward the vestibule.

Throwing her hands in the air, Zoe looked back and forth between her parents. "I told you!" she exclaimed angrily. "Who thought this could go well?"

"Judge, please," Simon swept his hand toward the chair the judge had vacated. His voice was both persuasive and respectful. The judge stopped walking and pivoted to meet Simon's eyes. Simon stared back steadily. "Yes, it is hard, but we thought you might want to be involved, or Rafael might, at least. You're right, they are too young and this is not something I ever expected or *wanted*. But, shouldn't we try to get to know each other?" Simon's face remained a controlled mask, belying none of the insulted frustration he felt. He was thinking that it might have been wiser to do as Zoe had begged and leave the Cordero family the hell out of it.

The judge was incredulous as he looked at Simon, his eyes narrowed. "You are really willing to let her keep this baby?"

Shrugging his shoulders, Simon admitted, "At first, I thought it was ludicrous, maybe even insane. But when it became clear that Zoe wouldn't consider adoption no matter what we said or offered or threatened, I came around. In my family, you play the hand you're dealt." He looked toward his pregnant daughter and smiled lovingly.

The judge further straightened his already straight spine, suggesting military training sometime in his youth. "If she were my daughter…" he began.

"We would do the same thing," Elena ended her husband's sentence definitively. She reached out and gently took one of the sonograms in her hand, her eyes misting. "A baby girl," she whispered. "We would do the same thing. We wouldn't give a baby away either."

Thoroughly exasperated, her husband stared at her, his jaw twitching. "Elena, come now," he said, "We must not condone this sort of thing. It's foolish. Let's go. We have no business here."

"No, we're not leaving, Jorge" she replied softly, her gaze shifting toward Simon. "May I reconsider that offer of a drink?" And then she looked at her husband and inclined her head toward the chair he'd been seated in. "Take a seat, dear. And do allow Mr. Feldman to get you a scotch," she directed, "maybe even a double."

40: It's About the Boys

Muscle memory controlled her actions as Ellen floated through the familiar motions of steering her car out of the Sister's Hospital parking lot. A feeling of being disconnected descended on her, as if an alien woman had moved into her body. Noticing the pulsating lights of a Lebanese bakery in the plaza off Main Street, she wondered how many times she had blindly driven past it. Fluffy, light snow continued to waft from the sky. It melted immediately off the streets but began to cling to pine trees and the wrought iron fence, ornate statuary, and tall headstones in Forest Lawn Cemetery. Driving slowly down West Delavan Avenue past the burial ground, the wispy white outlines of the tombstones looked like fat ghosts at a ball. How many of the thousands entombed here had followed their hearts' path, she wondered.

It was close to ten when she pulled into her driveway and sat, staring at the house. There had been a time when she loved it tenderly, groomed its gardens, sanded and painted its porch railings, and power-washed the spiders out of its eaves. Tonight, all its charm had evaporated. It was only a house, after all, and she felt her attachment to it fading like the snowflakes melting on the sidewalk. Ellen was confident that there would be no interrogative greeting party as there had been three weeks ago when she came home from the Riverside Inn. Before leaving for work this morning, she positioned a note prominently on the kitchen counter announcing to all that they were on their own for dinner; she would be home *very late*. *Very late* was underscored in red marker.

As she tucked her keys into her purse, she noticed the blinking light on her cell phone announcing a missed call. Late in the afternoon, Julie left a brief voice message bowing out of their next few running dates. In an anxious voice, she'd explained that her sister-in-law was having an emergency surgery and Julie was booking the first possible flight to Seattle to be there for her brother and his family. She expected to be back next week, hopefully in time for book club.

Okay, Ellen thought, sending "be safe" wishes into the ether. It was a reprieve not to run with Julie in the morning, not to face so soon what was sure to be her friend's robust disapproval. Every betrayal, even fictional ones, catapulted Julie back into those dark, lost days when her marriage had unraveled. Admitting to an affair with Ty might be a lethal blow to her friendship with Jules, Ellen realized, although *not* acknowledging it would require some unsavory ducking and dissembling. Actually, not owning up to this affair would require lying to her friends, and, far worse – to her family. Ugh. And then, like a fog lifting off in a strong morning sun, she knew with certitude: continuing on this path was *not* something she would do. Despite its intoxicating allure, it was wrong, sleazy. Lying was not something she could live with doing. A relationship with Ty would not go forward. Instead, she would soldier on in her marriage, giving her boys the stable home life they deserved while maintaining her self-respect.

The other message on her phone was from Ty, who had texted simply: "Wow! Awesome pix! Hope you come to see them soon." Her reaction was visceral and immediate, as if his index finger was slowly tracing the line of her collarbone. She shivered, savored it briefly, and blew it away. Slowly and sadly, she texted him: "Sorry, no." She deleted his message as she entered her dark foyer.

Flipping on the light, Ellen noticed a crack in the plaster, snaking from the dusty antique ceiling fixture across to the stucco wall and down to the oak door jamb of the closet. How long had that been there, she asked herself. A house can sit on its foundation perfectly comfortably for forty or sixty years and then, suddenly, the earth exerts such pressure that knife-thin fissures open up, or a closet door suddenly won't close, or the concrete porch separates an eighth of an inch from the house, allowing seepage that will eventually cost thousands to repair. Those imperceptible shifts can be so costly.

As hoped, William was nowhere to be seen. Relieved, Ellen hung her coat in the hall closet and wandered into the kitchen, hoping a glass of chardonnay would smooth the edge off her raw feelings. A nonstick frying pan sat on the stove's back burner, whitish grease congealed around bits of onion, pepper, oregano, and ground beef. The concoction smelled wonderfully Italian and reminded Ellen that she hadn't eaten since her apple and cheese cubes at noon. She wished Cole's emerging interest in cooking were matched with some interest in cleaning up behind himself. She would point it out to him in the morning.

A bottle of chardonnay was tucked behind the half-empty gallon of milk on the middle shelf in the fridge. Expertly, she uncorked it and poured herself a generous glass, admiring its delicate lemony hue. Underneath the hand-written note she had left on the counter in the morning, she noticed a message from Jonathan in bold red marker: Cancel Friday wrestling meet. I QUIT!

That will be a story she understood as her younger son materialized in the kitchen.

"Hi, Jonathan," she said in a light voice. She held his message in the air. "I was just coming upstairs to see you. What's up?"

Jonathan was bare-footed, wearing torn jeans and a loose Grateful Dead t-shirt. His freshly washed hair hung in long brown strands around his face and dripped down the back of his neck. He looked like a wild thing, Ellen thought, bracing herself. His expression was *not* carefree. Shoving a small pile of mail and magazines out of his way, he launched himself onto the kitchen counter and sat facing her, his legs jiggling.

"I want to quit! Simple. I *hate* wrestling. But turns out you can't just tell coach you're done. You need a parent's signature and guess what Dad wouldn't do?" Her son spat the word "dad" out and paused for breath and effect. "Sign the effing form! No, oh, NO! He had to tell me what a freakin' loser I am, that only *losers* quit!" Jon's face was contorted with hurt as he extended a crumpled permission slip to her, hand trembling.

Suppressing her frustration with her husband, Ellen fished a pen from the junk drawer and signed the form without hesitation. "I'm sorry," she said, trying to soothe him. "What happened? Didn't you used to like wrestling?"

"Can't talk about it!" Jon shook his head vigorously as he reclaimed the form. "Thanks, I *will* tell you the whole sorry-ass story sometime, promise, just not now. I have a ton of homework and it's too stupid!" His long strides covered the dining and living room in seconds and he took the stairs two at a time.

"Shit!" Ellen muttered, taking a hefty swallow of wine. Gently, she returned the bottle to its place in the fridge and turned to find herself face to face with her husband, leaning against the door to the basement stairs, his arms laced tightly across his chest.

Will's eyes were hard and his voice was low, on the verge of menacing. "You signed it? After he told you that I refused?"

"What the hell?" Although she had devoted two decades of her life to avoiding arguments with him, Ellen stepped resolutely toward him, hands clenched. "He hates wrestling. *I* hate wrestling! You don't give a crap about wrestling. This is a no-brainer."

Snorting, he shook his head. "I have no respect, no respect whatsoever, for quitters."

"And you apparently wasted no time beating him up with your expert opinion," Ellen snapped, stopping about three feet from William and working to keep her sudden fury in check.

"As *you* apparently wasted no time in undoing. Classy how you back me up!"

"Oh, so this about *you*, about *your* feelings! Wouldn't want to mistake it for some concern about what's right for our son!" Ellen challenged, raking her hair with her fingers.

If he registered a new resolve emanating from his wife, William didn't heed it. "The boy should suck it up! You don't quit in the middle of a season just because you don't like something," he bellowed, the veins on his forehead and neck pulsing.

Ellen extended her arms, palms up, as if embracing a universe. "Of course you quit, if you hate something. Why not? What sense does it make to force a kid to do something that's *voluntary* that he's discovered he doesn't like? It's not like he wants to drop out of school and join a commune!" It made no sense for William to be this angry and rigid about wrestling, Ellen thought. He'd not been to a single wrestling match, not ever.

"I won't have it. Period. Quitters make me sick." His voice was booming through the small house. Picturing her sons having to hear it, Ellen felt sick. "Jonathan does not deserve this. What are you doing?" she whispered angrily, hoping to change the volume, if not the tenor, of their argument.

"He should not be given permission to quit midstream. Learning to finish what you start is how you build character. And you should not undermine my authority." William was still leaning against the door to the basement. The room felt claustrophobic and hot. The color of the walls, a buttercream that Ellen had spent weeks last spring deciding upon, seemed sallow and flat. Her perky calendar of strutting bantam roosters had large x's through the days she had taken vacation in order to prepare the upcoming Thanksgiving feast. *I hate this,* she realized, I hate everything about this.

"So," she taunted, "You're saying we should've stayed in Vietnam because we started it, even though we were always going to lose that war in the end?"

"That's a stupid thing to say. It has nothing to do with Jon dropping a responsibility," he shouted.

Their footsteps pounding on the stairs, Jon and Cole poured together into the kitchen, faces strained and pale. They had never looked more like brothers, with their skin pulled taut over their nearly identical facial bone structure. Their brown eyebrows were knit together and their shoulders were squared like mirror images of each another.

"Can you dial it down?" Cole asked in a carefully modulated voice. He was staring at his father, chin thrust outward at a challenging angle. Cole was now taller and quicker than William. He had never before inserted himself into a parental argument.

The father's face registered shock, as a painful recollection of his own parents' septic marriage seeped into his awareness. "What?" he asked softly, struggling to calm himself and back away from the memories of his own youth, when he had never challenged his father or defended his mother. Pushing those memories away, he said "Fuck it!" and turned from his family, stomping down the cellar stairs.

A strained silence fell over the threesome left in the kitchen. Romeo sidled in and began to weave himself around Ellen's ankles, filling the air with plaintive mewing. Juliet quickly joined them, jumping on the counter and contorting herself so that she could lap a drop of water from the faucet without actually getting into the sink and getting her paws wet. Ellen picked her up and hugged her, wiping what she hoped was an inconspicuous tear off on the cat's soft fur.

"All right then," Cole pronounced. He fake-punched Jon affectionately on the shoulder. "You okay?" he asked his mother.

"Yes, thank you," Ellen said, formally. It was unnerving to see Cole step into a peacemaker role, although he seemed quite natural in it.

"Bed, then," Cole pronounced, turning to leave. Jon hesitated, torn between staying with his mother and scurrying off under the newly protective wing of his brother. Ellen tipped her head slightly, encouraging him to follow Cole. She wanted to be alone.

41: Airports

Trying to book a convenient flight from Buffalo to Seattle on a moment's notice is difficult, Julie quickly discovered. Though the Buffalo-Niagara Airport is large enough to handle international traffic, it's not a hub to anywhere. If you need to fly to the west coast, you must often begin by flying toward the Atlantic. After an hour of searching Internet travel sites, Julie booked a flight to Seattle that took her first to Logan International Airport in Boston, and then to Milwaukee. The flight was expensive and prolonged, at nearly thirteen hours, but she would arrive at 5:30 in the morning, pick up her rental car, and be at her brother's house in just two more hours. He could then spend the day with his wife and fragile newborn at the hospital and she could enjoy her dear, precocious niece.

USAir Flight 1912 roared into the calm skies over Buffalo just after six in the evening, heading due east. Squeezed into a window seat at the rear of the plane, Julie watched as the rooftops and then the lights of her urban home disappeared into the murky darkness. The New York State Thruway receded into colorful pinpricks of light streaking across the mostly rural terrain. She fished out her notepad and stared unhappily at the few sentences she had written so far for her *Mariner's Cove* piece, due in just one week. She nibbled on her pen's clicker and looked for inspiration at the nearby passengers. *Maybe there's some way to incorporate flying into the new ending*, she thought. Now and then, she peered out into the darkness to watch an illuminated schmeer sparkling in the distance far below and she wondered, am I over Syracuse? Could that be Albany? There was a long patch of dense blackness, possibly the Adirondacks. Writing was a challenge as she tried to keep her elbows from jiggling the snoozing teenager shoehorned into the next seat.

After an hour in the air, the pilot's youngish voice crackled urgently over the public address system. "Good evening, ladies and gentleman! I'm going to ask everyone to take your seat and buckle your seat belt. We're preparing for landing in about twenty minutes. There will be some minor turbulence, and I'm sorry to inform you that most departures out of Logan have been delayed due to an extreme weather system moving rapidly up the eastern seaboard. We'll have extra personnel at the gates to assist you with your connecting flights if you need them. Thank you for flying with us; we hope you've had an enjoyable experience, and have a great evening in Boston!"

Like anybody was likely to have a great evening after *that* news, Julie grumped to herself. A pit was forming in her stomach as she contemplated her best-laid plans going up in smoke. Or rather, down in snow. And then the plane began to buck like a carnival bronco, riding turbulence almost to the tarmac before it leveled out and made a rocky landing. A man seated in front of her was audibly praying and cried, "Praise Jesus!" as the plane taxied smoothly down the runway. Others clapped. Julie hoped her flight was slightly delayed. She didn't think she could board another plane until she'd had time to metabolize a Xanax.

Flights weren't just delayed, the departure board was covered with cancellations in anticipation of a snow and ice storm barreling up the coast with its sights set squarely on Boston. Dismayed, Julie slowly reconciled herself to spending a night in the airport, while hoping fervently that her rebooked flight at 7 in the morning would actually get out of Logan. Arriving suddenly, the storm swirled around the airport, bursts of driven snow and sleet battering the huge windows like artillery fire. She texted her brother with the bad news and purchased a bottle of water, some overpriced cashews, a book, two magazines, and a pink fleece blanket at the bookstore on the concourse.

The terminal was jammed with frustrated fliers, all feverishly needing to be somewhere else. Toddlers fussed, teenagers stared glumly at the floor and adjusted their iPods, business travelers barked urgently into their iPhones, and long lines formed in the ladies' restrooms. A night on hard plastic airport seating seemed as miserable as it did inevitable. She could even less imagine trying to sleep on the grungy floor, although some tough travelers were using their coats and backpacks to stake out yoga-mat sized land claims.

At last, she found an available seat next to an older, primly dressed woman who was engrossed in a novel. She dug *Mariner's Cove* and her notepad out of her luggage and added them to her bag of goodies. After stowing the carry-on under her seat, Julie settled in, covered herself with the pink fleece, and surveyed her choices of reading material. Although she was exhausted, she fully intended to stay awake and read all night and sleep on her cross-country flight tomorrow. Skimming *Ladies Home Journal,* she was briefly intrigued by an article about Meryl Streep's cooking secrets (dash of balsamic, zest of lime, don't be afraid of butter). Juxtaposed in the next section was an adoring feature on Hollywood's latest anorexic-looking actress, who probably hadn't tasted real butter in ten years. Shaking her head in exasperation, she commented out loud, "Talk about a double message!"

The woman in the adjacent seat looked startled, hastily gathered her things, and scurried away. *Did she think I was a crazy person just because I talked out loud?* Julie wondered as she slipped the magazine back into her bag and pulled out her new book, *Cutting Loose: Why Women Who End Their Marriages Do So Well*. The book was a feast of heroic stories about women who were able to thrive after getting free of their controlling, abusive, or otherwise worthless spouses. Julie read until the airport quieted and sleepiness finally, blessedly, overtook her. She slid *Cutting Loose* back into the bag at her feet. Her hands cradled her purse under the blanket. Slowly her head tilted forward and all her facial muscles relaxed into sleep.

Within minutes, the adjacent seat was claimed by a veterinarian en route to a conference in Milwaukee who had been rebooked on the same morning flight as Julie. He had a bag of books and goodies from the same concourse store and he, too, eventually drifted off to sleep having placed it at his feet.

When the public address system crackled to life at 5:30, Julie awoke in a disoriented fog. She'd been in the middle of a vivid dream about flying to Egypt to buy silk for her new upholstery business. Her neck hurt, her face felt gritty, and she was desperate to brush her teeth. All around her, people were waking up, making calls, stretching and steeling themselves for the day's travels. A group in matching bowling shirts called raucously to one another across the concourse like crows at dawn. Quickly gathering her things, Julie marveled that the fellow in the seat beside her could sleep through so much commotion. A quick glance at the departure board revealed the good news that most flights were on time as the storm had merely glanced off Boston and rolled out to sea. She freshened up as best she could, bought a cup of coffee and a low-fat granola bar, and headed for her gate.

Boarding was painless, although she felt pangs of jealousy upon hearing the flight attendant offer the first class passengers their choice of coffee, juice, and warm muffins. Grimacing, Julie angled her body, luggage, and book bag so as to sidle past the attendant who was pouring juice for someone. At her end of the plane, it was a cattle car with every seat taken by last night's displaced passengers, most of them worse for wear. The middle seat on an airplane should be reserved for small children, Julie believed, as it is simply impossible to get comfortable in such narrow straights. But that's where she sat. The man in the window seat on her right was already tapping away on his laptop and shortly, a family of four filled in the rest of the row and began loudly reviewing all facets of their dreadful night in the airport.

Julie consoled herself that at least she had a good book to finish, a new magazine to read, and maybe even some fresh concepts to weave into her rewrite of *Mariner's Cove,* possibly something to do with flying, Egypt, or silk. The first item she extracted from her bag from the Logan concourse store was a glossy publication called *Welcome to Bovine Veterinarian.* "What the hell?" she thought. Splashed with photos of placid Holsteins grazing in emerald valleys, it was pitched to vets who specialize in cows. The tagline promised "leading-edge information to improve your marketing to beef and dairy clients." Had the clerk given her the wrong magazine by mistake last night? Wouldn't she have noticed it before this? How could a thing this specialized even be for sale at an airport bookstore?

Reaching again into the plastic bag, she wrapped her fingers around a hardcover book entitled *Strong Medicine.* Now she looked more carefully into the bag and confirmed a dismayed suspicion that it was not hers. No *Mariner's Cove,* no notepad, no *Elle,* no cashews. Reddening, she realized that, in her rush to get to the correct gate, she scooped up the bag belonging to the sleeping fellow next to her. Inside the jacket cover of his book was a printed email from a friend encouraging him to buy the book because "it's written by men who know divorce and the hell we go through. It tells how to act for the benefit of our kids and promises that we'll get to a better day with integrity and resilience...strong medicine for our devastated psyches." Wow, she thought. What does this guy mean by "devastated psyches?" At least she had his email address and could likely mail his belongings back to him, with profuse apologies.

With no headset and a three-plus hour flight in front of her, Julie took a deep breath and opened *Strong Medicine*. Its message was the male equivalent of the book she had been reading, full of nicely phrased exhortations coaching men on how to buck up, own up, and gracefully let go. That some men felt so hurt and blindsided when their marriages imploded or exploded was a revelation. Maybe some men really were as vulnerable, and as nice, as Nathan seemed to be. She had been struggling to believe in him. As she sank into the book's message, she felt a shift in herself, a little opening to the idea that perhaps she didn't need to spend the rest of her life armored with a distrustful view of all men.

With a burst of energy, she began to write a new ending to *Mariner's Cove* on the back of Hariri's email:

> *Paula died, leaving a huge void in Claire's world.*
> *What would she do with herself now? She could never sit*

still, never relax. She went nuts fixing up her house and updating her stuff. For weeks, she obsessed about reupholstering her furniture. Could she do it? Though her prior sewing experience consisted mainly of making curtains, she found a pattern and bought thirty yards of brilliantly colored Egyptian cotton. When her couch and chair were dressed in their snazzy new covers, she noticed how tired her painted woodwork looked. Could she fix that, too? Why not? She slathered stripping chemicals on the white front door until noxious fumes filled the house. She decided to move her birds onto the safety of the back patio. It was a lovely spring day and she imagined her little star finches would enjoy the fresh breeze ruffling their feathers. The pair fluttered and chirped in response to the chipping of the sparrows in the pines.

When Claire went back to stripping the door, the tiny hen hopped off her perch and dangled upside down from the thin wire at the top of the cage. Her mate settled into his usual position, asleep on the uppermost perch, his red face tucked into his breast. As the hen jostled her wings, the cage jiggled slightly and its diminutive door swung open. The hen's attention was instantly fixed on the open door. She had spent her whole life in a cage. Silently, she glided to the open door, somehow understanding the peril of drawing attention to the open hatch. Distending her tail feathers, she flexed her neck and launched herself

forward and upward. The hen was flying, flying! Her
wings beat harder and harder, as she ascended over the
low bushes in the back yard, a streak of red and yellow
with a miniature speckled cape.

   Claire happened to look out the window as her
tiny bird vanished into the green leaves. She'd had the
bird for three years and she was fond of it. But its launch
into freedom, which would almost surely doom it, seemed
like a signal she had been waiting for: a sign that it made
no sense for her to stay in her cage. She suddenly
understood that the only honest thing she could work on,
her only tolerable choice, was to get free.

Julie stopped writing and closed her eyes, pondering her
next words. It made sense for Claire to break away from her
marriage, but how would she do it? Thinking of her own long
struggle to disengage from Eric, who, long after their divorce still
needled her in ways that sent her spiraling into self-doubt, Julie
recalled the final tipping point. It happened last spring, at a school
play. Stephen had a minor part and Julie, ever polite and
thoughtful, was approaching Eric and his parents in the lobby in an
effort to be civil to her ex-in-laws.

   In a voice so low only she could hear it, Eric sneered
derisively, "Is *that* what you're wasting my alimony on?" He was
staring at her ring finger where she had replaced her wedding band
with a lovely gold band set with Stephan's birthstone.

"What?" she asked brightly, although she had heard him perfectly well. "What was that you were saying?" she sought his mother's eyes and interest.

"Nothing!" Eric mumbled.

He's a coward, she realized, a coward! *His* alimony, my foot! Thereafter, whenever he tried to belittle or undermine her, she begged him to repeat himself, over and over, feigning an inability to hear him. With his verbal bombs defused, Eric's power over her finally evaporated.

The man to her right started to snore lightly, snapping Julie out of her daydream. Looking at the words she had penned, she recognized that fictional Claire's husband isn't her real ex-husband. She didn't need Claire to mete out justice on her behalf, nor was Claire really in a position to do so. A resolution that vindicates what I stand for, Julie thought, is for Claire to be honest with herself, and then with Philip. So Julie picked up her pen and described Claire telling Philip about the bird flying away, about her envy of it, and about her need to end their marriage because it was a sham, and she had been unfaithful. Julie tried to imagine how Philip would respond, because he didn't actually have a leg to stand on either. She decided he would probably be pissed off because he had sucked it up so many years before, but those aren't grounds you can save a relationship with. So he did the only thing he could do, he let her go.

Julie sat back, satisfied. This was the right ending for her; not actually happy, but honest. The pilot announced the imminent (and untroubled) landing in Milwaukee. She was desperate to stretch her legs and find a ladies' room. As she exited the plane, deep in the throng of economy class travelers, she spotted a man standing just beyond the exit gate, holding aloft a copy of *Mariner's Cove*. She smiled shyly at him and the vet grinned back.

"We seem to be from opposite planets," he said, handing her book bag to her.

"Oh, I'm so glad you waited here," she said warmly. "I think you'll like this book you bought, or at least I did!" She offered his bag. "It was interesting food for thought. Our planets may not be as far apart as we think."

They shared a coffee before Julie boarded her next flight, the one that would safely deposit her in Seattle later that afternoon.

42: Running it Down

Ellen slept fitfully, churning back and forth between glimpses of the exquisitely libidinous photo shoot with Ty and the boorish confrontation in her kitchen with her husband a few hours later. After stomping angrily away, William spent the night in the basement. Nor did Ellen descend to his hidey-hole to sort things out, as was her usual pattern. Instead, she chugged another generous glass of chardonnay, took an Ambien to knock herself out, and crawled between her sheets, grateful to be alone. By five in the morning, though, she was fully awake with but a slight headache and an excess of nervous energy. She decided to go for a run.

Though winter was more than a month away, November's short days and the bitingly cold winds streaming off Lake Erie had transformed running outside from mere sport into a test of personal endurance. Nevertheless, Ellen loathed running on treadmills in stuffy gyms ("It's like running in a closet") or on an indoor track, which she found crushingly boring. With no need to reconnoiter with Julie, she jogged east on Forest Avenue and then loped north following the gentle S-curves of Delaware Avenue. The snow had stopped overnight, leaving an artist's white filigreed tracing on the neighborhood's tall old trees and steep gabled roofs. It was pretty but cold, so bitter that her eyes welled with tears. She felt bracingly alive, released from a fugue state, confronting her life clearly in the shadowy dawn.

She pictured her husband, William Lincoln Palmer, firstborn son of William Washington Palmer and Patricia Butler Palmer. William's younger brother, a banker in Hong Kong, was named Andrew Jackson Palmer. Their baby sister had been christened Jamie Madison Palmer. When Ellen was first introduced to the Palmer clan, she thought it exotic that they had inserted presidential names into the children's given names. Now, she wished that she had recognized it for the pretentious posturing it truly was. In reality, William's father was a self-aggrandizing bully and his mother was a mouse, albeit a mouse that sometimes gnawed through important wiring or left foul pellets on select aspects of her children's psyches.

Feeling disloyal for having such an unkind view of her deceased mother-in-law, Ellen remonstrated herself. Wasn't the woman first and foremost a victim, always turning herself inside out trying to anticipate and placate her domineering husband? And yet, should it not be acknowledged that often one generation's victims morph into the next generation's villains, passing along their demons in the same wrapping as their DNA? Whenever Ellen asked herself what was *wrong* with her husband, a question that was especially vexing to her this morning, she ended back at the beginning: imagining what growing up as the oldest son in the

Palmer household must have been like for him. The children were taught that they were special, destined for great things, possibly even presidential things, yet the household's equanimity could be upended for the most inconsequential of provocations, such as a poor grade, a burnt pork chop, a too heavy sigh. Eventually, the children grew callouses, all three of them honing an ability to defensively control any situation before it controlled them. This insight took a dozen years to fully form in Ellen's awareness and by then, she was adept at what she now saw as her dance of denial.

A familiar wash of resigned sadness began to settle over her but this time, Ellen pushed it back. "No!" she shouted, startling even herself. It was time to stop allowing the legacy of William's past to be the architect of her present. Pumping her fists rhythmically as she ran, Ellen heard the squish-squish of her Nikes pounding the wet sidewalk, left-right, left-right, and the loud in and out whoosh of her breath. The street was momentarily deserted, the city hushed, not even disturbed by the distant barking of dogs. Hearing herself, feeling her body in motion, she felt whole. It was a new and liberating sensation.

Like a chant, she began to syncopate her thoughts with her steps. "He is who he is." Left – right – left – right – left. "He is who he is, he is who he is. It's not mine to change. It's not mine to change." Right – left – right – left – right. "It is what it is." Reversing course abruptly, she stretched into long, hard strides. It was urgent that she reach the house before William left for his office. Everything was so simple, so clear to her. The moment had come when she must end the charade of her marriage. Not for the sake of their sons, not because of the drummer, but because it is what it is – not a marriage, not a partnership, not even a friendship; it was poison and she'd been feeding it to herself long enough.

William was standing at the kitchen sink, slurping the last of a cup of coffee when she burst into the house, her cheeks flushed from the bitter cold. "Oh, hey," he said in a conciliatory tone, "You got out for your run awfully early!"

"I'm not, I'm not going to live like this any longer," she declared, struggling to catch her breath, and beginning to strip off layers of running gear, starting with her purple neoprene gloves and soaked shoes.

Shaking his head in agreement, William said, "Yeah, I don't understand how you run in this crap anyway."

"Oh, no, no, no. I mean I'm not going to live *with you* like this any longer!"

He stepped back and looked at her impassively. "Okay. I've been thinking maybe I was a little hard on Jon last night."

"It's not about Jon," she gasped, unwinding her scarf and unzipping her jacket.

"What now?" he said sharply, straightening his back.

"Us." Ellen looked at him calmly.

He rolled his eyes and glared at her, "Oh, here we go. Your laundry list of my imperfections!"

"Ha!" Ellen half-laughed. "It doesn't matter. Your imperfections, my imperfections. It doesn't matter! You are who you are. You aren't going to change, nor should you be expected to." Pulling off her insulated pants, she grabbed the back of a kitchen chair for support and set her jaw firmly. "I want a divorce."

The blue ceramic Buffalo Bills coffee cup that William had been holding slipped out of his hand and into the sink, where it shattered. "You're just pissed off," he sputtered, "you'll get over it."

"Actually, I'm not mad at all. I'm calm and relieved! It's over! And I would prefer to stay here and not disrupt the boys' lives, but if you can't let that happen, then we'll just sell."

"You are crazy. You need to get a grip." His ruddy face was flushed and his eyes glittered. "I have a meeting. We'll talk tonight." He grabbed his coat and briefcase and stormed off, leaving the shards of his favorite cup smashed in the sink.

"Bullshit," she sputtered, getting out a plastic bag for the broken bits of cup.

43: Brian and Maggie, Session Two

Maggie and Brian passed the days between their marriage counseling appointments in tense détente. Reluctantly, she got rid of the weed on her property by asking Ellen to hold it for her. It seemed a necessary gesture: that, or move out and she didn't want to leave her family or her home. However, sleep instantly became a cat-and-mouse game, as she tried, unsuccessfully, to transition to herbal sleep aids, which did nothing for her. Finally, her physician prescribed some sleep meds that knocked her out all night and half the next day. It was not a happy compromise. For his part, Brian, finding himself distracted and on edge, was deeply relieved that he didn't have any huge or complex cases going before the judge this month. The citizens of New York State would not have gotten his best work, and his excellent focus was something he had always prided himself on.

Finally, they were back in Dr. McLaurin's office. After settling into the same seats they had chosen during their first session, the psychologist shared that she felt that each of them was a strong and resilient individual but that their marriage was at a critical juncture. She needed to know their level of commitment to moving forward together.

Her first question aimed to open them to more honest and mutually respectful communication. "So you've had some time to think about what you want and need out of marriage counseling. I'd like to hear where each of you is today."

Brian looked at his hands. He had thought about removing his wedding ring, but he hadn't taken if off. Still, he felt that things were falling apart in front of him, and this was something he could never have imagined. He loved his wife. She was a good mother. He had been a good husband. A good father.

He began addressing Dr. McLaurin: "I just don't get it. How could she keep drugs on our property? I could be *so* screwed. We could *all* be so screwed. What is so special about weed that she would put that much risk on our whole family?"

"Please ask your wife directly," Anna suggested, tilting her head toward Maggie.

"Why?" Brian said to Maggie.

Despite her endless mental admonitions to stay calm during this hour, Maggie fired back shrilly, "It's *not* a big deal. It just helps me sleep. Really, Brian, you're being so melodramatic! You'd think I'd killed someone or something."

"Are you trying to kill our marriage?" Brian asked pointedly.

"It doesn't have to have anything to do with our marriage. It's about me, about what I need. But you don't care about that!"

Angry lobs were volleyed back and forth, with occasional redirects from the marriage counselor.

Brian: How can you say that? You wanted to move to the country, we moved to the country. You always get what you want. But drugs in my house? I can't bend that much.

Maggie: There we go. You're the lawyer, I'm the criminal. Why did you even come here today?

Anna: Maggie, I'm glad you brought that up. Brian, could you share your ideas of how marriage counseling can help you and Maggie?

Brian: I don't know! How the hell should I know?

Anna: In your mind, what does help look like?

Brian: Help would be that Maggie gets it, that she understands why I'm upset.

Maggie: Oh, I *understand* all right. You have made your case repeatedly. I just don't think it makes any fucking sense!

Anna: Could you say more about what you understand? Tell Brian more about your understanding of why he feels upset?

Maggie: He's upset because he wants to believe that everything is perfect in my little world, but when he found my weed, it sort of, sort of blew that fantasy out of the water. And he can't stand it when he doesn't control things.

Anna: So how accurately did Maggie sum up your view of things?

Brian: She's dead on that it made me angry to find marijuana in my house. I could lose my job, we could be ruined! That's not *me* being unreasonable, or being some asshole who just wants to control his wife.

Maggie: Brian, that's crazy. I had a tiny amount of weed, at most a misdemeanor. Plus, no one's looking to arrest you or me and I don't normally even keep it in the house. Sooner or later, they've got to make it legal. You're not going to lose your job. They *love* you at the DA's.

Brian: It is a huge risk. There's no difference between the house and the barn, by the way. It doesn't matter where on our property you keep it! Why would you take such a huge risk?

Maggie: Because I need to sleep! Weed makes it possible for me to sleep.

Brian: That's not the only thing you can take to get to sleep. There are a million things that would be legal and safe and wouldn't convey to our children that being a dope addict is a hunky-dory solution to life's dilemmas.

At that, Anna sat up in her chair, theatrically placed her right hand on top of her left hand in a *t* shape and called "Time!" Maggie and Brian stifled their next screeds and stared at her.

"Okay," she said authoritatively. "You've covered the same basic territory three times. I'm completely certain there's nothing, *nothing,* you're going to say about the specifics of Maggie's weed that you haven't already said. So just allow that to be the facts, okay? You've each stated your case fully. You each know, fully and well, the other's position and feelings." She paused while her antique clock ticked loudly.

Maggie noticed that the table lamps were beautifully finished in a deep bronze glaze. Afternoon sun glinted gaily off them in stark contrast to the despair she felt gnawing at her heart. Sweat began to trickle down Brian's forehead. His hands were clenched like baseballs balanced on his thighs.

Anna continued, "Now, I would like you each to think for a minute about the *deeper* things you haven't yet said to each other. The things that go to your pain, your disappointment, or your loss."

Her chest rose as Maggie noisily drew in air and held it. Brian studied the carpet.

Anna continued briskly. "I'm going to ask you each to speak that truth and withhold any judgment you feel about what your partner says. Just *hear* it. Imagine that you are listening to a long-lost friend, somebody you care about and really want to hear from, somebody you're not already in touch with. And don't repeat *anything,* not one single thing that you've already said. I'll give you a few minutes."

Instantly, Brian crumpled over himself and put his head in his hands.

"It's alright," Anna encouraged kindly. "Say the things that you have not said, the things that must be said."

Maggie reached for a tissue and dabbed the corners of her eyes as she watched her husband, uncharacteristically quiet and clearly in pain.

Brian spoke to the carpet. "For the first couple of years, after going through two bouts of her being sick, it was like I was living on borrowed time, waiting for an inevitable catastrophe.

Planning for how I'd deal with the kids, when Maggie got sick again. Hearing the word *widower* in my head, first thing in the morning. As I was lathering up my face to shave, I would think, *widower*. Then it started to fade, maybe two years ago. I dared believe we had beaten it. Except she," he looked at his wife, "except it seemed like you were never really going to come back. You were different and you wouldn't talk about it."

Maggie opened her mouth to speak, but Anna stepped in. "No, please let him finish."

Brian nodded and unclenched his hands. "Then this amazing transformation happened and you came back to us,. You even got turned on to me again. You started waking me up for sex! Now I guess that was because you were stoned and, Jesus, I feel like such a fool."

Maggie shook her head vigorously causing her earrings to jingle. "So the rules," she challenged, "are that I can't say anything about what he just said? I can't respond to that?"

"No, please do not," Anna responded compassionately. "Speak your own truth. Let Brian's stand just as he spoke it."

Crossing her arms so that she was hugging herself, Maggie paused. When she finally spoke, her voice was hoarse. "Death stalks me. Every weird twinge, every odd freckle, sends me into a tailspin. I don't want to live like this. I think *I'm* the fool! Because, logically, death stalks everyone. It's one wrong step off the curb, one time when you're in the wrong place at the wrong moment, one random clot floating loose in your brain. So weed is just a bridge back to the place where I can relax. It isn't about you, Brian. I still love you, I want to be your wife, I like sex with you, but…"

She stopped and stared at the floor. Dr. McLaurin motioned to Brian to just wait. Finally, Maggie spoke again. "It's not that I don't want to talk about it. I desperately want to talk about it. What I get is that you want me to say I'm all better, that the cancer is just a memory, like a trip we took ten years ago or something. It's not! It's with me every second of every day. It's a monster lurking around all my corners."

Anna held her hands up again in a "stop" gesture. "You've both just said some deep and important things." She paused for a full minute. "Now there's another rule. Don't talk about what you've said here for at least two days. For 48 hours, just let yourselves be aware of what each has shared."

She stood and ushered them out. "I'll see you next week."

44: In Accord, November

In sharp contrast to the wintry blast that exploded over the book club's excursion to the Outlet Mall, the third Thursday of November dawned sunny and almost balmy 45 degrees. Most of the residual snow that hugged north-facing slopes had melted back into the earth, revealing dull clumps of grass against a backdrop of barren trees. As the early evening closed in like heavy drapes around them, the book club women gathered at Maggie's, settling into her comfortable living room where a wood fire crackled cheerily from the cast iron stove. Maggie offered an assortment to please every palette: cranberry-walnut scones, chocolate-almond torte, hummus with toasted pita, thinly sliced Gala apples neatly circling a pile of aged Canadian cheddar cheese cubes, Blue Mountain coffee, and a selection of tea and tea-wannabes.

"Good Lord! Look at all this," Julie laughed. "It's going to take a couple of extra miles of running to make up for what I'm going to do to myself in the next five minutes."

"Yeah, what exactly are we doing with all this food?" Hannah asked. "I mean, *really*! Could we call a truce?"

Nonetheless, they piled treats on their pink china dessert plates and gathered in a close circle. When all were settled,

Hannah squared her shoulders and cleared her throat. They looked expectantly in her direction. "Before we get to our raison d'être, I want to bring you up to speed about Zoe. She *is* going to have, and keep, her baby. A girl, she's having a baby girl. Simon's building them a little suite in the attic so they'll have room. There's a program for teen moms at one of the schools and she'll enroll in that, *with* the baby after she's born." Hannah's face looked both soft and sad. "So no party hats or sparklers, but we're going to help her make it work. And I have settled down and think I can live with this. We've met the boy and his family and that's going to be a challenge, but Simon's been great!" Trying to smile, she relaxed back into her chair and shrugged. "What else could we do?"

"Whoa! Grandma!" Julie raised her coffee in a toast.

"Yes, damn it!" Hannah toasted back. "A good decade earlier than I'd have wanted, if anyone asked me, but of course…"

"Wow!" Ellen drew the word out slowly.

"That's it, really."

Logs shifted and crackled in the wood stove as the women sat in momentary silence.

"Sorry, I guess I don't see how you can support that," Maggie said pointedly. "Couldn't you have nudged her?"

"Are you kidding?" Hannah retorted. "We did everything we could to *nudge* her but, after all, she was already so far along! If she had come to me the day after that stupid, stupid party, I would have had her at the pharmacy for Plan B in about a minute-

and-a-half, let me tell you, but she didn't, and now she won't consider placing the baby for adoption."

"To me, you're doing the right thing," Julie placed her hand on her heart as she leaned toward Hannah. "How is Zoe feeling?"

"Poor girl's having the full gamut of pregnancy symptoms," Hannah said, "but her attitude is totally changed and we've had some amazing conversations. Instead of fighting me on everything, she's looking for maternal guidance, and taking it. It's going to be a hard road for her, and us, but not an impossible one. Though I reserve the right to flip out periodically during the next five months while this thing happens." Her friends nodded their assent. "Or the next twenty years, whichever," she added.

"You got it!" Ellen said simply, appreciating how Hannah landed on her feet no matter what the crisis.

A dog-eared copy of *Mariner's Cove* lay on the coffee table. Maggie picked it up. "Okay, so, we had quite the little assignment after our last book club. Anybody else struggle with this?"

Julie was first to respond. "I suffered! I reread that epilogue a dozen times and the thing that kept bugging me was the way Claire just stayed in that victim role. But I wasn't sure how to believably push her out of that, you know? What would jar her free? So here's what I have." She fished a typed paged out of her purse, cleared her throat, and read the ending she had penned on the flight between Boston and Milwaukee. When she was finished,

Julie smiled and looked at her friends expectantly. "So, that's what I've got!"

"I love the whole bird thing!" Ellen said softly. "Flying the coop! But what about Charles? You don't see her hooking back up with Charles?"

"No way! That's over. He's an idiot. Before I came up with this, I thought long and hard about letting her get revenge on him for the way he dumped her, twice, but if she's really going to evolve into her own woman, and if the story's really going to have an ending that satisfies *me,* she has to let him go. She has to stop defining herself based on the men in her life." Chin up, Julie was definitive.

"So she doesn't get involved with anyone after she leaves Philip?" Hannah queried.

"Oh, she has relationships, absolutely. But none where she gives up her whole self again."

"All right, I can't help but ask," Ellen sought her friend's eyes, "is this a reflection of how things are going with that guy you were dating, Nathan?"

"We've been on several dates, actually," Julie acknowledged. "And you know what? I'm enjoying myself. But if he doesn't call again, I'll be okay with that too. I worked too hard figuring out how to stand on my own. I'm not throwing that away ever again!" She stabbed a pita crisp into the garlicky hummus and sat back.

Smiling, Maggie raised her coffee cup in a toast. "Good for you! I loved the bird thing, too. Poor little bit, though. It won't last long! But kudos for writing it down in a real story. I couldn't quite get that together. But I did think about it. And came up with a roughish outline for how I wish it had ended." Maggie unfolded a piece of lined notebook paper upon which she had written several points. She summarized:

- The sister finally gets the words out to tell Claire that Philip cheated on her.
- Claire is angry and humiliated yet humble because she knows she's no better than he is.
- Claire confronts Philip and they have a massive blow-out of a fight, dredging up crap she's mentally collected all the way back to their first date, and some crap he has stockpiled, too. All their anger and disappointment with each other gets splayed open like a gutted fish.

"Ew!" "Gross!" the listeners murmured.
Maggie nodded and continued:

- There's a painful separation. Then, each is surprised to be missing things about the other, habits they took for granted, stuff they liked, ways they relied on one another.

- So they see a marriage counselor and end up reconciling and there's a new, scary, exhilarating honesty between them.
- They grow up and each one owns their own shit. They stop laying it on each other. That includes especially the big shit, her crippling death fears, his fear of being abandoned, stuff like that.

The group grew still, each grappling with the image of "the big shit, her death fears…stuff like that." Breaking the spell, Maggie laughed, "Relax, gang, it's a *good* thing that happens! In my version of a perfect ending, Claire and Philip grow old together, they're at peace with what they have as a couple. They're both decent people. The story shows that, in how they take care of the sister. They've just never been real with each other, Claire all obsessed about the past, and Philip, well, I'm not sure what his deal is but I am sure that if you drilled into his psyche deep enough, you would find a whole universe of thought and feeling going on there, too."

"So marriage counseling saves the day?" Ellen asked.

"Oh, my God, yes," Maggie enthused. "Marriage counseling, and how it opened them up to each other. If any of you ever need a referral, this shrink that Brian and I have been seeing is just amazing. Although she kind of doesn't *do* anything, yet she's getting us to listen to each other, which I would have said we did already but I would've been wrong."

"That's wonderful," Julie smiled.

"It is." Absently, Maggie retied her scarlet scarf and smoothed the fringe on her chest. The grandmother clock in the corner chimed half-past the hour, drawing their attention to the display of five large, framed Brinkman family photographs Maggie's brother had taken. In the first two, Maggie and Brian were leaning into each other with their babies or toddlers in their arms or on the laps. Then, the children, gap-toothed and gangly, sat or stood between them. In the final picture, Maggie is wearing an elaborate turban and the children, well groomed and taller, are standing like sentinels on either side with their arms around her, while Brian is slightly off to the right. She gestured at the wall. "Time to update our gallery!"

Finger-picking her curls as if preparing to be photographed, Hannah smiled. "Yes, definitely. So, in Julie's perfect world, Claire is happy on her own while in Maggie's, Claire reconciles to the husband after the truth comes out. I got to give it to you, Ellen, this rewrite thing is turning out to be pretty interesting. Here's what I came up with." She pulled a notebook out of her huge purse and sifted through some handwritten pages covered with cross-outs and arrows leading to scrawled revisions in the margins. Finally locating the version she wanted to share, she began: "*Hannah's New Epilogue.* Sorry, that was corny. You can tell I spend a lot of time in a middle school. Here goes, really:

338

Put yourself in the operating room for a miracle. Neurologists implant electrodes into Paula's brain and they function perfectly. They don't cure her disease, but they reverse the downward spiral of her symptoms. As she grows stronger, she yearns for the day when she can finally check out of the group home. People expect her to settle near Claire and Philip, but that's the last *thing she wants. She's had more than enough of them. The desert beckons; she flies off to Arizona.*

With Paula gone, Philip and Claire are lost without their mutual caregiving project. Their whole rhythm of coexistence slides into chaos. Claire is restless and depressed. Feeling important, virtuous even, was the balm that she had slathered over her conscience. Now, she questions her whole existence and starts picking fights with Philip. Then she moves out, confusing the hell out of him. She won't even talk to him, because she can't really explain herself even to herself.

Claire and her best girlfriends go winter camping. They get snowed in, drink a boatload of wine, get stoned. Then the fights start – stupid arguments that seem to be about petty things but are really about everybody's insecurities. They all end up needing to forgive each other for some hurtful things that were said in haste. It's hard for Claire to realize that she is so human, so flawed, so dependent on others, including her friends, and yes, her sister and her husband. But realizing that truth allows her to, as the Buddhists say, be in the moment.

So, of course, the snow melts, the plows get through, and everyone goes home. Claire goes home to Philip, full of apology.

Philip steps up. Not only does he make peace, he secretly buys tickets. Days later, he asks her to go for a ride, ends at the airport, and shows her airplane tickets to New Zealand. Claire has always wanted to go there but he has always resisted – too expensive, too far, too crazy. They fly away and have a fabulous time. The affairs are never revealed to one another; their infidelities are like an undiagnosed virus that went away, made irrelevant by all the new, good energy between them, the new memories they build together.

Hannah looked up self-consciously. "That's it. Now I'm going to change my name to Pollyanna!"

Laughing, Julie agreed, "Yeah, let's rename ourselves the Pollyanna Club. I want to replace my Accord with something sexier anyway."

"It feels really good to hear you giving Paula a new lease on life. How sweet is that!" Maggie gave Hannah a thumbs-up.

Julie resumed, "But you'll never convince me that people can cheat like that and have it go away. It's not the flu! Do you really think their affairs become irrelevant?"

Hannah shrugged. "I don't know. The years pass, maybe as they get older, they actually do gain some perspective, some appreciation of each other. After all, dumb things people do aren't the only side of them."

"That sounds pretty good to me," Maggie commented. "No one's nominating those characters for sainthood."

Julie said pointedly. "Okay, Ellen, that leaves you. What do you have?"

Nervously jiggling her ankles and rustling her pages, Ellen explained: "Before I read my new epilogue, I have an announcement. Ummm," she pursed her lips and looked around the room at her expectant friends. "Um. I'm actually staying at the Home Coming Suites until I can move into a little apartment I just rented on Sterling Avenue. My marriage? Well, I've moved out. I've left Will."

Shocked expressions rippled across the room. "I just had one of those moments where everything came clear. It's like you live with those little cracks in the plaster for months or years and suddenly, you can't tolerate them one more second!"

"What? Wait! You've left William?" Hannah stammered.

"Holy God," Maggie breathed.

341

Her friends stared in silence, so Ellen continued. "So that's what happened. We had another one of our fights and I saw that it was always going to be like that, and I had to end it. After William went to work last Friday, I just flew around the house, taking this and that to get me by. It's amazing how much you can pack, and how much you can leave, when you just have to get out!"

"What about Jonathan and Cole?" Hannah demanded.

Ellen looked at her hands, trembling in her lap. "Of course, that's the hard part. They're staying at the house, at least for now. He's being really ugly right now but my hope is that William will get over being such a dick and I'll move back in with the boys. If that doesn't happen, I do have rooms for them and they can decide where they want to live. They say they understand, but Jon's kind of dazed and Cole says he doesn't know if he wants to go to college after all. I feel horribly guilty about them." She wiped her eyes with a tissue. "Sorry, been crying a lot. But if it weren't for the boys, I would've left Will eighteen years ago. My suitcase was all but packed when I got pregnant."

"Hell, I didn't know that," Maggie muttered.

"It's not something I've ever been proud of. I've tried, I've really worked at my marriage, but when you're not both willing to work at it, it's kind of hopeless. *This* is my one life. There's a thin sliver of a chance that I could be happy. I have to take it." Glancing around at her friends' concerned faces, she felt relieved to finally share this.

Julie, an unpleasant comprehension dawning in her awareness, asked: "What do you mean, *you're taking a chance to be happy?* Are you saying you're having an affair?"

"Not yet, but I probably will be. Ty, that guy from college, is definitely someone I'll see. After I get a formal separation. So here's what I think should happen in Mariner's Cove." She already held the pages in her hands.

Hannah's eyes sparkled like coals in her face, but she said nothing. Maggie wondered if it was too late for the Palmers to benefit from marriage counseling, but sensed something resolute in Ellen and refrained from recommending it.

"I just don't understand," Julie said tentatively.

"I'll tell you anything you want to know after you hear what I've written," Ellen replied. She cleared her throat and read:

Epilogue: 2 years later. Loneliness is a killer, a slow, languorous killer. While the world's population explodes toward eight billion, loneliness stakes out big dark spaces where it thrives. It devours your energy, shrinks your soul, twists your thoughts so you say and do and think things that make you a prickly stranger to your very self. And still it demands more; it is insatiable. It clamors to be heard and when you listen, it tells you that you are worth nothing. It calls you an idiot. It laughs when you stumble. Which is why what Claire did made perfect sense.

Eventually, she could not survive within the straightjacket of her own sad loneliness.

So one day, one more day when she had done all the right things, gone through all the appropriate motions as caring sister/loving wife, she stopped to gas up her Accord. Paula was in her last days, in a coma. There was nothing Claire could do for her. Unbidden, thoughts and images began to pour into her. She didn't have to go home! She had a credit card and a full tank of gas. Why go back there? There was no longer even a fish that needed tending, the goldfish having expired shortly after their child left for college. She could be utterly free!

The awareness of impending freedom was honey-sweet. She decided not to just disappear from her marriage without a word. Why not speak her truth finally? There was nothing, nothing Philip could say or do that would change her mind. So she went home and poured herself a glass of L'Ecole No. 41, a luscious red merlot she had been holding for a special moment. And waited for Philip.

While she sat sipping the merlot, she Googled Charles, who popped up on a social network site in seconds. Relationship status: single. Quickly, she texted him: "Are you still there?" She downed another glass of merlot. By the time her husband finally pulled into the driveway, she was packed and had booked a flight for later that night. Charles would be picking her up in San Francisco in the morning. Her heart was literally fluttering in her chest. She was laughing as she eyed all the things she had collected over the years, all of the things she would no longer dust and carefully place back on their shelves. Glass figurines and lovely raku vases, watercolors and good cookware; she didn't care a whit about any of it.

"Going somewhere?" Philip dropped his keys and wallet on the counter and cocked his head toward her suitcase.

"Yes! I'm leaving. It's over."

Philip snorted. "Bye."

His snort smarted. "I'm sorry, Philip."

"Yeah, save it! Nothing about you says sorry.*"*

Claire turned to leave. Then she turned back and sought her husband's eyes. "No, I really am sorry. I'm sorry it's taken so long. I'm sorry we've wasted so much of our lives. I'm doing what I need to do, finally. And I hope with whatever time we have left, that we each get to live a little."

He stood there in rigid silence, in his tailored suit and new white shirt, svelte and self-satisfied. Claire saw her partially full wine glass on the counter and staved off the urge to fling it at him. Instead she spoke again. "I want to amend what I just said. I hope with all my heart that we each get to live a lot."

345

Then she picked up her valise and walked out into the crisp new air.

Acknowledgements

Deepest gratitude to my daughter, Katharine Miner, for the extraordinary editing, intellectual rigor, and boundless enthusiasm she brought to this manuscript. I am also profoundly grateful for the wonderful support, wise commentary, and persistent encouragement given by my son, Daniel Miner. Heartfelt appreciation is due to my editor/friends: Ramona Pando-Whitaker and Sarah Blackman, whose expertise and exactitude were invaluable; and to my brothers, Mark, Jery, and Lee Chambers, and my brother-in-law Jim Miner, for their provocative and on point feedback; to my thoughtful readers: my father Glen Chambers, my niece Lyla Menkhaus, Holly Richardson of the Lakewood, NY, indie bookstore *Off the Beaten Path,* and to my friends Nancy Callahan, Pat Anzideo, Ann Servoss, and Cheryl Bell, for their gentle feedback and patient nourishment throughout this process. I am grateful to my publisher, Mark Pogodzinski and his brainchild, No Frills Buffalo, for providing a launching pad for local writers. And finally, to my husband Edwin Miner, loving thanks for everything.

Made in the USA
Coppell, TX
24 September 2020

38287375R00193